THE SWORD OF SHADOWS

THE SWORD OF SHADOWS

ADRIAN COLE

WILDSIDE PRESS

THE SWORD OF SHADOWS

Copyright © 2011 by Adrian Cole.
All rights reserved.

Published by Wildside Press LLC.
www.wildsidebooks.com

The Weaver of Wars first appeared in a slightly different form in *Weirdbook* magazine, No 23/24, 1988.

At the Council of Gossipers is a revised version of the story published in *Dark Horizons* magazine no 21, 1980.

Dark Destroyer was first published in a slightly different form in *Swords Against the Millennium*, Alchemy Press, Autumn 2000.

DEDICATION

For enduring support, hugely appreciated:
Dave Holmes
Dave Brzeski
Bob Covington
Roger and Rod

CONTENTS

Part One	THE WEAVER OF WARS	11
Part Two	AT THE COUNCIL OF GOSSIPERS	35
Part Three	ADRIFT IN DELIRIUM	47
Part Four	DARK DESTROYER	63
Part Five	THE SLIVER OF MADNESS	91
Part Six	AMONG THE BONES OF GIANTS	113
Part Seven	GATE AT THE EDGE OF REASON	151
Part Eight	IN HOLY HEDRAZEE	171

EXORDIUM

So, I begin once more this history of the dark man, pawn of the shadow gods who turn universes on their axis.

Though I sense the darkness coiling about my lonely retreat and imagine that I hear its measured breath, yet I am not molested. Perhaps the war that rages between the gods distracts them from a mere exile such as myself and my recorded impieties. For I know that it never ends, this god war, merely ebbing and flowing like an ocean, its tides washing the shores of human existence, re-shaping them sometimes as no more than an afterthought.

Wars and wars within wars, these are the things of which I must speak now. Gods fall, gods rise, some die, others live on and, like the tide, come again. The power of gods fluctuates, surging, breaking, dispersing.

The greatest of them may be humbled by the oceans of change, while even the least of those creatures that catch the tide at the flood may benefit. We all cling to the debris of hope. Even the outcasts, the condemned.

In this spirit I begin this history again.

—**SALECCO,** flotsam on the tides of Fate

PART ONE

THE WEAVER OF WARS

> *The Dark Gods had been strict in their control of the Voidal and in their manipulation of him. Part of the curse with which they had burdened him was that he should befriend and be befriended by no man.*
>
> *I have written elsewhere of how Elfloq, craftiest of familiars, had sought to overcome this censure by emphasising that he was not a man and thus immune to reprisals. While some remarked on this insouciance with amazement, others were far more sceptical, seeing in the dark union a hidden purpose that would ultimately serve the Dark Gods.*
>
> *At this juncture in my history, where the very gods clash and shatter in the maelstrom of their wars, I must introduce another pawn in their ineluctable machinations. Though he, unlike Elfloq, was never a willing protagonist.*
>
> —**Salecco**, whose own memory of companions grows fainter by the hour

* * * *

Tyrandire, the Palace of Pain, moves secretly and silently through unseen tunnels between the many dimensions of the omniverse, traversing any of them that its grim master wishes to visit. A minute moon, perfectly circular, colder than terror, Tyrandire speeds on its way like light, sometimes lingering like a biting frost. The energy that charges this oval missile is greater than that of any sun, indeed greater than the energy contained within an entire universe, for it is the will of the outlaw god, Ubeggi the Deceitful. Where Ubeggi seeks to go, his Palace of Pain takes him. He has many missions, all of them selfish, all of them corrupt, for the Weaver of Wars exists solely for his own amusement and he delights in knotting together the workings of more thoughtful gods or undoing their orderly tapestries of fate. All the gods know of Ubeggi, and when his Palace of Pain nears their own haunts in the omniverse, they curse him, knowing that his mischief will be upon them.

* * * *

Inside the Palace of Pain, Ubeggi entertained several visitors. (Those who came here could not rightly be termed guests, for Ubeggi admitted no equals.) These seven beings stood in an ovoid chamber near the heart of the Palace. Before them was no more than a shimmering image encased in a globe, a projection of a laughing face, though the laughter that shaped the face distorted its lines cruelly and made of it a mockery of amusement. Ubeggi often laughed, but his laughter was unique to himself, for others read into that laughter only terror.

Those who now stood before their master were not ordinary beings. They were creatures that had once been men, but whom Ubeggi had warped into hybrids for his own purposes. Blue-skinned, hairless, hunched as though they always walked in fear, they resembled demons, and indeed their nature was much akin to those evil beings. They had no hands, only a clutch of five small sickles where there fingers should have been. Those sickles were said to be capable of cutting in twain the web strands of the smallest spider.

"Well, my pretty Gelders," came the voice of Ubeggi from the globe. "What have you to report? Tell me of the places you have visited. What seeds of ill have you sown?"

At this, each of the Blue Gelders growled a short report: each of them had visited one of the many dimensions, searching out information, studying kings and empires, monarchs and dictators, sowing discontent, or noting where it simmered, ready to be brought to the boil. Ubeggi would evaluate all the news that his spies brought him and from it would initiate some new campaign of terror, aimed at bringing into conflict whole empires and even gods, for he was eager for new sport. It gave him the greatest pleasure to destroy the reputation of gods and turn their worshippers away from them.

As the last of the seven finished his report, Ubeggi nodded, musing on their words. "So, Cattapermennon still builds a star empire in Gorzendoom, does he? I think I shall let him consolidate his conquests a while longer. Shaddar H'mmil and his vermin grow stronger in the Well of Odak, too? And Aacrol of the Oceans grows weaker, does he? But, no, he is too feeble to warrant my attentions. Age will decay him, not I. I like the sound of the rebellion on Alendar. I've half a mind to spoil the Bloodwight dominion: Androzael grows fat and lazy there." Ubeggi deliberated long, but somehow none of the reports he had received filled him with the zest for a campaign.

"Wait, though. Were there not eight of you in the cell that I sent out?" he said. "Who is missing?"

The Gelders looked at each other unhappily. One of them spoke. "Orgoom, master. We awaited him as long as we dared without rousing your impatience, but he has not returned."

"From where?"

"From the universe of the Tree Citadel, Verdanniel," replied another.

Ubeggi mused on that. "I sent Orgoom there as an afterthought. Life on Verdanniel is not accustomed to war — the turmoil of growth, certainly — but a war as we know it would risk destruction to the great Tree and thus to all Verdanniel. And Verdanniel is little more than a gardener! He controls his subjects with great care. I wonder how my little Gelder has gone astray."

None could answer that, having been on other errands.

"A riddle, then," smiled Ubeggi. "Some good has come of your work. I will set to solving it. It may yet lead to a new game." With a final chuckle, he dismissed the relieved Gelders.

* * * *

Orgoom, in fact, was no longer in the universe of the Tree Citadel, to which his master had sent him, though he had of late been there, prying into its secrets and its intrigues. Curiously he now found himself floating in a most unique fashion in what appeared to be a void in space. Distance had blotted out the stars. He knew this must be an illusion, for he could breathe and was not cold. To be sure, he told himself uncomfortably, he was floating in an illusion, which could well be the working of Verdanniel, the all-encompassing god whose being made up the universe of the Tree Citadel, angered by the work of Orgoom. This was strange, though, for Orgoom had done no open harm (aside from prying into matters social and political) and it was not forbidden for astral travellers to pass across the Tree universe.

Orgoom fixed his attention on a point of light that grew. Now he became cold, prompted by fear, for the light formed itself into a long arm of impossible dimensions. It reached from the depths of space on a thin, tenuous thread and the hand touched the Gelder's chest. Its touch was clammy, unhealthy, as though blighted by plague. Orgoom screeched as it slithered over him like a tongue. Courage was not his forte.

"You have been exercising your insufferable curiosity again, have you not?" said a disembodied voice. Orgoom shivered: it was harsher and even more suggestive of pain than even the laughing voice of Ubeggi. More hands came snaking out of the night from infinity, dabbing and teasing at his flesh. He writhed.

"Who are you?"

"We are those who do the asking. We are the Divine Askers."

Orgoom gurgled with an even deeper-rooted fear, for these invisible horrors were the inquisitors of the Dark Gods, who none dared oppose.

"Why were you in the universe of the Tree Citadel?"

Orgoom had to watch his words. He dare not seek to outwit the Askers, but he would be thrice damned if he as much as whispered a word against Ubeggi. It was for such reasons that the ugly, blue-skinned Gelder loathed his position in life. He would gladly have become a dung roach had the opportunity been given to him. Clearly, though, such an opportunity was not about to present itself.

"Collecting information."

"For some reward?"

"Quiet life is all I want!" insisted Orgoom.

"Yet your master, Ubeggi, seeks anything but that, Gelder. What, we wonder, does he seek in the universe of Verdanniel?"

"Never told me, Just sent me."

"For an informer, Gelder, you are remarkably tight-lipped."

"Ubeggi just says go. Find out things."

"And what did you find out?"

"Trouble brewing. Verdanniel's creatures have been attacked. By others from outside."

"Describe these others."

Orgoom was anxious not to conceal anything, certain that these Askers already knew what he did. Why must they toy with a flea such as himself? "Warriors. Looking for conquest. Want to win Verdanniel."

"So you expect Ubeggi to foster a war there? One that would likely destroy Verdanniel?"

"Don't know. Just do my duty. Collecting information."

"Duty? To Ubeggi or to the Dark Gods? You cannot serve both, for they oppose each other."

Orgoom felt his bowels loosening. Here was a pretty dilemma. It seemed he must make a frightful choice. But the immediate threat was obviously the one to avert. "I am forced to obey those who prod me, masters. Dark Gods are omnipotent. Their will is my deed."

Soft laughter came from around the floating Gelder, but it chilled him just as if it had been his master's. "Go back to the Weaver. Encourage war in the universe of the Tree Citadel. Do all you can to persuade Ubeggi into it. Understand? Serve him well, and remember nothing of this meeting."

Orgoom felt the awful hands slithering off him and withdrawing. He was not to have his brains clawed open after all. The words were riddles, but what gods or divine messengers spoke otherwise?

"Go back to Ubeggi? It is done, masters."

* * * *

Again Orgoom felt hands of fear pulling at him, tightening his insides. An audience with Ubeggi never bred comfort or relaxation. Orgoom and his fellow Gelders snatched what comfort they could in numbers. However, to be stood before the Weaver of Wars on one's own, that was something to squeeze one's bladder. Orgoom trembled as the face in the huge orb glared at him.

"So you have deigned to return at last, little Orgoom. What has kept you so long? You must have a considerable amount to report."

Orgoom made several attempts to speak, failing each time and lapsing into a growling monologue in which his tongue contrived to knot itself around his thick lips. He was known for his lack of eloquence, but in his current state of fear he had surpassed even that in incomprehensibility. He did not want to blab about the Askers.

Ubeggi was in a patient mood, amused by the gibbering. "Come, come, little Orgoom! If it were not for the fact that you are one of my most successful Gelders, albeit reluctantly, I'd have had you killed off long since. I've a fancy you'd like that, though! You serve me well, so why fear me now? Come, say what you must! What is it that transpires in Verdanniel's universe?"

"W-w-war's a-brewing, master."

"How intriguing. I should have thought it the last place in the omniverse for violence. Have the plants developed teeth?"

"No, master. Outsiders have found a way in. Gates must be weak," Orgoom stuttered. "Tree creatures worried. Can't stop flow."

"Outsiders, you say? Who? Who are they? Describe them."

"Warriors. Thin and nimble. Black and gold armour. Swords like needles. One each side. Mean to steal the wealth of Verdanniel. Steal the blood of the Tree. Use it to grow strong, like gods. Build up their own empire." Orgoom was not given to long speeches, nor over-use of words, which were a premium with him, one serving where others would have used a score. But Ubeggi had a quicksilver mind that could assimilate information from a thousand sources in an instant. Orgoom's scant words were enough.

"Black and gold armour? Swords like needles, to suck out the blood of Verdanniel. The Tree is Verdanniel, its sap a unique potion. With sufficient of it, a nation could become like an army of demi-gods! Good! Do these warriors have a lord?"

"Don't know," mumbled Orgoom.

"Did the name, Mitsujin, reach your ears?"

The organs referred to seemed to quiver for a moment, as though a sullen bell had sounded close to them. "Yes, master! Heard it whispered by the leaves and in the branches."

"Mitsujin!" sighed Ubeggi. "A most ambitious conqueror. I have been watching his rise. Already, for one so young, he has branded together the warring nations of his own world, Oshotogi, and spread an empire far across his dimension. Almost as great an empire as those of Cattapermennon and Shaddar H'mmil I spoke of earlier. Well, I had thought I might extend their triumphs, but this ambitious Mitsujin excites me more. He has found a gate into Verdanniel? How very singular. Oh, this is a fine tale you bring me, after all, Orgoom! What a worthy vassal you are."

Orgoom grunted, which could have signified pleasure or relief.

"I will elaborate some plans," mused the Weaver. "Perhaps I can open still more gates for Mitsujin. Verdanniel must be getting careless. Well, we must have you sent to the warlord. I have words for him that you must carry."

Once Orgoom was dismissed, some time later, his heart beat less violently. His brush with the Divine Askers had not come out, nor should it need to now. Yet who would next pull the Gelder's strings? He muttered curses to himself and wished again for the guise of a worm or roach in some remote universe far from all conniving gods.

* * * *

When the god Verdanniel first entered the small universe that was later to become the universe of the Tree Citadel, it was empty and no more than a void, a pocket of nothingness. Verdanniel fashioned a large world and upon this planted himself in the form of a sprawling treegrowth. Into the earth of the world he had created, Verdanniel spread his roots, and across the surface of the world he spread his shoots. Into the skies he diffused countless clouds of his seed, so that in time all the heavens were seeded and other worlds were born and pollinated. All life that spread throughout Verdanniel's universe was rooted in Verdanniel, so that all that happened there was known to the Tree god. To be spread so far and wide taxed the god, though, for he had never been as formidable as many of the other gods, and certainly not one who cared for conflict.

In the Tree Citadel, which was the heart of this universe, there lived the tree beings, which were fragile and delicate, for their purpose was not to go forth and conquer the universe, but to nurture it and tend its rampant growth. These tree beings were the hands of Verdanniel: their strength came from the very sap of the god and they partook of it to the exclusion of any other nourishment. Its properties were unique and gave the tree beings their remarkable powers, which included an enduring life and healing abilities.

Verdanniel had closed up his small universe by sealing any gates that had led into it (such gates between dimensions and universes being the prerogative of gods throughout the omniverse). Thus there was no reason for him to suppose that anyone or thing would ever visit his enclosed universe again. As time passed, Verdanniel came to rely upon his tree beings more and more, himself dreaming lazily, content to do little more than produce the sap which sustained his universe. It was this sap that had drawn the attentions of Mitsujin.

The warlord had heard about it through legends, of course, but had never thought to find a key to the closed universe of the Tree Citadel. That he did so came about by chance (if one is naïve enough to believe in such a preposterous concept). Universes may be closed, but the one common link between them all is the astral realm, which is admittedly only accessible to certain gods and beings, such as elementals and familiars.

A certain tree sprite of Verdanniel used the astral to speed a long journey and was abducted by wraiths loyal to Mitsujin, whose allies numbered among them all manner of beings. It was this tree sprite that provided the eventual lever, which forced a minor gate into Verdanniel's universe. Hence the conqueror from Oshotogi sent his minions in to gather what sap of the Tree they could, for it would make supermen of his warriors. Now the warlord prepared to enter the universe of Verdanniel himself.

* * * *

The dark man opened his eyes, then closed them against the unaccustomed glare. Was this no more than a continuation of his confused dreams? But then he knew that it was not, for the unique sense of total awareness that came with each new entry into one of the many dimensions permeated his entire system. Gently he opened his eyes again, adjusted them, and sighed. Through a vivid green canopy of leaves, he could see a remote blue sky. This was not one of the darker dimensions, for looking about him he could see healthy vegetation. He stood upon a firm wooden rampart that appeared to be part of a living branch.

His first thought was, why was he here? Who had brought him out of the dream regions this time? No doubt the Dark Gods were behind it, for he was ever their pawn and they had thrust him into the many dimensions when it had suited them. He had no control over that, though he yet sought a way. Otherwise it could have been the scheming Elfloq, the winged familiar who had never been averse to goading both men and gods into invoking the Voidal before now. But there was no sign of the squamous little figure.

The Voidal decided it must be the work of the Dark Gods. Until he had performed some grim, unwitting deed, he must remain here. His memory had been partially restored, and he had an abrupt vision of the terrible landscape of Vyzandine, volcano world of the fallen god, Krogarth, where he had lately endured the rigours of a hellish battle. Instinctively he examined his right hand. It was his own, restored in the aftermath of that terrible death struggle. So, the Dark Gods had kept their word. The Oblivion Hand, their hand, was no longer his burden.

However, in spite of the tropical humidity of this place, he felt a shiver: someone would likely die because of his coming, to feed the needs of his hidden masters. He felt the living wood beneath him stir like a branch in a breeze, as though it had read his troubled thoughts. Something fluttered nearby on wings as thin and brightly hued as a butterfly. He looked up to see a number of beings like plants. They eddied around him closer and he saw that they were hemispherical sacs with clusters of bright pink petals spreading from their tops: these pulsed gently and acted as wings.

"Who are you, and why have you come to Verdanniel?" the whispering voices asked him. He knew at once that it was these flying things, their words a susurration, an echo inside his head.

"How did you enter the universe of the Tree Citadel?" came another voice.

The dark man shook his head. "I cannot answer any of your questions. I have little control over what happens to me."

He could sense the floating creatures trying to probe what must be held in his mind, but they trembled with puzzlement, for it could be no more than a pool of dark turmoil to them, as it was to him.

"You must come with us to the Hollow of Thought."

He had no alternative, and besides, no riddles could be answered until he had acquired certain information. The hovering tree beings floated around him, edging him along the wooden ramparts of this strange place. As he walked, he discovered that he was on a fantastically interwoven highway of thick branches, none of which appeared to be attached to a visible trunk. Above and below him much of this peculiar arboreal architecture was obscured by thick fronds and leaves, together with an abundance of exotic blooms and flowers that shone with colours of every conceivable hue. The dark man had never before seen such a breathtaking display of vegetation. Somehow it seemed to be part of one colossal parent plant.

There were places along the vertiginous journey where water fell from above, and in the curves and dips on the branches pools of trapped moisture had formed. The air was clamorous with the cries of birds, the plumage of which vied in splendour with that of the foliage. From far below him, the dark man could hear the answering hoots and shrills of yet more indigenous creatures.

Soon the hovering plants stopped. Before them the tangled framework of branches parted to form a natural clearing. Above was a circle of clear blue sky, ringed by waving leaves, while below all was lost in a hazy distance where the endless branches and shoots tangled anew in an artificial floor. In the centre of this clearing rose what at first appeared to be a green column, but which was in fact another plant, like an unripe trunk. A single branch, no wider than two men, grew outwards towards this silent plant, ending yards from it like an unfinished pier. The dark man realised that he was expected to walk out over the dizzy drop and stand before the plant. He did so.

As he waited, balanced on the very edge of the branch, a number of translucent tendrils undulated across to him. He fought the urge to defend himself or run from them and waited. They tickled across his face, gentle as a lover's hands, then softly parted his hair, affixing themselves with infinite care to his scalp.

"You do not fear me?" It was a question, as well as a voicing of surprise.

"I do not fear that which I know nothing of," replied the Voidal.

"A unique reply, for men usually fear most what they do not understand," mused the mental voice.

"I am not as other men."

"Indeed? My children would seem to agree, for they tell me that your head is full of screaming colours and thoughts that conflict and drift apart. But you do not have the appearance of a madman. Have you, perhaps, been touched by some god?"

"I fear so," nodded the Voidal. "I am used."

There was a long pause, as though the two minds were studying each other. That of the plant seemed to sigh. "The mysteries locked within you remain closed to me. It must be, therefore, that you are what you say."

"Who are you?" the dark man asked.

"I am Verdanniel, god of this universe. You see now why your are a puzzle to me. What other god or gods have you brought into my realm?"

"Their names and identities are as much a secret to me as my own. If you cannot read the answers for yourself, Verdanniel, I cannot tell you."

This was apparently good enough for the Tree god. "Dark things are happening in my universe. Events transpire here which are not rooted in my designs. This is strange, for all that occurs should be through me. You are not the first recent intruder."

Across the drop, the dark man saw leaves unfolding above him. From out of their centre depended a stalk, upon the end of which dangled a light green pod. It opened as it swung over the drop. Inside was what appeared to be the body of an imp, blue-skinned and inordinately ugly. Its hands terminated not in fingers, but in five small sickles.

"Is this an accomplice?" asked Verdanniel.

The dark man shook his head at sight of the motionless figure, which was either dead or unconscious. "I have no recollections of this creature, though my memory is incomplete."

"It came to the Tree Citadel with a prophecy. That my enemies would have aid in destroying me, aid from outside. It said that some evil god would assist in my destruction. Are you that god?"

Ripples of unease spread throughout the Voidal's frame, for it was conceivable that the Dark Gods had brought him here to destroy Verdanniel. "You must seek the answer to that in the mind of the imp," he replied, "for again, I cannot answer."

"I see that I must." Verdanniel lowered the dangling pod and set it down upon another jutting branch, close to that which sustained the Voidal. The imp was not dead, for as the pod withdrew, he stirred, then sat up dazedly, staring around in horrified amazement. The first words that passed his lips were gruff and obscene. He rose to his feet and hissed at the air creatures, his sickle-fingers zipping through the air in several wild passes.

"Do you know me?" the Voidal challenged him.

On seeing the black-garbed man and the tendrils about his head, the imp drew back with another curse. His sickles were before him defensively. "Who are you? Tree god?"

"You prophesied that one would come here — am I he?" said the dark man.

"Who is your master? Say who and I'll say if I know you."

"Say, rather, who is your master," demanded the Voidal.

The imp spat accurately over the lip of the branch. "Don't know you, nor you I. No words for you, or the trees!"

Verdanniel's voice returned to the dark man's head. "So it would seem you are not allies."

The Voidal shook his head. "I think not."

"Lost!" called the imp. "Never wanted to come here. Let me be."

The Voidal spoke softly to the Tree god so that the imp could not hear his words. "Release him. Perhaps he will lead you to his master, if he is here."

"You are the only interloper in my universe, save for the minions of the warrior lord, who seek my lifeblood."

"Who are they?"

"You know them not? They serve Mitsujin, a conqueror from another dimension who has ruptured a way into me. He seeks my precious sap which would strengthen his armies a thousandfold."

"Then this imp must be his slave —"

"Not so. The prophecy of the imp was intended for the ears of Mitsujin, not for me. The promised aid was for this intruding conqueror. The evil god that seeks my downfall promises aid to Mitsujin."

The Voidal began to feel that perhaps he had not been sent here to destroy Verdanniel after all. More likely the Dark Gods had set him up against this Mitsujin. But who was it that was to aid Mitsujin?

Verdanniel read each thought that passed coherently through the Voidal's mind. "Perhaps, dark man, you will aid *me* and stand with me against this conqueror from Oshotogi?"

"If I am able to do so, I shall. Tell me all that you know of the intruders."

"Very well, but first let the imp go. His flight may teach us more."

The Voidal gestured to the blue-skinned being, who growled something before skulking along the branch out of sight.

* * * *

The forest stretched out along the very crest of the low hills and spilled over the last of them like a long green wave, dipping down to a wide valley floor where the trees ended. The valley became a plain that spread for miles into the hazy distance and from that haze there arose tall mountains — or so they seemed. The army that was encamped in the forest at the foot of the hills looked out at those barely visible mountains across the plain and knew that they were not mountains at all, but the remarkable sky-piercing entanglements of the Tree Citadel, that colossal vegetable structure that was the very essence of Verdanniel himself.

In his tent, the warlord, Mitsujin, spoke confidently with his chieftains. He had entered Verdanniel's universe with a fanatical horde, personally coming to mastermind the draining of priceless sap from the body of that vast, tranquil god. The gate that had punctured the perimeters of Verdanniel's universe had been widened. The Tree god had been caught unawares by the blight that had been used and had acted too late to halt the torrential flow of Mitsujin's warriors. The warlord, his veins afire with the belief that his own passionate gods would be with him, would stop at nothing. He would succeed, or die gloriously in battle and thus sit alongside the terrible gods of Oshotogi.

A shout from outside brought Mitsujin to his feet. He was lithe and alert, the twin blades at his sides always a mere second from his grasp. He snatched aside the flaps of the tent.

"Someone crosses the plain — alone," came the message.

Presently Mitsujin and a heavy escort stood on a knoll overlooking the dip in the landscape that reached as far back as the distant Tree Citadel. The warlord could see the tiny figure in the distance. He motioned riders out to it.

Soon they returned, escorting the surly, blue-skinned Gelder, Orgoom.

"Words for Mitsujin, no other," spat the Gelder, apparently contemptuous of the countless blades that surrounded and menaced him.

Mitsujin stood before him, dwarfing him. He glared down, face an emotionless mask. "Well?"

"I serve Ubeggi, the Weaver of Wars," began Orgoom.

Mitsujin's heart gave a lurch, for he had heard of this fearful warrior god. But his face remained like stone. He waited.

"Ubeggi seeks the fall of Verdanniel. Will aid you."

This appeared to be the entire message. Mitsujin considered it, then gave a hint of a bow. "You must excuse my impertinence, voice of Ubeggi, but why should such a divine overlord aid a mere maggot of the soil such as I?"

"Ubeggi asks only that you swear fealty to him and no other, once you have conquered here. Discard the gods of Oshotogi, for all gods are the enemies of the Weaver of Wars. One by one he will eliminate them," Orgoom concluded with a hawk.

A muted roar went up from the yellow and black ranks of the warriors who heard this blasphemy. Mitsujin stilled them all with a motion of his hand. He indicated his tent. "Please enter," he told Orgoom. "We will talk further privately."

Orgoom grunted, confident that his master's will would be enforced. No one refused to serve the Weaver of Wars, least of all those whose very existence thrived on conquest, for Ubeggi was generous to those who did his killing.

As Mitsujin and the Blue Gelder went into the tent, the warriors went back to their waiting. None noticed the plant creature drift upward on a breeze and float far away towards the remote Tree Citadel, the words it had heard still clear in its mind.

Some time later Mitsujin emerged from his tent. At once he called all his chiefs to him and they gathered before a small hill at the edge of the forest to hear his words. The warlord stood with legs apart, arms on hips, glaring almost insolently at his men as though daring them to challenge him, even though he had not yet spoken. Behind him stood the surly Gelder, his features puckered in a permanent scowl.

"Hear me!" Mitsujin roared in a voice that would have shouted down the wind. "I have reached a decision. We are to march on the Tree Citadel and take what we will of its vital juices. Verdanniel will gather himself to oppose us, and there will undoubtedly be a bloody battle. Many of you will die."

This was greeted with cheers, for the men of Mitsujin were eager to die for their wild causes.

"To die in such a battle would indeed be glorious, but far greater the glory if we triumph. We must do so! Vaster rewards await us should we drink deep of Verdanniel's precious sap. Then we would be truly invincible. Is this not a prize worthy of any endeavour, and of any price?"

The reply was unanimous in its agreement.

"There is one who will secure our victory. The greatest god of war in the entire omniverse! To find favour with him, to be chosen to serve him, imparts riches beyond belief. Is there a warrior here who could resist such an honour? Is there a warrior here who could name a greater honour?" Mitsujin shouted defiantly at them, his face drawn into a veritable mask of war, his manner terrible to behold.

No one dared to speak. But the silence was eloquent.

"We knew that it was time we rose above our past. In Oshotogi we were heroes, smiled upon by the gods there. But see! We have outgrown our old home. We reach for greater glories. We have outgrown the old gods! They have no power here. If we triumph over Verdanniel — when we do so — we shall be *greater* than the old gods! We need not die to stand beside them, but living, stand over them. We have been watched and are favoured by the Weaver of Wars!"

The warriors thought on this, many nodding, some keeping their faces absolutely impassive. Mitsujin did indeed resemble a god, as though he had only to lift his hand for mountains to fall. In his own mind, he was a god already.

"Are we united?" he cried. "Do we wish to become more than men? Will we acknowledge the frightful might of Ubeggi and swear fealty to him? Will we accept the glories he will heap upon us? Climb from your modest stations with me and we will stride among the stars! Accept the terms!"

If there were dissenters in all that massed gold and black, their doubts were lost in the savage shout of compliance from the majority. The warriors chose to stand with Mitsujin, and thus Ubeggi: the glories of conquest were like an aphrodisiac to them.

Mitsujin turned to the Blue Gelder. "Go back to your master. He has our answer. We dedicate our coming victory to him."

* * * *

The Voidal stood upon a high place, looking out from the last of the branches at the flat landscape so far below. Verdanniel had had him brought here to the outer ramparts of the Tree Citadel to let him look out over the world and see the coming of the enemy. It was as though the dark man stood on a high mountain ledge, studying the colossal drop to the lowlands. Green earth spread away to hazy distance, like a detailed map. There were low hills and a small range of mountains some thirty miles across the plain, stained dark by plentiful forests. It was there, said Verdanniel, that the enemy was gathered.

All around the Voidal the plant beings hovered in the air, as thick now as windblown seeds. They would be the Tree God's defenders, but they had such little strength for conflict. The dark man sensed the despair and acute anxiety of the Tree god, for Verdanniel had never designed his world for contest. It had never been anything but peaceful.

"I must revitalise powers within me that I had thought never to use again," said Verdanniel. "I came here and built this universe to escape the strivings of my fellow gods. Their constant warring appalled me; they were never satisfied with the powers they had. I am afraid that my own powers are devoted now to creation, nurture and healing. This Mitsujin frightens me to my very roots."

"And you say that the Weaver of Wars is the most powerful of all the gods?" the Voidal asked, having heard the report of the plant being that had drifted across the great plain from Mitsujin's war camp.

"Perhaps. He is at least the most reckless, the most bellicose. If Ubeggi is to aid the conqueror, my very existence is threatened. I cannot guess what Ubeggi will send against me."

"Why should this god seek your death?"

Verdanniel sighed deeply. "It is his only purpose, to destroy all those around him, or bend and warp them to his will. To undo the works of others. All gods delight in creation and are driven from within to perform wonders. But Ubeggi is driven by a lust for destruction. What others build, he will pull down. In this he is alone, but nonetheless powerful for all that."

"You speak as though you are already doomed," said the Voidal.

"I will fight. For the lives of my offspring."

"Are there no gods who will aid you?"

Again Verdanniel sighed. "I chose to live here in isolation from them all. I spurned them and their war-like ways. They would certainly spurn me now if I called upon them for aid."

"And yet," mused the Voidal, "the Dark Gods have sent me here. For what reason, do you suppose?"

"I have been alone with my universe for timeless ages. Your identity, your past, are unknown to me. If I knew these secrets, I would impart them to you, even though that would seem to be angering these Dark Gods. Yet I do sense that you are here to aid me, rather than to contribute to my undoing."

The Voidal nodded. "The Dark Gods seem cruel and unwavering in their purpose. Yet my fractured memory suggests that those they destroy work for evil ends. Perhaps they seek to undo Ubeggi."

"All gods curse him and seek to destroy him, for he seeks to destroy them."

The dark man mused on that. The riddle would not be answered until the battle began. Below him now he could see movement on the plain. Like a mighty column of ants, the vast host of Mitsujin was approaching.

"I will begin it," said Verdanniel. "If I attack them before they reach me, surprise may yet unseat their initiative."

The Voidal studied his right hand. It had remained as it was when he had first opened his eyes here, his own hand. He lowered it, instinctively fitting his palm to the grip of his sword. He looked down at the weapon, noticing it for the first time. He knew that the Dark Gods possessed thirteen blades, each with a powerful property. Often when he woke in one of the many dimensions, he wore one of them at his side. And this blade? His hand tightened on the haft, which was cold. With a certainty, he knew that this was the Sword of Ice, though why it should be so was yet another riddle.

Down on the plain, Mitsujin rode proudly at the head of his army, his confidence ablaze like a sun, his destiny assured. Verdanniel was a peaceful god who had done no more than sleep for millennia. What could such a bloated vegetable offer in the way of resistance to such an oncoming army of fanatics? Mitsujin was soon to know.

The Voidal saw the van of the army clearly now. At the feet of the Tree Citadel something strange was happening. The land was flat, but odd hummocks were moving across it like ripples on a pond, very slowly.

These grew in number to become a procession of barrow-like humps, spreading outward to meet the front ranks of the army. Verdanniel was defending himself.

Mitsujin was the first to see the green waves approaching. His horse reared up as though sensing some awesome, primal force at work. It looked as though huge burrowing creatures were coming upon the army. Mitsujin drew his gleaming blade and whirled it defiantly. The first hummock shook the earth and then its crest split open like a ripe fruit. From out of it shot a curling root, three times thicker in the middle than a man's waist. It flicked across the heads of the warriors and lashed down at them. From a score more of these undulating hummocks, tendrils burst, lashing at the army with their slender whip— tails. The warriors cut into them wildly, relieved to be in a battle, thriving on the confusion.

Only the savage ferocity of the fanatics saved them from a terrible mauling by these whiplash roots. Men tumbled from their steeds as the ground heaved like a sea swell. Mitsujin sought a high place on which to rally his men, but the ground kept altering. He was forced to defend himself. The roots, however, cut up easily in spite of their girth. Verdanniel strove to keep as many of the tendrils attacking as he could, but they were being systematically hacked apart, Mitsujin's army organising itself efficiently under its many chiefs.

The Voidal sensed the agony coursing through the entire Tree Citadel as it sent out these roots to defend itself. Presently he noticed two new factors in the battle. Firstly, a dark cloud scudding quickly across the battlefield, fanned by an astral wind. From out of this pall dropped scores of figures. Secondly, the Voidal saw what looked like a small moon hovering high up in the blue, a silent observer.

The leaves around the Voidal trembled with fear and the bough on which he stood shivered. "Fire elementals!" said Verdanniel, horrified. "And above us, Ubeggi watches like a hawk preparing to dive. There is nothing more destructive to me than fire!"

"I must join the battle," said the Voidal. "Can your creatures set me down amongst the fray?"

Verdanniel marshalled a number of his floating creatures and the Voidal caught hold of the tendrils that hung beneath them. He clung on as they drifted out over the great drop, spiralling down with their human load.

Mitsujin gave a hoarse shout of joy when he saw the terrible allies that Ubeggi had sent him. Taller and thinner than men, the fire elementals sliced about them with blazing rods that charred and burned the roots that were still bursting up from the earth. The elementals took a frightful delight in setting ablaze the roots, driving them back into their burrows.

The earth was scorched and fires began to lap forward in a yellow tide towards the Tree Citadel, the base of which was now no more than a mile away.

The Voidal dropped down in the thick of the battle, pulling out the Sword of Ice. It was evident now how he must use it. The warriors around him were too busy defending themselves to question him, thinking him another of the allies sent by Ubeggi, for they expected no men in this world, only Verdanniel's creatures. The dark man made his way through the dead and the struggling to one of the fire elementals. It stood a head taller than him and its scaled armour steamed.

The Sword of Ice hissed through the air and cut deep into the trunk of the snarling being, drinking deep of the elemental energy. The fire fiend screamed in a terrible fashion as it felt all the heat sucked out of it by the blasting fury of a frost colder than the void between universes. It turned a look of concentrated agony on the man who had seared it.

"Voidal!" it spat, collapsing. The dark man rushed forward to the next of the fire elementals, but already they were wary of him and the devastating weapon he bore. Verdanniel's roots were all slithering away in retreat, crippled by the fires, but from the skies there now fell countless numbers of the tree creatures. From small sacs beneath them there burst clouds of poison seeds. Choking cries of alarm went up from the warriors beneath. Fire elementals tossed blazing balls up at the clouds and sheets of flame engulfed many of the creatures.

Several of the fire fiends converged on the Voidal, their glowing rods thirsting for him. He cut at them with the Sword of Ice and they drew back in mad-eyed horror, knowing its colossal power. Two more of them died in shrieking agony as they felt the killing bite of the ice weapon. But one of them ran in behind the dark man in triumph and crashed his rod down on the Voidal's shoulders. Flames licked upwards at once and in a moment the Voidal had become a human torch. Yet still he attacked. Astounded, the fire elementals pulled away. Mitsujin's warriors fled from the burning man, waiting for him to fall, but he did not. He could not.

Holding his weapon before him, he let it suck into it the flames that formed the blaze about him, and like a candle snuffed by a breeze, the fires disappeared. In the vacuum, it was clear that the Voidal was unmarked. It was not to be his fate to perish here, just as he had known. He looked up. Many of the fire elementals had taken to the air, buzzing like angered hornets. They vented their anger and frustration on the clouds of plant creatures, frying many of them, sending the scalded vanguard back to the Tree Citadel in a second defeat. Beyond the elementals, the Voidal could see yet more clouds of them bursting in from the astral, fanned by the anger of the Weaver. The Voidal could never hope to stem the flow. Verdanniel needed far more help than he could provide.

From the ranks of the warriors, Mitsujin came into view, swords a-gleam. He stared at the Voidal, his face a malign war mask, emblazoned with killing fury. "Who are you that opposes us?" he snarled.

"Go back through your gate to Oshotogi and ask forgiveness of the gods you have deserted," the Voidal answered.

Mitsujin sneered derisively. "Go back! When we stand on the brink of victory? Ubeggi favours us now. See, his eye watches us. You go back to your Tree lord, man of shadows. Tell him that when we have drained him, we will make of him the greatest pyre in history!"

The Voidal shook his head, stepping toward the warlord. To kill him might end this war, for the warriors would almost certainly disperse like a serpent with no head. But as he moved, he recalled a part of the Dark Gods' decree: he could not die, neither could he kill. He had destroyed the fire elementals with the Sword of Ice, it was true, but could he kill a man? On his bizarre wanderings, he had struck down other creatures, but never a man. Did Mitsujin know this?

The warlord met the Voidal's attack with a grim smile. The Sword of Ice and the curved blades of the former met and clanged. Both swordsmen fought for supremacy, but they were too well matched. Around them the warriors watched, agog at the ferocity of the combatants, none daring to interfere. Although Mitsujin cut at the Voidal many times in that tireless contest, he could not make a killing blow, though five times he was certain that he had done enough to kill him. He drew blood, but the black cloak of the dark man flapped about him, obscuring the view of any damage inflicted. Likewise, the Voidal bettered the guard of his opponent more than once, but somehow his weapon never found its mark. What devious game were the Dark Gods playing?

As the fight dragged on, its pace still furious, the warriors were not prepared to lose the initiative given them by the fire elementals. They continued their drive on Verdanniel. The Voidal realised his error, for he would remain deadlocked with Mitsujin and thus be unable to protect the Tree god from the elementals, who were closing in. Ubeggi must be smiling. Mitsujin realised too, and it suited him well, for he was glad to keep this stranger at bay while the siege began.

Again the skies opened to disgorge another force, but this was very unlike the first. Great ghostly shapes towered up like spilling waves after an earthquake. In their aerial foam, frightful visages glared down upon the army, visages that were huge celestial mirrors of the war masks worn by the warriors. And the warriors saw in those baleful glares the familiar anger of the gods of Oshotogi. They had come to exact their revenge on those who had discarded them. The warriors looked to Mitsujin, but he was deadlocked impotently in the struggle with the dark man.

From the mouths of the gods came great shrieks of howling wind, which took the fire elementals and hurled them back across the plain for miles, shredding them into no more than wisps of smoke. Many more of them burst out of this world and back on to the astral, as much afraid of these gods as of Ubeggi's wrath. On the plain now, all was chaos. When the warriors of Mitsujin saw their vengeful gods blast aside the aid sent by Ubeggi, they broke their ranks and fled in every direction, most of them rushing back the way they had come. Verdanniel, still smarting from the fires that had threatened to engulf his outer ramparts, withdrew the last of his plant creatures. The army was breaking up before Ubeggi could send reinforcements, if he wished to. No one could know his mind.

Mitsujin cursed his erstwhile gods aloud.

The Voidal watched as they descended as hurricane winds upon the disorganised rabble that had been the army. Why did Ubeggi not act? Surely he would send forth some final horror to attack these gods. But the gods of Oshotogi went unchecked in their rage. Mitsujin's forces were totally demoralised, hundreds of them trampled to death by their companions. Mitsujin's name was screamed aloud as a curse. In the sky, the false moon that was the Palace of Pain disappeared.

Mitsujin turned to the Voidal. Now only the dead and dying surrounded them, for the army had already drained away like water into the earth. "Ubeggi has lied! Where is the honour in that! The Weaver of Wars is a false god to desert his servants like this! See, the gods of Oshotogi are jealous masters. They have won back their flock!" the warlord shouted above the scream of the winds.

The Voidal said nothing, watching the return of the towering cloud masses. Each of the six god-figures, sculpted in thunderheads, pointed down at Mitsujin. "You have chosen another god, Mitsujin," rolled a voice like thunder. "You perverted our children, and we will chastise them for their faithlessness. They will serve us anew, with more humility. But know this — you, we abjure. We leave you to your new master."

They said no more, but simply wafted apart, broken up by the breeze that replaced the dreadful hurricane blasts. Mitsujin watched them dissipate and laughed. "Hah! So they abjure me. And I them." He spun to face the Voidal. "I have failed. And you have triumphed. You drew me away from my purpose so that my warriors would founder on doubt. Who is your master, dark man?"

"I serve no man. I am the Voidal."

Mitsujin's voice changed on hearing the name. "*Voidal?*" he breathed, the word almost inaudible. Terror fought to grip him, but his self-control was remarkable. He kept his face still. "Then I could never have killed you. I should have know that when the fire failed to devour you."

"Nor could I have killed you," returned the dark man.

"Has Ubeggi the deceitful sent you, then, to shatter my army? Was this all a trick to wipe away my ambitions?"

"I fought for Verdanniel. Ubeggi did not betray you."

Mitsujin turned and looked up at the enormous mass of the Tree Citadel. "Then I will enter that place and take what I sought. Or will you stay me?"

The Voidal would have answered, but the air fizzed with sudden life. A group of figures stepped into view as though from nowhere. They were astral travellers. Blue Gelders. Orgoom was with them, skulking at the back.

They walked in silence to Mitsujin, enclosing him in a half circle.

"Mitsujin!" growled their leader.

The warlord held up his blades and faced the Gelders as though preparing to engage. "Why has your master failed me? Why did he not smite asunder the gods of Oshotogi? They are nothing beside his powers!"

Sickle fingers flexed and gleamed.

"Ubeggi does not manipulate his servants like pieces of wood," said the spokesman. "He merely sets the board. The pieces must move themselves if they are to amuse Ubeggi. Those who win honours, receive even greater from him. It is not Ubeggi who has failed, but you, Mitsujin."

"I?"

"Your minions fled. If they had truly renounced the gods of Oshotogi and sworn loyalty to Ubeggi, they would have mocked the winds of your old gods, as you did. But they were fickle. True to their old gods when challenged. Such are not for Ubeggi. Why should he aid them? They had their chance."

"I remain loyal, willing to serve."

"Ubeggi knows this. You are to come with us."

The warlord's face was blank, though his mind worked furiously. Could this be further deceit?

It was the dark man who supplied the answer. "Forget your dreams of conquest, Mitsujin. Go with these and you will become a pawn for all their words. They say Ubeggi does not manipulate his servants, Look at *them*! They serve him and pander to his every whim. They are no more in command of their fate than am I."

Mitsujin scowled deeply. "Is this so?" he snapped at the Gelders.

"We are highly placed among Ubeggi's servants," said their leader. "To become a Gelder is to become one with Ubeggi."

"*To become* — I am to *become* like you?" gasped Mitsujin. "I am a warrior! A man! Am I to be emasculated, mutated!"

"It is an honour to be a Gelder."

Mitsujin spat contemptuously.

Orgoom, who had been silent, gave an involuntary grunt. The others turned to him. "Honour!" he said under his breath. "Curse, more like."

"It would seem you have a turncoat in your midst," the Voidal told the Gelders.

They glared at Orgoom, flexing their sickles. "Be silent, scum!" hissed their leader.

"Silent too long. Let me be a worm, or a beetle, or a clod of earth. Not Gelder," Orgoom went on, muttering to himself.

"Well spoken," the Voidal told him. "What say you to this, Mitsujin? Are you still eager to rush to the glory that awaits you?"

Orgoom shuffled close to the towering warlord. "Want to spend eternity skulking in dark places, feeding on offal and the curses of the omniverse? Want to be loathed more than vermin? Want to be a puppet, not even finding the comfort of death?"

"You've said enough!" snarled the leader of the Gelders and he jumped forward, tiny blades reaching out to punish. But one of Mitsujin's blades flashed up and met the sickles. Sparks danced.

"I'll answer you with steel," Mitsujin told the Gelders.

Orgoom seemed to be mumbling to himself. "I was a man once. Greedy. Thought I'd snatch power. Made me a Gelder. Gave me these blades. Made me do foul things —"

The Gelders began to laugh, but the sound was a disturbing gurgle in their throats. "Since you spurn us, warlord, we'll deal with you here." Their sickles opened and closed as they prepared to cut Mitsujin to pieces. Orgoom drew back, wanting no part of this.

Mitsujin answered the ugly laughter with a laugh of his own. His weapons were ready. He expected no quarter and no help from the Voidal. The dark man and Orgoom watched, for this was Mitsujin's fate, not theirs.

"We will not kill you, warrior, but cut away your manhood and leave you for the worms." More of the Gelders were appearing, as though Ubeggi had sent them from an invisible vantage point. A score of them closed in on Mitsujin and set upon him, but he attacked them with astonishing speed, slicing off hands and heads with either sword, howling with defiant joy at the contest.

Orgoom and the Voidal were not to remain onlookers, for another group of Gelders approached them.

"You cannot die, Voidal, until your appointed time. But we are assigned to meet out a punishment for your part in this abortive war. We will take from you that which the Dark Gods did not." They laughed, making crude gestures. The Sword of Ice readied, and in a moment he, too, fought furiously. Orgoom stood beside him, suddenly committed himself, for he had rejected the abysmal life he had led.

The three of them fought bitterly against terrible odds. Mitsujin hewed down innumerable Gelders, but was badly sliced by the slashing sickles that cut the air in efforts to hamstring him. The Voidal was also badly cut, his blood soaking the earth where he fought. Orgoom was nimble and fought well, skipping away from death, cheating it at every wild swipe. But he was not a prime target. The Voidal knew that he, himself, could not be maimed, but Mitsujin's life did hang in the balance. The warrior was glad of that, though, preferring death to the frightful punishment of the Gelders.

At last it was over. The Gelders abruptly drew off, fifty of their dead and crippled littering the plain. Perhaps Ubeggi was satisfied and tired of the fight, for the Gelders began to disappear, drawn back to the astral.

Mitsujin and the Voidal regarded each other, both ripped and blood spattered. The Voidal could see that Mitsujin was dying, his chest torn and gaping.

"I remain whole!" snarled the warrior. But he fell to his knees and looked up at the towering mass of the Tree Citadel. "I have rejected my gods and have been rejected by them. I have spurned Ubeggi's cruel life. I have sought the downfall of Verdanniel. Yet I ask of the Tree god, if he hears me, a last favour in life." He addressed this to the high ramparts overhead.

A voice drifted across on a light breeze, tired and heavy with unaccustomed pain. "Ask it."

"I am soon to die. Let me lie here and feed the earth. Let my blood help to atone for the ill I have caused."

Verdanniel answered. "It shall be so."

Mitsujin then placed the haft of his largest sword in the ground and fell upon it. His blood watered the charred earth as his life leaked away and the forgiving earth rose up to meet and embrace him.

Orgoom looked around him nervously. The real import of what he had done rushed in upon him like sudden nightfall. "Not for me such an easy exit," he mumbled.

"Nor for me," said the Voidal.

They heard a movement among the dying Gelders. One of them rose up, covered in its own blood. "You are cast out!" it spat through its pain. "Both of you! You are loved by none, rudderless and damned! The seas of Chance shall wreck you throughout eternity. Steer clear of the Weaver of Wars, if you can, or he will mete out to you a curse more terrible than any that has ever tortured your dreams before."

Orgoom rushed over and kicked the body, but the Gelder was already dead. The impetuous gesture amused the Voidal. This Gelder possessed an extraordinary spirit. Could there be stubbornness here to match that of the persistent Elfloq?

"Chance?" said the dark man. "No, it is not Chance that moves me. I would that it were. Though I will seek ways to win the favours of Chance."

Orgoom, who never smiled, tried to do so. "I'll take what Chance flings in my face. I'll sail her stormy sea gladly."

The Voidal nodded, then turned away in the direction of the Tree Citadel. Orgoom watched his back, then popped into the astral and to his freedom. The Voidal felt the sudden onset of exhaustion, wondering if he would reach Verdanniel and succour there, or if he would sink down into sleep, doubtless to awaken somewhere far, far from here.

Even as the thought took hold, he began to fall. The Dark Gods had acted for good here, he realised. They had thwarted evil. It was not the first time. They opposed evil and their own darkness was not symbolic of it, merely a cloud of mystery about them.

Did I once perform some great evil? He wondered. The crime that I committed, for which they punish me.

Sleep lapped over him. Already the dreams were beginning, smothering the lost secrets anew.

PART TWO

AT THE COUNCIL OF GOSSIPERS

> *In such a simmering cauldron of chaos as the omniverse, who should one trust? Gods, demi-gods, Man, the creatures that serve, where does faith begin and caution end? Indeed, can one trust oneself?*
>
> *The Gods know well enough our weaknesses. Being so armed, they manipulate us easily. As they do our humblest of servants.*
>
> *They certainly knew the mind of Elfloq, regardless of its extraordinary deviousness. And there is no denying, a familiar never changes it scales.*
>
> —**Salecco**, no longer trusted by anyone, probably for good reason.

* * * *

Lost somewhere in the impenetrable vastness of the astral realms lies an old world of dust and shadows that no longer has a name, a world that was once firmly rooted in one of the many dimensions, but which now has faded not only from human memory but also from corporeal existence. On the astral realm it is real enough, though even here it fades like a neglected memory, or a simple act of no significance beyond recall. Its very obscurity and lack of character have, however, paradoxically won for it a small if occasional band of adherents. These gather here but rarely, having no wish to advertise their coming, or their activities. They are by nature and purpose secretive beings: indeed, their lives are devoted to secrets and the gleaning of forbidden knowledge. Only on the rarest of occasions do they share these secrets with other than their masters. Their visits to this remote extremity take the form of unique gatherings, Councils, for it is for the express purpose of bartering their gleanings that they come. Between themselves, they have no other coin but knowledge, its metal usually of the censored kind.

* * * *

It was at the *Inn With No Sign* that Elfloq first came upon the Blue Gelder.

This hostelry, if one could describe it so grandly, nestled, so to speak, in a cranny of the astral realm that was truly off the beaten track. Its lack of hubbub and babble suited the withdrawn nature of its customers, most of who came here to escape a dreary life and find solitude of a kind. Elfloq, however, called in from time to time on the off chance that he might just turn over a stone that would otherwise be unmoved.

The familiar found himself drawn to the Gelder almost at once. He knew a little about these beings and even less about their grim master, mostly from rumour and hearsay. Curiosity being one of the great motivators in Elfloq, it naturally prompted him to study the Gelder from the tiny bar, but he was conscious that it was more than this that had snared his attention. Elfloq, not himself being beautiful, discounted the Gelder's stunted physique, his resemblance to a blue-skinned demon. The Gelder was evidently in something of a state of confusion, not caused by his surroundings, as Gelders used the astral more often than the real dimensions, but by some internal conflict that lent an air of unusually heightened dejection to the being. This seemed doubly extraordinary in a Gelder, beings that were noted for their lack of emotional display.

"Pardon my rudeness," said Elfloq, mindful of the dreadful miniature sickles that were the Blue Gelder's elongated fingernails. "I see that you sip refreshment alone and ruefully, and appear to be in no hurry. I likewise have some time on my hands. May I join you?"

The Gelder nodded and muttered a gruff affirmative. Elfloq perceived at once that he was neither suspicious nor guarded. He appeared, rather, distracted.

"Of course," grinned the familiar, "I have better manners than to ask your current employment. That is your master's affair entirely. But I notice your diffidence. So out of sorts for one of your, ah, talents. Have you, perchance, fallen upon harsh terrain, so to speak?"

The Gelder sighed, an even sharper indicator that something was highly amiss. "Harsh? Not sure. Obscure, yes."

Encouraged by the fact that the Gelder had not simply dismissed him with a vicious swipe of those blades, Elfloq extended the conversation. "Your next move presents dilemma?"

The Gelder, typical of his kind, was not given to loquaciousness, but Elfloq was not put off by this, recognising a natural trait rather than an arbitrary one.

"Well," said the familiar, sharing the mood, "I am also in a dilemma. My master, a rare being indeed, often severs himself from me in such a manner that I have to spend all my energies merely seeking him, or word of him. A tedious business and an absurd waste of my talents."

"I have no master," said the Gelder bluntly. "Freed from him."

"Just so? Well, well." *This is indeed odd for a Gelder.* "I have been in such circumstances myself. An unstable predicament for such as you and I. So — you seek a new master?"

"None! Stay free. They are cruel. Find a dark world, live there. Stay."

Even more surprising, thought Elfloq. "Stay? Life will be short for you. We cannot survive without masters."

"Was once a man. Changed by evil power. Not like others of the astral places."

"Even so, life will take no pity on you. Who will protect you?"

"Better free than to serve the Weaver. That was bad."

Elfloq, a master at masking his emotions, feigned indifference. "Ah. The Weaver. Would that be the Light Weaver, or perhaps Stormweave of —?"

"Ubeggi," said the Gelder.

"The Weaver of Wars," added Elfloq, heart racing. *Then this horrific being does exist!* "You say you were freed by him?" Elfloq had actually heard the Gelder say that he had been freed *from* his master, a dimension of difference, but he continued to play at being naïve.

"Released by another," corrected the Gelder. "No retribution. Orgoom is free. Strange, to control myself. It has been long. A man long ago."

"What a blessing, to direct one's own steps! Who does not wish for such a pass? But, forgive me again, why should anyone take up your case and free you from so terrible a being as the Weaver of Wars? Does Ubeggi so tamely countenance the manumission of his slaves? Or was there a bargain struck?"

"Neither. Power did it. Immeasurable power."

This time Elfloq's inner excitement spilled out in nervous movement. "Immeasurable? Surely you exaggerate."

"Dark, fearful."

"Dark? Could it be that my very master — I mean, that is to say —" Elfloq looked furtively all about him, but no one in that remote place paid him any heed. He controlled his dancing nerves. "A dark man, perhaps? Green-eyed and bearing an ebon-hafted blade?"

Orgoom stared at him, then shuddered at the memory. It was answer enough.

Elfloq pondered this. This was becoming worryingly like one of those many coincidences that threaded his life. Except that coincidences tended to be something very different. *In which case*, he wondered, *who is weaving what?* When he spoke again, it was to steer the conversation elsewhere. "Your past is doubtless intriguing. But you must look to your future. You must savour it, as it is yours alone! Free — the very thought! You are uniquely blessed among our kind. It would be detestable to think of your not capitalising on your opportunity. Let me offer you advice — freely and gladly."

"Well?"

"I am bound for the Council of Gossipers. You know of it? It is held only occasionally. But there we of the astral exchange news, fables, tales, histories, spells, whatever we can. Why not bring your story along? Deliver it to the Council, sparing no detail, and to you will be imparted such knowledge as you need to construct a solid and curse-free future. Well?"

"Why should you help me?" replied Orgoom, suddenly unleashing suspicion that had evidently been slumbering within him like a guard hound.

"Your story intrigues me. I would hear it all. But naturally I could not expect you to impart it to me for nothing. You must profit by it."

"Said too much already."

"Enough to captivate me. But, you see, I have almost nothing to tell you in return. My own life is so dull. But at the Council — why, we can feast on stories. I will spin yarns that will win me a share of the spoils."

Orgoom evinced a little more animation at this. "Why not?" he said at last, with another of those eccentric sighs, though there was no semblance of a smile.

Elfloq remained baffled. Could it be this easy to manipulate the Gelder? Yet without further ado their irregular companionship was struck and they set out for the Council of Gossipers.

* * * *

As they traversed the astral limbo, Elfloq, whose perceptiveness had been honed to the finest edges by a life of danger and skulduggery of an often insolent nature, began to notice the subtle stirring of some colossal force around him, as though he passed through the chasms of an immense heart, its pumping a deep undercurrent to the entire astral realm and probably well beyond. It did not, he thought, presage an immediate or even imminent presence, but took the substance of some far-flung dimensional disturbance. Of course, he himself had been embroiled in more than a few of these himself. Extreme caution was, therefore, a constant necessity. Even so, his instincts warned him of something abnormally immense, cosmic, implying somehow the inescapable involvement of many things, no doubt himself included.

He thought of his master, and of the Oblivion Hand, which the Voidal had sought to cast from him. Did it yet stir, crawling back inevitably to him? On Intercelestis, he seemed to have won free of it, as Orgoom had won free of his master. But the Dark Gods were fickle. And what of the Sword of Shadows, the key to the Voidal's soul? Elfloq had been warned from pursuing it, and yet its mysteries lured him, never far from his mind.

He said nothing about any of this to the Gelder. It seemed that a hard life had had an opposite effect on Orgoom, blunting his senses and narrowing his insights, so that he was aware of little of the external worlds, apparently withdrawn and introspective. Elfloq, who had good reason to prefer his own faith in divine interference rather than blind coincidence, may have done better to question his meeting with the Gelder more fully, but his hunger to reach the Council of Gossipers and his greed to unravel more secrets hampered any possibility of cool objectivity.

* * * *

Familiar and Gelder threaded through wispy veils of mist until at last Orgoom looked down and drew in a breath at what he saw. They were above a world, closer to it than he would have guessed, and on its obscured surface could be seen one particular object, raised up like a hill of the most unseemly proportions.

"Ah," grinned Elfloq, "the Egg of Echoes. Once laid by a messenger bird of the Blind Gods of Allwang. Petrified now like stone, its embryo long since grown to adulthood and departed. Which is just as well."

It was certainly an egg, but one such as Orgoom had never dreamed of. Its size would have laughed at a substantial palace, castle or fortress, and human engineers would have been at a loss to design and build its twin. The Gelder fought an impulse to contemplate the dimensions of the creature that must have produced such an egg.

As they dropped closer to it, its arc grew and Orgoom saw what he took to be innumerable tattoos and designs all over it, but closer inspection revealed these to be miniature cracks, as if time would at last have its way and disintegrate the vast shell. Elfloq led them to a jagged orifice down in the central shadows, and they went inside.

Internally it was lit by living creatures: hundreds of them lined the walls high up, and if Orgoom had been more travelled, he would have recognised tiny starflies from Emberdoom, fireweed from Xenidorm's hot worlds and lightworms, all of which cast a shimmering glow like a thousand candles. The immensity of the Egg of Echoes shrank in this ethereal light, so that the gathered host of the Gossipers' Council did not seem so small. This varied multitude perched, sat and hovered about a central area, a tapestry of eon-toughened wood, the last tree of the world of the Egg. In the shadow it seemed to rise up like a canopy of girders that held together the sweeping, concave walls.

Elfloq guided Orgoom to a place on one of the countless branches, wrinkled and bare of leaf like the skin of an impossibly old crone. They looked and listened. All manner of familiar, elemental and underling had come. Already the self-styled masters of the Council had taken their places and were running things as they saw fit. Foremost of these was Ecclesiastro, a tall and skinny familiar of one of the much-vaunted Priest-Sorcerers of Jagg-Illgash, a particularly powerful world of old magics. The respected familiar (he was taller than most and could claim to have possibly the most exalted master of them all) was talking now in a piercing voice that reached every inch of the cathedral-like eggshell. He struck Elfloq as being almost human, which was doubtless one of his mantles of power.

"I am delighted to see such a great number of you, brethren. How you slip your masters' bonds to be with us always amazes me, but there it is. Welcome. Let us hope we may all benefit from this particular Council. We will begin, as is traditional, with major issues, and after that you may squabble among yourselves, as is also traditional." There was polite laughter at this: no one dared to argue with Ecclesiastro, and besides, they were all notorious hagglers, their prerequisite for survival. "Then you may extort from each other whatever particles of information you may."

Elfloq turned to Orgoom with a wry grin. "And now I suggest we each take a turn to nap. It will be a long time before someone decides to offer what he knows of events in the many dimensions. No one likes to be first. This is one occasion when it is a positive advantage to be last."

Orgoom shrugged. "I will speak if it will be of benefit. Must leave soon. Too big a gathering to escape ears of the gods."

Elfloq's tiny hand clapped over the Gelder's ugly mouth. "Say no more! Everyone has enchanted ears in this place!" he whispered fiercely. "You know much. So do I — in my way, that is. But we'll not toss it away for trifles. There is richer profit to be made. Bargaining is a skill, nay, an art form. I pride myself on my mastery of it. I mean to leave here with a library of fresh knowledge. You are part of my collateral. And I yours, for you shall be rich, too. So — listen, say nothing, and wait!"

Orgoom nodded, but for the first time Elfloq saw craftiness in his eyes (and who should be more qualified to recognise it?). Orgoom did not like being bullied in his new life of freedom, but he was not a fool and appreciated the value of knowledge in an omniverse draped in shadow.

Elfloq smiled. "My friend, trust me. Our tales will please the Council. If I did not know so, I would not have brought us here. To render up tales of no merit, thus cheating the Council, brings a heavy penalty and much discredit."

"Penalty?"

"Better not to dwell on such things. Go to sleep."

Orgoom grunted, beginning to get Elfloq's measure. But he closed his eyes, feigning sleep, though listening hard. The familiar's prediction proved accurate, for silence had fallen. After a protracted period of coughing, stretching of wings, shuffling of feet and claws, yawning and clearing of throats, some of the more powerful familiars came forward. Each spoke for a while on certain topics, mentioning gods, human sorcerers, mages, kings, warriors and all the convoluted workings associated with them, laying bare secrets, strategies and magical concatenations that were not approved for universal consumption.

They spoke of the clandestine marriage of Sisthric the Beautiful, a devastatingly powerful demi-goddess, to the young mage Holec, whose powers were already on a par with the lesser gods and who would certainly make himself immortal through his union with Sisthric. They spoke of the growth of the Reptilians, a race of quasi-demons spreading like a plague down in the hidden dimensions of Dourdreg, the Deepwells and Tyrrica. And they spoke, with ever growing concern, of the apparent linking together of many dark occurrences, small and large in scale, that more than hinted at an overall and terrifying will. Indeed, as each new speaker addressed the Council, fragments of this awesome puzzle slotted together ominously so that a grim picture began to form, thus justifying the efficacy of the Council.

Elfloq felt an internal writhing of his abdominal organs. This frightful pattern shaped by the various speakers was unquestionably linked to his premonition of earlier and made it the more worrying. There was indeed a cloud forming around the omniverse and it was thickening.

Ecclesiastro had decided to speak himself. "My learned colleagues have done right to unburden themselves of their secrets. I, too, can shed light on this spectre that seems now more substantial than was first realised. My own master, Robanda Nodrin of Jagg, has shied away from the implications of what lies outside us. It is not a power from *beyond* the many dimensions, but one that seems to exist in *all* of them. Like a single nightmare that has become many nightmares, each more evil than the last. Individually these terrors are powerful enough — combined they threaten omnipotence. And the gods are so single-minded, how could *they* combine? How could their vanities permit them this?"

"Then how," said another respected familiar, "can such chaotic forces as these evils we have described themselves combine? Are they not less stable?"

"Have you not listened, Ratcarve? Have you not stepped back and looked at the overall picture depicted by all our contributions? The drawing together of these innumerable evil forces is evidence that such a unifying will *is* at work. Like a shattered mirror repairing itself. It may take many ages, but if it should draw together all its disparate shards, then it will mean the complete and total recreation of the omniverse itself! It is not for me alone to ponder the implications of this. Your own minds can no doubt grasp the horror of it for themselves."

Another speaker rose. "But surely the gods know of this. Surely they, too, are already at work, counteracting these dark activities?"

Ecclesiastro nodded. "We must look for evidence. I think we may have heard some already. Who now will come forward and tell us of brighter things? Who knows of the whelming of evil? Whose masters have served Light of late?"

Several familiars hopped forward to speak of such things, but they talked of small matters, minor things that seemed insignificant compared to the growing advances of darkness described previously. Elfloq noticed that Orgoom, for the first time since their meeting in the *Inn With No Sign*, had become quite excited, seemingly unable to contain himself.

"I must take my own turn now," the Gelder said, and would not be forestalled.

"Wait —"

"My story has importance," said Orgoom, getting up.

Elfloq could not prevent him and had to be content with one swift warning. "Under *no* circumstances mention the name of the one who saved you from Ubeggi. They will kill you," he hissed, easing into a deeper shadow.

Orgoom stiffened, but nodded, for Elfloq had not been totally ungenerous to him. The Blue Gelder now had the attention of the Council and they bade him speak. He went on then in his stumbling, truncated way, to tell of how he had once been a Blue Gelder of Ubeggi, the Weaver of Wars, and had been one of his most useful spies and torturers, though always against his will. He told how the infamous Weaver had planned the downfall and destruction of Verdanniel, the Tree God. This evil act, obviously quite in keeping with the other evil acts noted by this Council, had been thwarted by the intervention of a strange being, a dark man who had not only blunted Ubeggi's offensive, but who had also insured the salvation of the Tree God and his self-contained universe. Ubeggi, furthermore, an immensely powerful god, had not reared up from defeat as expected to smite those who had thwarted him. Orgoom went on to explain that he had been freed from the bondage of serving Ubeggi, and that to his utter amazement the Weaver of Wars had, as yet, taken no steps to punish him.

In the gloom, Elfloq nodded to himself. It was this curious puzzle that had attracted him to the Gelder, for the immensely destructive power of Ubeggi was well known.

The Council of Gossipers was mightily impressed by Orgoom's story. "Well, well," said Ecclesiastro, "this is heartening, most heartening. A force that could negate Ubeggi. But surely the Weaver can only have turned his attentions elsewhere temporarily. He would never accept defeat. Indeed, is he possible to defeat? This must be a mere tactical manoeuvre. Which gives us something to ponder. But, Gelder, tell us more about this dark man —"

"It seems to me," said Elfloq, cutting in very quickly as he hovered down to the very heart of the hearing, "that it must be the Dark *Gods* who have taken a hand in this affair."

There was a unified murmur of amazement. One did not speak lightly of the Dark Gods.

"Ah, Elfloq. Why am I not surprised that you were lurking out there somewhere in the half light?" nodded Ecclesiastro, and there were many knowing smiles. "The Dark Gods, you say? How are they involved?"

"I learned but recently that they are not the evil masters of the night, as is commonly supposed. Not evil at all."

Grins turned to grimaces at this. Ecclesiastro scowled as if the batrachian familiar had said something highly offensive. "What *are* you babbling about?"

"On Mare Serenis I helped to save a dying water sprite from tragedy and for my efforts he taught me that the Dark Gods are the gods of Justice. They are Punishers, but they are opposed to this gathering of evil." Elfloq waited a brief moment, long enough to assure himself that he had wrested all attention from Orgoom, who, he felt sure, had been about to speak of the dark man.

"Are you certain?" said Ecclesiastro. "This is contrary to all understanding of the Dark Gods."

"Indeed, I am. They stand in the shadows of anonymity, not the black cloak that symbolises evil. And they would seem to have shown themselves at work many times of late. Furthermore, always they oppose the evil powers that are rife. Why, they spared me from as heinous a servitude as that of the Gelder. I was once the familiar of Quarramagus — and who here has not heard of that vile sorcerer? — but the Dark Gods saw fit to tear down the Csarducts who he served. I, alone, survived that debacle. Now I am between masters, it is true, but as I am experienced and versatile, I will doubtless be taken up by some important earthly mage ere long."

This brought more laughter, and Ecclesiastro waited for it to die down. "What else do you know about the Dark Gods?"

Elfloq, seduced by the limelight, then recited a number of stories that he claimed to have heard which involved the Dark Gods and of how they had defeated the armies of evil, on the Uttermoor, in Nyctath the All-Night and on Vyzandine, where the volcano god, Krogarth, had fallen. Not once did he mention the Voidal, but he made oblique references to a dark being. He said enough to convince the gathering that forces were at work to oppose the welling threat of nightmare.

"Well, you seem to have given us hope," said Ecclesiastro, relieved.

After this there was much discussion, during which Elfloq was able to hustle Orgoom away from the centre of things and back up to a lofty, secluded branch. "You have said all you need to say," whispered the familiar. "And we have both paid our dues for what we have learned. No one will deny us that."

"Little value," grunted Orgoom disconsolately.

"You are mistaken. Priceless," avowed Elfloq.

"I go now. Find new life. You promised me good future. Where?"

"Ah, yes, that I did. Well, things may not be so easy now, my friend, in view of the tumultuous things we have heard. The omniverse in upheaval! No one may now retire to a peaceful place. No such place will exist soon. No — you need a master, someone to give you causes to follow, causes that will help to hold back this onset of nightmare."

Orgoom frowned suspiciously. "You will select him?"

"Perhaps. But let us leave here before we discuss such a delicate matter. It is not a thing we are obliged to share. Give nothing away without payment. Vital rule."

Orgoom was grumbling again, not entirely at ease in the company of the wily familiar, who now seemed to be a cauldron of contradictions. But they flew out of the giant egg and back across the astral wilderness.

When they at last found somewhere discreet to rest, Elfloq spoke again. "There are wise men who say that everything, every grain of dust, has its appointed place in the scheme of things, even the humblest of familiars, the meekest of Gelders. Others say that it is for each thing to make a place for itself. How do you view such things, Orgoom?"

Orgoom merely shrugged.

Elfloq went on thoughtfully. "You see, I was not content to be an object placed here and there by the whim of others. I, by certain actions not outside my own influence, have, like yourself, won a degree of independent motion. But I am not powerful. Only with power can a thing move for itself. So proximity to power is of the essence. True? Well, I do have a master. He is elusive, as I said before, but he holds a key to power. *Colossal* power. You, yourself, have felt it like a wave passing, for your path and his have already crossed."

Orgoom merely scowled deeper, framing a hideous visage.

"The dark man you met on Verdanniel's world. He is the Voidal."

"*He* is your master?"

"Yes! I must find him. Now more than ever. You can help me. It is vital."

"Why?"

"If you do, I will see to it that the dark man takes you into his service, as he did me. He will not be able to refuse such a thing."

"Why?"

"*Why*? With the entire omniverse in turmoil! We all need to stand by the strongest. And did my master not better Ubeggi? It was my master of whom I spoke to the Council, though not by name. No name is more accursed than his. Yet it was he who has thrown down so many evil powers, albeit at the behest of the Dark Gods, who use him as their instrument. Where else could you find such power?"

Orgoom murmured something unhappily. There was to be no peace for him after all. He recalled the dark man, who had terrified him, in spite of his sense of justice, his sympathy for Verdanniel.

Elfloq was peering out at the astral mist. That brooding cosmic shadow of earlier remained. It could not be long before it made itself manifest and left some painful claw mark etched on the physical fabric of the omniverse. "So, are you with me?" he asked the Gelder.

Orgoom shrugged once more, resembling a waif far from home. "I follow."

Elfloq grinned. "Follow? No, not this time. You must lead. If we are to find the dark man, we will have to pick up the twisted threads of his life where you left it."

"Verdanniel?"

"No. I have a feeling, and it is a very positive feeling, that Ubeggi will be searching for the Voidal. Probably watching him."

"So?"

"Forgive me, but if we can find the Weaver, we can find my master."

Orgoom let out a hiss of terror. "The Weaver! Madness. Seek him? I want many universes between us!"

"Come, come," said Elfloq. "The path to power is not strewn with flowers! Be bold, as I am." He was quite beside himself with fear, but as on numerous occasions before in his life, determination somehow got the better of it, though in this instance it was by the narrowest of margins.

"Go to Ubeggi?" Orgoom was repeating to himself, shaking his head.

"I don't mean openly," snorted Elfloq. "There must be secret ways. Somewhere where we could sneak in and steal the odd conversation, clues to what we seek."

Orgoom sniffed. "If we are caught, the suffering would be unimaginable."

"I would rather not dwell on that."

But the Gelder seemed suddenly to have made the first momentous decision of his life. "Secret ways. Maybe. Ubeggi took from me my manhood, made me a Gelder. He owes me something for that. So — we go to him!"

Elfloq's ugly grin widened. "Just so."

"I will find Tyrandire, the Palace of Pain."

Elfloq winced at the reference. But he preened himself, delighted. Fortunately it did not seem as though it would be too difficult to manipulate the Gelder. But as they flew upwards into the astral heights once more, Elfloq wondered just how rudderless Orgoom was, and what dark powers might, after all, be moving him across their celestial board.

PART THREE

ADRIFT IN DELIRIUM

I have written before, in my history of the dark man, of tapestries and the weaving thereof. There is a skill required for the undertaking of this highest of art forms that the gods constantly seek to perfect.

Fate is a complex subject, and where several powers weave their own unique creations, inter-weaving or crossing over the destinies of lesser creatures, considerable care has to be taken in the working. Enmeshing several tapestries requires a singular purpose, a unified approach. The results of such fusion can be extraordinarily vivid, dazzling and enlightening, enriching the omniverse.

But the gods often tend to work for themselves, regardless of each other's efforts.

This results in confusion and there are dangers, as any weaver or indeed, artist worth his paint pots would explain. To mix all colours results in no colour at all, a final darkness, the ultimate colourless mass.

Inevitably, there are forces at work that strive for such a Lightless state of affairs.

—**Salecco**, great believer in the concept of one loom at a time

* * * *

Those who travel the astral realms usually do so alone, hurrying diligently at the beck and call of their masters, or flitting furtively among shadows, prowling or lurking, dashing guiltily, or gliding in secret silence. No one travels openly or innocently, at least, they do so under extremely rare circumstances. Of course, the astral realms thrive on chance meetings, passing discourses and apparently random conferences. Gossip here is as common as the mist: indeed, some say it is the mortar that binds the astral. There are recognised meeting places, mostly well known, frequented like bustling markets, as with the Gossipers' Council. But for one to travel in company, although not unheard of, is usually considered burdensome and inexpedient.

Stranger still, therefore, that an astral frequenter such as the wily Elfloq — such a singularly independent familiar — should wander the astral murk in the company of another being. Even stranger, that this other should be a reticent Blue Gelder of uncharming mien and surly temperament. But so it was. However, it must be added that although the two squat figures crossed astral distances in company with each other, they did not do so in harmony.

Orgoom, the Gelder, had actually become quite animated for one so habitually taciturn and glum. He was flexing the hitherto atrophied wings of his own independence, metaphorically speaking (as he did not possess physical wings). Annoyance had goaded him from his shell (a similarly metaphorical attribute). Annoyance that had become anger and at length, heated wrath. Elfloq's remonstrations added to the flames of the quarrel, threatening to make a pyre of their recent companionship.

"Can't find Tyrandire without help!" snapped Orgoom for the dozenth time. He had resigned himself to returning to Ubeggi's grim stronghold, in spite of hideous misgivings.

"Quite so," whined Elfloq. "But is it absolutely necessary for us to visit Mindsulk? No other place in all the many dimensions can sport such a concentration of beings who would delight in doing me harm of the most painful kind."

"For me also. But Mindsulk full of Gelders. News of Ubeggi. You want to find Tyrandire. Then Mindsulk first." Orgoom spat loudly, a habit that he was perfecting, implying that nothing would change the veracity of his statement. Evidently he was growing impatient with the familiar. He was by no means bound to Elfloq, although it seemed to the Gelder that Elfloq possessed enough knowledge to win for them both positions of relative comfort and security in this capricious omniverse. The Gelder was, nevertheless, tempted to part company and travel on alone.

Elfloq sensed this as readily as if it had been shouted. "Orgoom, you are right, of course. I am a coward, though not without reason, but there it is. I must come to terms with it. So, lead on to Mindsulk. We must first cross the swamps of chance before we can sit on the isle of rewards."

Orgoom snorted at this distorted poetical remark (a very loose rendering of a more classical piece) and forged on ahead now that the argument was at an end. Behind him Elfloq grimaced and gave a shudder or two. Mindsulk! Great Gods of the Earthbowels, what a sink of horrors. It was a bleak and remote place, a huge bastion of crags upon which a grotesque accumulation of buildings adhered as if they had been tossed there by some peevish god unable to satisfy his creative whims. These poor architectural rejects had soon become the welcome abodes of the dregs of the omniverse, where evil thrived and blasphemous plots abounded. Elfloq had had occasion to go there only very rarely and each time had been extremely fortunate to come away intact.

When they began to draw close to the obnoxious crags of Mindsulk, Elfloq insisted that they do something to disguise themselves, a course of action that readily appealed to Orgoom. The Gelder was all for Elfloq using a spell to give them different forms, but Elfloq rejected this outright, knowing that the dark magics of Mindsulk would strip such illusions bare and draw attention to them.

"Simplicity is the key," he said. "We must procure ordinary rags. There are places at the edge of Mindsulk where we can do this. We won't be questioned. There are more disguises in this place than an inn's cat has fleas. Let us find the house of Witweave."

This visit was shortly undertaken, but Orgoom, who had used Mindsulk regularly when in the service of the Weaver of Wars, did not trouble himself by wrapping up and shielding his face. Elfloq, on the other hand, padded himself under a thick cloak and pulled tight its heavy cowl, walking bent double, which made him even more squat than he already was. He kept strictly to the darkest shadows of the dingy streets as they sought a large inn well known to Orgoom.

"Perhaps," suggested the familiar, above the thundering of his heart, "it would be sensible for me to await you outside, where I can watch out for any enemies that might be drawing near."

"Enemies already inside," growled Orgoom and pushed open the wooden door. Elfloq reluctantly shuffled in behind him. The familiar had been in some of the most notorious dives in the omniverse, but few of them came close to this stifling melting pot of virulence. For certain, no individual in here was doing the work of anyone but the vilest of masters, bent on the destruction and damnation of sanity in the many dimensions. The place was barely lit by a few, thick candles, themselves almost intrusive, black-hung and austere, though filled with mutterings and harsh laughs, sneers and growls. There was a veritable host in here, jammed together, each individual leaning close to another in order to stifle what they were saying: secrets were dark, their consequences terrible.

Orgoom looked around him fairly brazenly, while Elfloq cringed behind, not unlike a cat in a yard full of rabid dogs. Shortly Orgoom had the scent of two other Blue Gelders who were hunched over a low table with a very tall being whose shaven head dipped between pinched shoulders on a peculiarly long neck. His head was the more obtrusive as its dome had been dyed a savage shade of red.

"News there," Orgoom grunted to Elfloq and squeezed through the packed company to the table. Its occupants stared up at him angrily, but Orgoom, who was accustomed to the uncivilised ways of his blue brethren, merely pulled up a stool and sat. Elfloq stood miserably behind him like his diminutive shadow and was, mercifully, more or less ignored. His terrors of this place had been barely lessened earlier when Orgoom had explained that Gelders were all very much alike and often did not recognise each other.

"Greetings, fellow Blue," said one of the Gelders. He was a fat fellow with a face like murder. "Going outwards, or back to our master with word?"

Orgoom helped himself to the acidic Mindsulk wine with a theatrical hawk. "Out. No specific task. Nosing."

The tall being, who was loftier than any normal man, though seemingly human, towered over Orgoom. His long nose dipped down as if it would jab into the Gelder's mind, spear information and draw it out. "Learned anything?" His voice had the effect on Elfloq of claws being dragged down the surface of a mirror.

"About what?"

The tall one scowled, ugly enough to petrify demons. "About *what*! How long have you been away from Ubeggi? Only one thing occupies the Weaver now."

Orgoom remained calm, though inwardly he was juggling possibilities. No one had recognised him as the Gelder who had lately escaped the services of Ubeggi in highly suspect circumstances. The Weaver, it now seemed, had relented his decision to take no action in the matter.

"Been far off. Remote dimensions. But no news. You?"

The fat Gelder snatched back the wine jug and guzzled. "It's no use, Snare. None of us knows enough to satisfy Ubeggi. May as well be hunting mist."

Snare made an animal sound in his throat. "We'll see. I have arranged to meet someone here. He may know more than all of us. I fancy he will lead us to this thrice damned dark man."

Elfloq was mentally gnawing over the bone of the name Snare. It had summoned up disturbing connotations. Could this be the shunned mystic who was reputed to command servants of the pits that few others dared summon?

"If only we could get our claws into that ugly little brat Orgoom," chirped the other Gelder, flexing his sickle fingernails. "He'd know where to start the hunt."

Snare leaned even closer to Orgoom. "What about you? Have you come across that traitorous pig-swill on your distant travels?"

Orgoom belched and looked away. "Word reached me. He went very far. Serving a new god — very powerful. More powerful than Ubeggi."

Snare laughed and many heads turned at the frightful sound. "*More* so! How absurd. Where was this?"

"Beyond the Lostways."

"As remote as that, eh? Still, I doubt if that little bag of droppings could tell us anything. Waste of time looking for him."

The fat Gelder spoke up. "Did you hear what Orgoom did in the place of the Tree God, Verdanniel? He allied himself to some grim being and aided him — *aided* him — to upset the war that our master had instigated."

"I heard a little."

"And where did this dark man, this Voidal, go?" said Snare. "The entire Gelder company is searching for him, to say nothing of all Ubeggi's other agents and hirelings. Come, speak. Say what you know!"

Orgoom had a mind to turn upon Elfloq and spit in his one peeping eye. They had come here for news of the Voidal only to find that everyone was looking for him, including Ubeggi! And Orgoom had only consented to go back to Tyrandire in order to find out the Voidal's whereabouts.

"Into the air," he said to Snare. "Like a dream. Strong power."

Snare gave a gusty snort of disgust. "You're no use to us. You know nothing. Teeth of the Dark Gods, does *no one* have word? Ah, who's this? A breathless young Gelder comes to us. Hey! What news, offal?"

Another Blue Gelder was indeed struggling to reach them. He was slight and short of breath, full of live nerve ends and eyes like small moons. "I do have word. But it is not good. I am afraid to send it to Ubeggi."

Snare shot out an arm like the tongue of a lizard and dragged the young Gelder across the table. "I'll pin you to the rafters! Give the word to me and *I'll* pass it on. Well?"

"I was lately at a Council of Gossipers," began the young one.

Snare let him go. "Really! A useful place to glean news. I was not aware that one had been convened, although several of the mages who send their slaves to those gabbling markets have set up means by which to keep me away. Well?"

"Great events are unfolding in the omniverse. Terrible powers are struggling to subjugate all of it. Darkness blends with darkness. Light gutters like a candle near to its last glow." This all came out in a rush, garbled and frenetic.

Snare growled. "Slower, slower! And speak plainly. You are a Gelder, not a wretched poet! What has all this to do with the Voidal?"

"At the Council I heard a small familiar speak. A strange creature, who said that this Voidal had, according to rumours, often foiled the workings of gods like our master, Ubeggi. This familiar said that he thought the Voidal was a servant of the Dark Gods and that they oppose all evil and seek to overthrow the creeping shadow that is threatening the entire omniverse. I am afraid to tell Ubeggi that his powers are threatened."

Snare pushed him away derisively. "You've said enough. The Dark Gods, eh? It's true that they are considered powerful. Their names are ineffable. But what is this about darkness blending with darkness?"

"All darkness will be one," said the Gelder, nodding frantically. "And light cannot be one. The gods never agree and never share power."

"Indeed," nodded Snare, with an even more unpleasant laugh. "But why should we be dismayed by your news? If there is to be colossal strife, Ubeggi is allied to the dark. Perhaps these gibbering rumours you have heard refer to his own coalescing powers. Even the Dark Gods have their limits. I doubt that Ubeggi fears them."

"Take care," hissed a voice behind him. "Take very great care, Cruel One."

Snare swivelled, hands ready to rend, like some primordial beast. But as he caught sight of the man who stood there, face deep in shadow, his expression changed, smugness seeping into it. "Ah, you are here. Come and sit. Take wine with us."

The other shook his invisible head. "No. I am impatient."

"Come! Sit. I insist. Listen to how the Dark Gods are to fall."

"You underestimate them, as I once did. For that impudence they stole my face, the most beautiful face in the omniverse, and replaced it with vileness. I know their powers. I will say nothing against them."

"Come, come, Shatterface. We all seek the same goal for now. This man they call Voidal. And I know how desperately *you* seek him. Destroy him and you win back your true face, eh?"

Shatterface remained motionless. "Destroy? Again you underestimate. You do not *destroy* the Voidal, any more than you put an end to eternity."

"Then what?"

"It is his mind, his knowledge. What he knows of himself. I must destroy that. The Dark Gods will reward me. Once I tried to win the prize, but in Nyctath, forgotten dimension, I failed to plunge the Sword of Oblivion into the Voidal's heart. I am permitted to try for him only twice more. After that, if I fail, I shall be as I am until the omniverse rots."

"Ah, but this time you have allied yourself to far greater forces. My promise of aid from Ubeggi was not an idle one."

"This Gelder here spoke of a familiar. Did the familiar have a name?"

The young Gelder thought for a moment, then nodded. "It was Elfloq."

Shatterface emitted another hiss.

"You know him?" said Snare.

"Yes! The dark man may not be so vulnerable, but that infernal familiar *is*. Elfloq is the servant of the Voidal. Some demonic alliance has come about between them. If we can find Elfloq, then we can weaken the dark man, I am certain."

Snare chuckled. "Well, well. Then it will be simplicity itself to comb even the omniverse for a paltry familiar. His powers will be minute."

Elfloq had listened to this with the greatest of palpitations. He felt himself seated on the very brink of madness and terror, as though the Oblivion Hand, which he once been forced to bear upon his back, had clamped down over his heart, squeezing it. He had met Shatterface once before, and it had been a dreadful encounter that yet haunted the familiar's dreams.

"When I find this Elfloq," avowed Shatterface, "I will spend every day teaching him the billion paths of agony."

At this, Elfloq surreptitiously nudged Orgoom, his elbow clearly stating that it was time to be moving on and away, far away. Orgoom now understood for the first time the true magnitude of the loathing Elfloq's enemies had for him. He cursed the familiar secretly for having dragged him into what must surely be the most unbalanced of conflicts.

"I go," he said, getting up quickly. "Much to learn." No one moved to stop him. Clearly he had nothing valuable to add to the conversation.

As he struggled away from the table, though, he found his path deliberately blocked by yet another presence. It was man dressed in a grey cloak, the hood partially thrown back to reveal a narrow face and steely eyes that were disturbingly cold. He carried a long dirk and with this he tapped Orgoom on the arm, easing him aside so that the smaller form of Elfloq was revealed.

Snare saw the face of the stranger and their eyes met in recognition. "Ipsol! This is a pleasant turn up. Word had it that you had been imprisoned."

"On Murderers' Mountain, no less." His weapon stretched forward and caught at the cowl that hid Elfloq's features. "I have walked a varied path since my fortunate escape. Later we can discuss it. For now, I am curious to see what this pile of rags will reveal, for I have developed a keen sense of smell in relation to *familiars*." So saying, he deftly flicked aside the cowl, to leave the hapless Elfloq exposed for all to see. In such a crowded space and smothered in his cloak, it was impossible for the familiar to spread his wings and flit up to the low rafters.

"As I thought," said Ipsol. "Your pardon, Snare, old comrade, I had not intended to intrude on your discussions. But I overheard certain comments and for a moment thought you were about to lose the very object of your desire."

Shatterface had recognised Elfloq instantly. He reached forward, bringing the mask that covered his own face into the candlelight. "Some god or other has indeed smiled upon us. *This* is the very same familiar of which we spoke!"

"This is Elfloq?" said Snare, and when Ipsol nodded, Snare's vulpine features screwed themselves into a ghastly semblance of a smile.

"My dear sirs!" protested the familiar at once, watching the tip of Ipsol's blade as if it were the head of a particularly poisonous snake. "I assure you that you are letting your imaginations have their head. I, Elfloq? To the furnaces with such a notion. Why, I know him, of course, vile rogue, never to be trusted. I admit, too, that there are certain superficial resemblances between us. Facially, it is arguable, I am not unlike him, and have indeed been mistaken for him on numerous occasions —"

Snare yanked him across the table and leaned over him like an avalanche about to smother him. "Shut up," he breathed. "The Skulk of Illhallows is no fool."

Shatterface stiffened. "Neither am I to be misled, familiar. I have good cause to remember you. Where is your master?"

"I — I have none. He died in an alchemical fire —"

While Elfloq's totally unconvincing tirade was in progress, the young Gelder was staring for the first time at Orgoom. A flicker of recognition abruptly ignited his bizarre face. "Oh, excuse me, fellow, but did we not once converse together in our master's service? I would not have known you, but you are famed among Gelders for your favour with the Weaver. You are Orgoom, are you not? I saw you at the Council. It is an honour to meet you again." He had not spoken loudly, but it was enough to divert the attention of both Snare and Shatterface.

"Orgoom!" they hissed in unison.

The Gelder muttered an unpleasant curse. Needless to say, it was entirely ineffectual in this company.

Elfloq saw the final wave of disaster about to crash down. "Again, sirs, you do this fellow an injustice," he piped hopefully. "He is Ugrang. I am sure the Weaver himself would confirm it."

Snare smiled the smile of a reptile about to lock jaws on its meal. "Why not? An excellent suggestion, familiar. Let us all go before Ubeggi. I am certain that he will be delighted to discuss the future with you both. Ipsol, will you join us?"

The assassin put away his blade with a shake of his head. "Thank you, but no. I owe this creature something for his attempt to swindle me recently in Cloudway. But you are welcome to him, Snare. I'm sure whatever you intend for him will more than redress the balance." He inclined his head in a bow.

"Another time, then," said Snare.

Orgoom was scowling his most repulsive scowl at Elfloq, but the latter had already closed his eyes. The inevitable was, well, unavoidable.

* * * *

It was the most extraordinary hall that Elfloq had ever visited and unquestionably the most disturbing. Its many marbled columns were pink hued, its carpets a deep crimson — indeed, everything in it that could be was a variation on the colour of blood. Elfloq noticed that Orgoom was not at all moved by this. He had been here before, of course, but even so, to pay no heed to the sanguineous surroundings suggested a coldness of heart that disturbed Elfloq even more. In fact, Orgoom did not seem particularly flustered by anything, which filled Elfloq with foreboding. Surely the Gelder should be quivering with fear at being here in the Palace of Pain, fortress of Ubeggi, from whom he had fled without repercussion.

Behind and between the two small figures stood the bowed form of Snare: Elfloq could smell the fear on him. Ubeggi may be his master, but the Weaver was, after all, a god and one of grim power. Shatterface had not arrived, and Elfloq wondered how the quasi-human being would cross the astral realm to Tyrandire. Shatterface had said that he was moved primarily by the Dark Gods, which seemed something of a contradiction.

In front of the three figures there was a placid pool, dark and scarlet, from which exuded a sickly, unpleasant smell. Beside it lounged several dreamy-eyed sylphs. They dipped silver cups into the pool and sipped at the liquid like tiny glass vampires. They smiled, Elfloq thought, at him, as if they waited only for a word to flit across to him and sample his flesh with those brilliant-white needle teeth. This thought did little to alleviate the wriggling of his bowels. Neither did the half-seen faces that he thought he saw rise and sink in the pool, contorted as though in torment.

Beyond the pool was Ubeggi himself. He was contained within a huge globe that was fed by countless vein-like tubes and from the unique head of the Weaver of Wars reached out dozens of filaments that appeared to be feeding from the milky body of the globe. These filaments were transparent and the liquid that pulsed down them was the colour of the liquid in the pool. Elfloq decided that the globular head was a projection, for it seemed to have no visible body within the globe. Ubeggi opened a huge, lascivious mouth, like some enormous fish inside its tank, and spoke. The voice came clearly through the globe's sides.

"The prodigal returns."

Orgoom made no movement and said nothing. Elfloq, however, fidgeted as he had never fidgeted before. The result of all his quivering was a little torrent of words that gushed from him at almost unintelligible speed. "I have been abducted in error, ultimate expression of divinity."

Ubeggi's head shook and the redness about him glowed like the embers of a fire that had been fanned. He was laughing, not angry. His eyes seemed to throb, but they were opaque and fathomless, just as his thoughts were.

"Be quiet, Elfloq. I know about you and where you have been. You serve the Voidal, the man I am seeking, the only being in all the omniverse that has ever withstood me and walked away unharmed. I allowed him this freedom merely because I wanted to learn more of him. And perhaps to use his powers for my own ends. Through you, and your dealings in secret places, I have indeed learned something. Your master is the pawn of the Dark Gods and they are dark only because they shroud themselves in secrecy. They are not evil, as so many of the dwellers in the omniverse believe. They are themselves the slaves of Light."

Elfloq's bulbous eyes were distending, which made them even more grotesque than usual. It seemed that Ubeggi was party to priceless knowledge. The guise of the Dark Gods, so long a mystery, was no secret to him.

The Weaver ignored Elfloq's look of stupefaction and went on. "I oppose most things, but most of all Light. I oppose order, peace, harmony, concord. I am the sower of discontent. The bringer of chaos. The Weaver of Wars. And why is that, eh? Why should I use my powers in such a way? Something deep within me moves me to be this way. Some inner restlessness of spirit. I obey no masters, only this perverse spirit within me. Have you not felt such desires yourself, little familiar? A hunger to control all that is about you? To make turmoil of it and guide it how you will? To wrest your own destiny from the gods who would mould it, just as your infamous master seeks to win his own destiny? Ultimate freedom, unfettered will!"

Elfloq was nodding furiously.

Ubeggi laughed again. "Of course! What could be more natural? We all wish to have such power. To obey the inner voice. To control fate, and that of others. We lust for power. All the power there is. To drink every last dreg and then to indulge ourselves in a wanton spending of it."

"What depths there are to your wisdom, divine essence," said Elfloq.

"We are of the same mind, you see," agreed Ubeggi sardonically.

"Darkness is blending," added Elfloq, praying that it was appropriate.

Ubeggi was nodding. "Oh, indeed it is. While the gods of Light go their divergent ways, proud of their freedom and refusal to subjugate others, the great darkness draws in. I serve no masters and have always sought to confound whomever it pleased me so to do. But we must all participate in the battle — the war — the better to wreak havoc. This war that comes upon us is the one that all wars throughout all the histories of time have been hurtling towards. For once I am aligned with its dizzying turbulence."

Elfloq gasped. "*You* are the one who shaped all this?"

"Would that I was! Such power! No, I am no more than a fragment of it. This irks me a little, for I have served none but myself, just as you have done. But in this I find that I am not my own master after all. I am no more than a footsoldier in the army of whatever shapes the omniverse. You see, little familiar, in the face of this horror, you and I are no better than each other."

Again Elfloq could scarcely believe what he was hearing. On an equal footing with Ubeggi! The idea was unthinkable.

"As for your master, the Voidal," went on the Weaver, "he is even less well placed. Aye, less so! For he is the pawn of Light, and in this war of wars, Light will fail. Darkness will snuff it out. I am sure you appreciate that."

Elfloq agreed vehemently. He was not about to question a single utterance of the Weaver's.

"So be it. You must cast your lot with Darkness, Elfloq. True Darkness, and not the sham darkness of mystery and ignorance. You must become *mine*."

This, then, was the awful truth. A test. Reject the Voidal and side with evil. If Ubeggi was truly more powerful than the Voidal and his terrible masters, Elfloq was caught like a flea under a thumbnail.

"I am yours," he said at once, trying not to make it sound too mechanical. His heart beat faster as it sensed the impending cracking of his bones.

"Really? So swift a decision? Well, we shall see." Ubeggi turned his attention to Orgoom, who looked even more sullen than usual. "And what of my runaway Gelder?"

Orgoom grunted something unintelligible.

"I never punished you for your treacherous part in the affair with Verdanniel. Did you think you were free of me? In your heart you must have known it would be otherwise. So you were swayed by the silver tongue of the familiar and thought you would serve his master, too? Foolish, but understandable. Yet you remain mine and must serve out your time with me. Do so and I *will* give you the freedom you so earnestly dream of. Serve me out, Orgoom, and I will make you again the man you once were."

It was not possible for the Gelder to radiate smiles, but Elfloq knew that he would have done so, had he been able. Ubeggi had offered him the greatest prize he could desire. The Blue Gelder's alliance was surely lost.

"I have a single task for you," Ubeggi told him.

"Will do it," said Orgoom, but within himself he was thinking that it was not wise to trust the Weaver. Ubeggi freed no one.

"So you are both eager to serve me. We shall see." He directed his unnerving gaze upon Snare. "And here is one servant who does love me and thinks only of my plans. Is it not so, Snare?"

The gangling Snare grovelled, a display that would have done justice to Elfloq at his most obsequious. "My heart and mind are books to you, master. You read them at your leisure."

"Always believe it. You worship awesome deities, Snare, and have become a master in their foul rituals, but I have the greater power. As I shall soon demonstrate to you. But where is the other? The fallen one?"

A figure stumbled groggily out of the shadows as if it had come direct from a dream. It was Shatterface.

"Welcome to Tyrandire," said Ubeggi. "But what is this that you have brought with you?"

There was a sword at Shatterface's side where before there had been none. Shatterface touched the hilt, but did not draw it, as if it were alive, a serpent not to be trusted.

Ubeggi was smiling hideously, contentment oozing out of him almost visibly. "Just as I calculated. Even the Dark Gods could not resist the temptation I set before them."

"What do you mean?" said Shatterface. Having once been a god, he had little respect for them, for the suffering imposed upon him exceeded any further pain they might inflict.

Ubeggi was too pleased with himself to correct Shatterface's manners. "I have been threading the warp and woof of a new scheme. You are all part of the tapestry. So, too, is the Voidal, and so are his unwitting masters, the Dark Gods."

Shatterface fingered the hilt of his weapon. "The Dark Gods have placed this sword at my side even as you drew me here. What blade is it? The Sword of Oblivion, that I carried before? Am I to sink it into the dark man?"

"Rest assured," said Ubeggi, "the Dark Gods do not love the Voidal. His fate is to serve them. To keep him under their sway, they must wipe his memory clean, for therein lies the key to the unlocking of his powers. Even I do not know what powers he once had. But I would not like to see them unlocked. The suppression of his memory suits me well. Thanks to the meddling of this small but significant familiar, the Voidal has recovered something of his memory. That must be changed. Therefore I will aid you, Shatterface. Even though I will be aiding the Dark Gods."

Shatterface stepped forward. "If I succeed in this, I will win back from the Dark Gods one half of my face."

"Succeed," said Ubeggi, "and *I* will restore the other half."

Shatterface gasped as if he had been struck. "Then by every god that listens, I will serve you well."

"Excellent! But there is more. It is not enough for me that the Voidal has his memory removed completely. That would satisfy the Dark Gods, of course. But I have a mind to punish the Voidal for interfering with my plans on Verdanniel. By so doing, I will be showing my teeth to the Dark Gods, who prompted him in that matter. I do not fear them as others do."

Elfloq shuddered at this. To his knowledge, no one had ever uttered such a thing before without drawing down terrible consequences.

"I want the Voidal imprisoned. Trapped and held in a place from which he can never escape, for he cannot be destroyed. I know of such a place." And the Weaver laughed gruesomely.

Shatterface shook his head, bemused. "Can that be?"

Ubeggi ignored the question. "There are certain dream dimensions where none but the mad or unwary set foot. Strange gods go there to conjure up their wildest visions, or to send out their nightmares. There is one such god looming on its boundaries now. A god that has come from a realm where none but his own kind dwell. Many are in chains, after an eon-old conflict. But this one has escaped the chains that bound him and plots the conquest of a universe. I have a mind to spite him. Have you heard, underlings, of the Great Old Ones?"

This meant nothing to Orgoom, who merely shrugged. Elfloq frowned for a moment in puzzlement. The name did not seem ominous. But then something at the back of his mind worked loose and he jumped as if bitten.

"Yes, I expected *you* to react, Elfloq. There is more knowledge stored in that junkyard of a brain than in a thousand libraries. The Great Old Ones, among the most hideous of beings in the omniverse. Certainly they are most offensive to look upon. No other gods communicate with them. Indeed, since their various incarcerations, it is not certain that they communicate with each other any longer. One of them, he that I mentioned, has cut himself adrift and lies semi-dormant at the edge of the dream dimension. His name is Ybaggog, the Devourer."

"What has this vile being to do with us?" said Shatterface.

"Everything," replied Ubeggi tersely.

Snare, silent until now, had visibly paled. "Ybaggog is spoken of in hushed tones only, master. He is said to rival Azathoth in power. Few of the crawling minions that serve these abominations dare speak his name."

Ubeggi nodded. "Quite. I want the Voidal imprisoned *inside him*."

Elfloq felt himself swaying, but gripped his reason tenaciously.

Ubeggi laughed again. "It should be a perfectly digestible meal for a god capable of swallowing universes."

Snare looked aghast. "But, master, how?"

Ubeggi was staring at the sword of Shatterface. "Draw out the Sword of Oblivion, for it is doubtless that blade. Plunge that into the Voidal and he will be helpless. Simple enough to give the dark man to Ybaggog after that. You, Snare, have been a high priest in the rituals of these dreaming gods. It should be a simple matter for you to perform a mass of sacrifice to Ybaggog. And who better as neophytes for your ritual than Orgoom and Elfloq?"

Snare was clearly troubled, but he bowed. "The Old Ones know me."

Shatterface had slowly drawn his blade, but was gazing at it in surprise. It seemed curiously alive and from it there issued bizarre sounds as if a veritable host of mad demons muttered and whispered, trapped within its steel, if steel it was. "This is not the Sword of Oblivion."

Ubeggi's wide eyes studied the weapon carefully. But then he gave a cry of pleasure. "No, indeed! It seems that we are truly aligned to the Dark Gods in this venture. It is the Sword of Madness. Plunge that into the Voidal and he will be truly undone. Evidently the Dark Gods have no further use for him. What do you say to that, Elfloq?"

"It must be as you say. The Voidal has served them well. Now his time is over. And he cannot be freed." Elfloq was thinking frantically. *Why? Because*, he answered himself, *the Dark Gods are afraid that the Voidal will regain his old powers, and they fear that more than anything else in the omniverse. Then,* he further mused, *he must be inching nearer his goal for them to reject him. Otherwise they would never aid one as deceitful as Ubeggi.*

"So," said the Weaver, "you now have no further reason to serve this dark man, nor indeed, to fear him."

Elfloq agreed at once.

"Then we are united. Let us begin." But Elfloq knew that it was not going to be quite that simple.

"Where are we to go?" asked Shatterface.

"To the dream dimension. One of its ancient towns will be an ideal place to meet. Snare, conduct Orgoom and Elfloq to Ulthar. Return them to me when the sacrifice is over and Ybaggog has been fed his unique meal."

Snare bowed low. "To Ulthar, lord."

Shatterface sheathed the Sword of Madness. "To Ulthar."

Elfloq's terror welled anew. The town of cats was about as unwholesome a town as any other he could think of.

"And Elfloq," said Ubeggi casually, "I have a specific task for you. Remiss of me to overlook it in my enthusiasm."

"I would be honoured."

"I am glad you think so. Well, as you now have no need to fear your master that was, you'll have no fears either of the various curses and spells surrounding him, which will soon be dissipated for all eternity. You agree?"

"Why, yes, ultimate one. Who should fear a madman locked inside the gut of a dreaming god?" Elfloq heard himself laugh flippantly.

"How well you put it. Before we can achieve anything, it will be necessary to bring the Voidal to Ulthar. Therefore, once you arrive there, I charge you with the simple, and now harmless task of invoking him."

Elfloq went rigid, but managed to twist his face into an ingratiating smile. Invoke the Voidal. The phrase repeated itself inside the tiny cranium of the familiar many times like an echo that would not die away. Once before he had had the audacity to invoke the Voidal, but it had been in Cloudway, the astral haven where it had been uniquely safe to do so. Yet the dark man had warned him never to invoke him again, otherwise the awesome penalty would be extracted in full.

"Snare will see that you discharge this duty," smiled Ubeggi.

Elfloq screwed up his courage and spoke. "But surely, divine one, if Snare is the high master of rituals, he would be the perfect one to summon my mas — uh, the dark man."

Ubeggi made a show of considering this. "Possibly. But it would make you superfluous. In which case, having no use for you, I'd have to cast you loose, with no master. I doubt if you'd survive long. Unless, of course, you would like me to make you a Blue Gelder?"

Elfloq shivered with nervous laughter. "No, no, you mistake me, most generous and gracious of gods. How could I not desire to serve you? I will be happy to summon the dark man in Ulthar."

Ubeggi nodded, smiling a most wicked smile. "Snare will see to it that you do."

"Be assured," said Snare.

"I am," replied Ubeggi. "I am indeed." Thus he dismissed the company. Moments later he had put them from his mind, together with the simple formalities that comprised their tasks. He turned his attention instead to far more engrossing matters, namely the pitting of the mad hordes of Zillraat the Ninth with the Howling Mages of the spellworld, K'nam-Paxl, which promised to be a war of devastating dimensions, affording the Weaver immense enjoyment. And it would no doubt thread more black strands into the gathering gloom that threatened the omniverse with its coalescence.

PART FOUR

DARK DESTROYER

In his strange travels, the Voidal visited many unholy realms and nightmare regions. There were reasons for this, which I will explore more fully as the history unfolds.

I have written already of Phaedrabile, a dimension of singular horrors, but in the conflict with Ybaggog and that repulsive god's inner terrain, lies a truly disturbing creation. Even more terrifying is the knowledge that it is but the edge of an entire pantheon of lunatic gods and their grotesque outpourings.

Many are the writings and annals concerning this most blasphemous of Powers, and in recording their histories, more than one devout scribe has succumbed to the insanity that permeates their very breath.

No one should consider himself or herself immune, least of all myself, but what follows needs must be written, no matter how deranged I may seem for having penned it. There are, I promise you, unexpurgated versions, but I have been guided by a need to balance the facts with a degree of restraint.

—**Salecco**, who believes himself not to have
lost his reason, though there is no one at hand to
confirm this.

* * * *

In Ulthar, the city of cats, two swarthy men sat at a table in an inn, talking softly and looking out through the window at the buildings of the city that dropped away below them. In the distance, moonlight fractured the winding river Skai and beyond that the shifting enigma of the dreamscape pushed forward like a silent bank of mist, tonight oppressive and alive with evil portents. Things flapped across the sky darkly and silently: the dreams of the inhabitants of Ulthar were not pleasant ones.

The first of the men wore a strange hat (as a priest might) and upon his cloak were sewn unusual figures with human bodies and the heads of varying animals — cats, hawks, rams and lions, marking the man and his colleague as travellers from the far South, whose mysteries were famous in Ulthar, where cats are sacred. In this high inn where the men sat, no one had spoken to them, and indeed the few patrons had already left, while all the cats that lived here — and there were many scores — gathered around them, purring and fussing like servants anxious to please. From time to time one of the men would reach down and dig with gentle fingers into the fur of an animal, or stroke its sleek coat. The silent innkeeper, Drath, was a little uneasy, but pleased, knowing that it was through these Southern wanderers that Ulthar had become a shrine to cats.

"There are signs here, too," said Umatal, taller of the men. He sipped at the strong Ulthar wine. "Everywhere."

"Just so," nodded Ibidin, his stockier companion, turning from the table to study the lower town. "Ybaggog's dreams are a far-reaching curse. Such dreams as flit about these skies are poisoned by this awesome god. I heard in the market today that seven men across the river were found dead in their beds, killed by the grim nightmares that beset them. It was unquestionably the doing of Ybaggog. These dreams are not confined to this realm, Umatal. They spread. It is murmured in hidden places that even the priests of the Old Ones are afraid for their gods."

"Say nothing of the Old Ones," replied Umatal. "Even in Ulthar, their ears catch every breath."

"How are we to be rid of the Dark Destroyer? What possible means are we to employ to thwart its purpose?"

"Its purpose! Pah! How can we comprehend its purpose?"

"Enough to know that Ybaggog is called, Devourer of Universes."

"We may have to sacrifice universes to kill him."

They said no more for a while, knowing that their own gods (and indeed, all gods that they knew of) went in fear of Ybaggog. Ibidin nervously chinked the silver coins in his pocket; he had not earned many this season, for few people in Ulthar wanted the benefit of his fortune telling. As the men subsided into their grim thoughts, more shadows crossed the moon. The men jerked up, a symptom of how afraid they were, for such nocturnal things were common in Ulthar and not usually worthy of concern.

"Something approaches," said Umatal, drawing back. Around him, fifty cats arched their backs and hissed in unison. Ibidin pulled a short, curved knife from his belt, lurching up from the table. Presently a small, squamous figure alighted on the windowsill and peered in with huge eyes. It was not unlike the frightful night gaunts, but was too squat and small, and a few moments were all that were needed to outline its evident trepidation.

"Begone!" growled Umatal, as if chasing off a wayward crow.

"Your pardon, masters," came the reply. "But is this the inn of Drath, sixth cat master of the northern heights?"

A figure had come out of the shadows behind the table, holding and stroking a cat, and with a smaller one perched on its shoulder. All the cats in the inn had subsided, purring softly again and gazing dreamily at the odd visitor. "Aye," said Drath. "What do you seek here?"

"I am Elfloq," said the figure, hopping in a frog-like way on to a table, narrowly missing a jug of wine. "Are these two lords your only guests?" He appeared to be searching out more guests with those bulbous, saucer-like eyes, though there were only the cats, creatures of which he did not approve. One of them extended an exploratory claw and came close to hooking it into the scaled hide of the familiar. Elfloq opened his wings in readiness to flit upwards to the rafters.

"We are not lords," said Ibidin. "But by the beard of Ozmordrah, what are you?"

Elfloq seemed relieved. "Then I am first." He kept himself out of reach of the cats, sitting birdlike in the windowsill, poised for flight if need be. "You must listen to me, for there is little time before they come."

"Who?" said Drath.

"Evil ones. Dreadful forerunners of an even greater evil. Dark and dire, foul and hideous to look upon — beings who will work frightful misery upon Ulthar and all the cities of the dreamworld."

"You babble, little frog," said Umatal. But his smile was very thin. "Who are these devils you speak of?"

"One is half-man — fat and blue-skinned, with hooked talons for hands and feet, and the face of a devil. He is shifty and foul-lipped — smelling of the gutters and with the eyes of a madman —"

"It seems to me," chuckled Drath, "that this description would easily fit yourself, apart from the hue of your skin."

Elfloq ignored this remark. "The other is tall, bent over and like a lean wolf with eyes that burn and hands that would rob the dead. His very presence fills the air with darkness, and he is a priest of the most abominable gods. His mother, they say —"

"Enough!" snarled Umatal. "Here, my friends, is yet another victim of the mad dreams that permeate this realm. He looks much like something from a bad dream himself! Away! Go out and annoy a street hound or one of the little wharflings on the Skai waterfront."

"I cannot leave. I am forced here by sorcery. I must wait for them," persisted Elfloq. He shuddered as he thought of the words of Ubeggi, the Weaver of Wars, from whom he had recently come. "But you have little time. I speak of real evil. These terrible ones are the slaves of something infinitely more vile. I speak of Ybaggog, the Dark Destroyer."

Umatal's hand shot out and gripped Elfloq by the throat, pulling him across the table. Cats screeched and leapt back, leaving fur dancing in the air. "Ybaggog!" snarled Umatal. "What do you know of him?"

"He sends his envoys here. They must be eradicated."

"How do you know of this?" said Ibidin.

Elfloq wriggled, but was caught like a hooked fish. "Ah — my master. He is a great sorcerer. He is engaged in a tumultuous cosmic struggle with Ybaggog, dedicated to wiping out the Destroyer's minions."

"Who is this master of yours?"

"He is known as the Voidal."

The travellers from the South glared at each other.

"Who?" they said in unison, baffled.

"Have you not heard of him?" piped Elfloq, struggling for breath.

Umatal and Ibidin shook their heads.

"That is because he shrouds himself in mystery and legend, so that he is not taken by his enemies, chief among whom is Ybaggog."

"There are a thousand sorcerers on every world. What makes your master so powerful?" asked Umatal suspiciously.

"Should you meet him, you would know at once."

"And where is he?" said Ibidin.

"Ah," said Elfloq, with what he intended to be a theatrical pause. "He waits without. Ready for the summons."

The men turned to the inn door, but Elfloq shook his head. "Not in this realm. He walks in the void between universes."

"Indeed?" said Umatal sceptically.

"Then call him," said Ibidin. "If he can help us, call him!"

Elfloq masked his terror at that particular thought, and shook his head. "I cannot, sirs, as I am his slave. It is I who do his bidding, not he mine. He would not obey me."

Umatal's eyes narrowed. "Why should I perform a convocation rite about which I understand nothing? I know of men who have summoned up demons and of the prices they have had to pay. You summon him."

Elfloq tried not to look as though some great beast were about to devour him. This was not working out at all well. Ubeggi had charged him with coming here and summoning the Voidal, but the familiar remained terrified of the consequences. In spite of his promise to Ubeggi, he was determined to trick someone else into doing this. "Very well, release me." They did so, and at once he flew up into the rafters.

Ibidin cursed and flung his knife, but in the darkness the blade lodged in a thick beam some feet from Elfloq's membranous wings.

"Send the cats after him!" said Umatal, pulling shut the window. Drath was loath to do as the tall man asked, but he did not argue. He ignited a number of candles, which threw a shimmering and vast shadow of Elfloq on the upper walls. Drath spoke and the cats uncurled. As one they gazed up at the familiar, anticipating an unusual meal.

"No!" cried Elfloq. "You are unwise to distrust me! I mean only to help you. Bring my master here. He will save you all. He will save all Ulthar — all the dreamlands — everything!"

Umatal nodded to Drath, who whispered something. At once the cat horde began leaping up on to tables, flowing out to the shelves and clawing for the beams that would lead them, by stages, to the trapped figure above.

"I will give you a last opportunity to prove your good intent," called Umatal. "Summon your master yourself."

Elfloq knew that he had failed, and worse, knew that he could not skip on to the astral realm as he would easily have done under normal circumstances. The spell of Ubeggi bound him to this inn until the Weaver's other servants came. But where were they? Elfloq felt doubly trapped: as soon as they got here, they would force him to invoke his master. The situation was not an auspicious one. The cats were already up on the beam and crawling along it upon eager bellies. There were many of them.

At that moment there came a heavy knock on the inn door. The men below cursed and Drath turned to them for instructions. The travellers looked up at Elfloq, who shrugged. The cats were motionless, all staring fixedly at Elfloq. Again the hammering on the door came, and then it opened to reveal a tall figure in a scarlet cloak and hood, a man who seemed to appraise the strange situation at once. He shut the door and bolted it, and as he came into the room, the cats drew back from him as if he were a wolf. They began to howl in their awful fashion, and nothing Drath could say would still them.

"You have chosen a bad time to visit this inn," said Umatal.

"You should thank me," said the stranger in a hard voice, one that was used to giving commands. He hissed something at the cats and they flattened themselves and amazingly were silent, a uniform movement that brought gasps of shock from the men of the South. Drath looked even more disturbed.

"Thank you?' said Ibidin. "For what?"

"Had you succumbed to Elfloq's wish and summoned the Voidal, you would doubtless have perished unpleasantly, along with this furry tribe."

"Then you are not the familiar's master?" said Umatal.

The scarlet-robed man shook his head. "No." He looked up at Elfloq. "Come down from that ridiculous perch, Elfloq. The cats will not harm you while I am here."

Elfloq obeyed. He knew the man to be a Divine Asker, a spokesman of the Dark Gods, those who used his master and who kept him chained to their own grim causes for whatever crimes he had once committed against them. It was not wise to dissemble with an Asker. But what in the many dimensions could one of them want here? Still, it had indeed been a timely intervention.

The familiar stood before the Asker, gazing up at him uncomfortably. Amazingly, the Asker put a hand on the familiar's shoulder in an almost affectionate way. He turned to the innkeeper and his guests. "Elfloq is known to us. He has a silver tongue, and I know how you value silver." The Asker took from his blood-red cloak a heavy bag and tossed it on to a table. It thudded down, the coins inside clinking. "Here it is in abundance. Take it."

Neither Umatal nor Ibidin moved, but their eyes filled with hunger.

"Am I not right in assuming that Elfloq would have been trying to inveigle you into summoning his master?"

"Your esteemed fountain of all holiness does me wrong," began Elfloq, but the tightening grip on his shoulder silenced him.

"My advice," went on the Asker, "is to take the silver and go back to your caravan. You are at liberty to remain if you wish, but be warned — those who next come in will not be kind. They are all the familiar said they are, and more."

Ibidin reached for the bag of silver, but Umatal snatched his hand away. They grunted their goodbyes to Drath and in a moment had left. The Asker went to a table and called on Drath to bring him wine. The cats shifted like grass before the scarlet robe, and soon were hardly visible at the extremities of the room. "Be easy, Drath," said the Asker. "None of this night's work need concern you. Elfloq! Sit upon the table here. I have matters to discuss with you."

Elfloq obeyed. Where were the others? "Master —"

A raised hand stilled him. As he sat before the Divine Asker, he saw the eyes for the first time. They had a sadness about them, as if a good deal of the original hardness in them had gone. "We have a little time before the others come." The Asker sat forward with a sigh. Elfloq was puzzled. This was not the way in which the Askers behaved — something was certainly amiss with this one.

"I think perhaps, Elfloq, you must have won a special place in the minds of my fellow Askers. Darquementi, our Principal Questioner, has spoken of you more than once. Does this surprise you?"

The Asker could hardly have got a more shocked reaction from Elfloq had he dipped him in boiling oil, but the familiar covered his distress. "Yes, indeed, master. Darquementi is held in great esteem." Elfloq recalled his brushes with the terrifying personage all too clearly.

"Most of the things you do are observed — most. There are times, I imagine, when our eyes are not on you. It is a busy omniverse. At the moment, much is transpiring. Strange forces are working, and we cannot see everything. Why should Darquementi be concerned about you, eh?"

"Because of my master?" said Elfloq, but at once wished he had not.

The Asker laughed softly. "Yes, your forbidden master. The Voidal."

"Though, of course, he — and thus I — are the slaves of the Dark Gods."

The Asker gazed across what seemed a vast distance. "I wonder." After a moment he had recovered himself. "Now, what is this business you are on for the Weaver of Wars? He sent you here to invoke your master, did he not?"

Elfloq knew better than to lie this time. "He did, knowing that it would be the end of me."

"Apparently he thought so. Well, it does not suit the Dark Gods that you should meet your doom in Ulthar — at least, not through the invoking of your master. However, it does suit the Askers that the Voidal comes here. The Dark Gods have work for him. Ybaggog must be destroyed. Otherwise he will bring to the omniverse an incomparable darkness."

"Given a little more time, I would have made the men from the South —"

Drath appeared, set down wine and then withdrew solemnly. The Asker smiled at the earnestness of the familiar. "Elfloq, Elfloq, have you learned nothing? You would have sacrificed those men needlessly."

"But the importance of the task —"

"Which is?"

"Destroying Ybaggog?"

"Is that the will of Ubeggi? To bring the Voidal here to destroy Ybaggog? No, little one. Ubeggi has other designs. Jealous of his power, he wishes to see your dark master locked away forever. And how will that serve your own ambitions, eh?"

Elfloq studied his feet uncomfortably. Did the Askers know everything?

"But what of justice? Do you not respect it, even a shade? The two travellers were harmless, reasonably good men. What sins they have committed may well find them out, but do they deserve to meet the Voidal's power? Of course not. I realise you acted out of terror, which is understandable. It is a typical ploy of Ubeggi. But you must be fair. Some other person must bring the Voidal here."

Elfloq leaned closer and whispered, "Drath?"

The Asker laughed aloud and slapped the table. "Stars of the Abyss!"

Elfloq shook his head. "No, not Drath. Foolish of me. You mean Snare, or that double-dealing worm, Orgoom."

"Oh, you have no liking for the Blue Gelder?"

"Betrayer! First he serves Ubeggi, then is freed by my master, and now he serves Ubeggi again."

"And yet he acts as you do, to save his hide. He bends with the winds of chance. Had he not done so, he would not have lived so long. Remember, he does not love Ubeggi, though he may take the guise of a willing slave to him."

"Snare, then! The vile demon-priest, Ubeggi's servant. Or that repugnant half-face, who now also serves the Weaver."

"Shatterface? Neither he nor Snare would be foolish enough to call up the dark man."

"Then who?"

The Asker took a hurried drink of wine and became silent for a few moments.

Elfloq stared at him. "*You* will call him? You? Ah, then as an Asker, you must have the power to revoke the curse that falls on he who —"

But the Asker was shaking his head. "No, I must take the consequences."

Elfloq was staggered. "You do this willingly?" This was a trick. There was some devious, underhand scheme running through this.

"I will do it," said the Asker. "I will tell you why, even though you may not believe me." He drank again of the wine, then pushed it away. "My name is Vulparoon, and once I was the highest of the high in the order of the Ascendant Mages. I was called to the Divine Askers and after a long initiation joined them and served at Holy Hedrazee. I did the work of the Dark Gods, the Punishers, and for a long time I did nothing to earn their displeasure. However, Darquementi remarked to me one day that I was considered a moderate, and that I did not seem to seek out evil and crush it as devotedly as one of my calling should. My absolute dedication was in question. I came before the Most High of the Askers, and I reeled under their probes. I was found lacking. The Dark Gods, they told me, are never to be questioned, always to be obeyed, and all that is done in their name is just and fair. Their enemies are to suffer, endlessly, until they decree otherwise. Just as your master, the Voidal, pays for his sins by walking eternity. Serve as an Asker should, they told me, or go from Hedrazee."

"They rejected you?"

"In a way. But you see, they are just. Even in sending me out, they have given me the chance to atone."

"For your sin of moderation, if it is a sin, they sent you here to invoke my master!"

"It was not an order. I do this of my own free will."

"Why not flee? You are free of them."

"Am I?"

Elfloq did not have to answer.

"I will flee afterwards. You see, I know the dilemma of the Askers. They fear this Voidal. It is not easy for them to keep him locked up inside the void they have made for him. They want him shut away, just as Ubeggi does. Devoured by the one who dreams out there, and whom all fear. If Ybaggog consumes the Voidal, I need fear no penalty for summoning him." He strode to the door and in a moment was gone.

Elfloq was surprised by what seemed to have been a genuine show of affection, something he rarely met. But he snapped out of his semi-trance and was about to pursue Vulparoon when he saw others arriving. Hunched in the doorway was the gangling Snare, a cruel smile on his white face. He was pulling at the ear of a Blue Gelder, whom Elfloq recognised at once as Orgoom, and Snare twisted the ear so that the unfortunate creature tumbled into the inn. He gazed around him, his eyes wide in fear, firelight gleaming on those terrible sickles that were his fingers.

"Greetings, master," stammered Elfloq, shuffling backwards and banging into a table. "All is as Ubeggi wished. My erstwhile master comes."

Snare spat, his eye catching the shadowed movement of Drath. "Here, innkeeper! Food and wine! The working to bring us to this place has exhausted me. Though you got here fast enough, familiar! Tried to flee my web, eh? Bruised your wings?" His long neck dipped down, his hideous face leering as though it would turn the very cats to stone.

"I wouldn't be so foolish," Elfloq answered with feeling. "I've waited patiently."

Drath quietly set cold meat and more wine down and Snare began wolfing the food at once. He scowled at the innkeeper. "Is this true? Or did he try to flap his way out of my trap?"

Drath smiled. "He wasted a little effort, no more."

Snare laughed bitterly, spitting out particles of food. He pointed to the familiar.

"To business! Invoke your master. Do it at once."

Elfloq had retreated as far as the window ledge and hopped up on to it again. "I knew how invaluable time was, master. Already he is summoned."

"Again!" snarled the tall one, rising and flinging a tankard at Elfloq. It shattered against stone and several cats hissed in the dark. As soon as Snare saw them, he hunched down as if about to be attacked. "Damn these creatures! Can't you get them out of here, innkeeper?"

Drath made no move to do so, but spoke softly to them.

"Ask him," said Elfloq. "Ask him if my master is coming."

Snare scowled horribly at Drath. "Well? Has he done it? Did he perform his disgusting ritual while awaiting us?"

Drath studied Elfloq for a moment, then nodded.

Snare strode to the innkeeper, mindful of the restless legion of cats that had been reforming since Vulparoon's exit. "So he's done it, has he? Then you'll know the name that he called on, eh? What was it?"

Drath ignored Elfloq's frantic mime behind Snare's long back. "I heard only one word."

"Yes?"

"Voidal."

Snare whipped round and fixed Elfloq with a withering gaze. "So you spoke the truth for once!"

"Of course."

"Excellent!" Snare turned upon the wretched Orgoom. "Time for you to earn your part in this, Gelder. Remember that Ubeggi has offered to restore you, to make you a man once more, if you serve him as you ought. I must go and prepare. Shatterface will soon be here. Wait for him and be sure that Elfloq does not try to wriggle away. There's more work for that scum yet." Snare guzzled the last of the wine and went to the door, kicking out at a cat that had strayed near him, and then was gone.

At once Elfloq rushed over to Orgoom. "Let us hurry away before Shatterface arrives."

But Orgoom barred the way, flashing his curled sickles. "We wait."

Elfloq drew back, appealing to Drath. "Tell him to stand aside."

Drath came to them. "I understand little of what is happening, but I spoke for you just now, familiar. Perhaps I was atoning for almost letting the cats have you. Now I am curious about your master, this Voidal, whom so many people wish to inconvenience."

"He is all-powerful. He will destroy Ybaggog, and after that, the Weaver himself. The Gelder is foolish to think Ubeggi is stronger."

Orgoom's face was set. "We wait."

"*You* wait," said Elfloq. "*I* wish to leave."

"Why?" said Drath. "Since the Voidal is your master."

Orgoom nodded. "You said he would be my master. I meet him and see."

The door opened yet again. Elfloq hopped back with an inadvertent squeak as the new visitor stepped forward. It was Shatterface. His steel helm gleamed, only the hellish eyes visible, his tall body encased in linked mail.

"You are expected," said Drath. "If you can do the things that your servant here promises, all Ulthar should welcome you, demon or otherwise."

Shatterface turned his mask upon the man. "Where is Snare?"

"This is not my master," said Elfloq, trying to inject a great deal of meaning into his voice, and indeed, Drath was quick to understand. This, he guessed, must be the last of the black envoys that the familiar had spoken of to the travellers from the South.

"Snare prepares way," said Orgoom.

"Quite," said Elfloq. "Why not sit and take wine?"

Shatterface did not answer, but he sat.

"Voidal coming," said Orgoom.

Shatterface turned to him like a hound at bay.

"Invoked already?" He wrenched out his sword, and it sang evilly as he pointed it at Elfloq. "You'd like me to wait, wouldn't you, familiar? I've not forgotten how your interference in Nyctath cost me my prize, the restoration of my face. I should cut out your vitals and feed them to you —"

"Better to go!" Elfloq cried. "Ubeggi's plans will come to nothing if the Voidal arrives and finds you."

Shatterface lowered the frightful weapon. "The Dark Gods have put this blade in my hands. It is the Sword of Madness. When the time is ripe, familiar, I will have your head for a lamp." He got up and marched away into the night.

"Strange company you keep," said Drath. "Who is he?"

"He was once a god," said Elfloq. "The most beautiful god of all, but vanity undid him. The Dark Gods punished him by destroying his face and by dispersing one half of it throughout the omniverse. Once they promised him they would return it if he helped them to destroy the Voidal. He failed them —"

"You were involved?"

"As a mere onlooker," Elfloq said modestly. "But I fear that the Dark Gods have given him yet another chance to strike at my master, with the Sword of Madness."

"Then if the Dark Gods and Ubeggi are united against your master," said Drath, "the odds would not seem to be very good, wouldn't you say?"

Neither of them had noticed the deepening shadow in the corner of the inn furthest from the embers of the fire. The cats stirred and arched themselves at something there, and Elfloq knew at once what had happened: the summons of the Asker had not gone unanswered. Orgoom drew back, more fretful than the cats. In a moment the darkness cleared a little to reveal a man sitting at the table, his attire blacker than that of the sky outside. Drath shuddered, recognising at once the power locked inside that form.

"Master!" cried Elfloq, hopping to the side of the Voidal.

"Elfloq? Have you been working your trickery again?"

"You wrong me, master, as always."

"Indeed? How did I come here? Where is this place?"

Drath came forward. "You are in Ulthar, the city of cats."

The Voidal nodded, though this meant nothing to him. He stared at the unhappy visage of Orgoom. "I know you."

The Blue Gelder was shivering, shaking his head.

Elfloq grinned. "Orgoom, master. You once saved him from Ubeggi's wrath. For which the Weaver has not forgiven you, but for which Orgoom repays you by going back to that vile heap of —"

"Yes, I recall some of my past, though it is often no more than a dream. Orgoom is a renegade? Was it you that summoned me, Gelder? If so, you may have cause to regret it."

"It was me," interrupted Elfloq at once.

The Voidal scowled at him impatiently. "Silence, imp. Who was it?"

"But it was me!" insisted Elfloq.

The dark man looked at him with mounting annoyance. "It could not have been you, Elfloq. I told you once before that if you ever summoned me again, it would be your undoing."

"Yes, master. Indeed you did. But it was me."

The Voidal stared at him for a long time. He knew that Elfloq was lying, for he understood clearly the complete terror in which the little familiar held him. Since the time he had done so in Cloudway, Elfloq would never have invoked him again, even under pain of a dozen grim deaths. They had shared too many dark deeds. No one knew more than Elfloq of the dark man's powers. The Voidal assumed that Elfloq, therefore, was hatching yet more schemes and lying for a deliberate reason. For the time being he would pretend to accept this. "It was you?"

"Quite so, master."

"I see. Then I am bound by the laws of the Dark Gods, whom I serve, to obey your wishes. What am I to do for you?"

"I will tell you," came the voice of Snare, grating along the walls of the night. He stood by the door, slick with sweat, panting with exertion. "Elfloq takes *my* commands."

Elfloq was at that moment sorely tempted to command the Voidal to destroy Snare, Orgoom, Shatterface and Ubeggi, but remembered barely in time that as he had not himself summoned the Voidal, he had no power to command him. Instead, Elfloq nodded meekly. "Yes. You must obey Snare. That is my wish."

The Voidal knew that this gangling, insect-like man, Snare, had not summoned him, but still he played along with Elfloq's ruse. There would be time to find out its twists — after all, the familiar sought power, but invariably unearthed useful secrets for the Voidal. What news would he have for him this awakening? "Very well. What am I to do?"

"I have prepared a place, Voidal. I have opened the walls of the dreamscape and made a place. There is to be a Mass of sacrifice. Elfloq and Orgoom are to be the neophytes. I am to be the priest."

"And what will you sacrifice?" said the Voidal.

"You will see. Let us go to the prepared place."

Drath watched them leave: Snare, the two small figures, and lastly the dark man, who had made no move, no sign of refusal, as if he had no real interest in the fate that the strange group had prepared for him. Was this enigmatic being going to be the saviour of Ulthar? If this could be true, then he was a man to respect. Drath had no respect for the hideous Snare, nor for the Blue Gelder, but had instantly taken to the triple-tongued familiar. He had taken the small one's side, and it had been the familiar who had come and warned them of the grim harbingers of the Dark Destroyer. Perhaps it would not be a bad thing to keep abreast of the activities of the party. Drath spoke to several of his many cats, and they slunk out into the darkness of Ulthar on silent feet, as fleeting and intangible as dreams.

* * * *

Snare had chosen his place of sacrifice with great care. Some miles from Ulthar was an open plain, called simply the Mutterings. It was dusty and sparsely dotted with scrubby plants and heather, as though the rocks spurned the advance of the woods around the city. In a natural hollow that faced the open plain, Snare had set up his half moon of spells, daubing rocks in his own blood, and in the centre of the chosen place he had sorcerously erected two huge monoliths and had set upon them a third block for a lintel. This gate, splotched in heiroglyphs and grotesque figures, faced outwards, an eye upon the plain. Those whispering creatures that Snare had invoked to help him prepare this place had withdrawn back to the grim regions from which he had conjured them, so that now all was silent, drenched by the bright glow of Ulthar's staring moon.

Into the hollow came the party. Snare went to the centre of the place and turned to the Voidal, who had made no attempt whatsoever to forego coming here. He seemed either bemused or intrigued and Snare wondered at his apparent obedience. Snare also wondered at the thoughts of Elfloq, who had as yet done nothing to hinder him. Ubeggi had warned him that the familiar was no trustworthier than Ybaggog himself — the Weaver had told Snare to destroy Elfloq when the working was done.

"All is almost ready," said Snare, who had now opened a pack and brought out a robe made of skin, embroidered with the same frightful things that were on the gate.

"There is one particular ingredient missing," ventured Elfloq. "The… uh…the sacrifice."

Snare laughed unpleasantly. "I have not forgotten. But first, there are places for you and Orgoom by those stones. Go to them." He pointed to some flat rocks at either side of the hollow and the two smaller figures went to them, both looking over their shoulders this way and that, as though from the hill behind them would arise any amount of demons and unsavoury acolytes of the evil Snare. Orgoom, whose face was so ugly to look upon that it was impossible to read real emotion there, appeared to be accepting this all even more indifferently than the Voidal. Elfloq doubted that his own nerves would hold out much longer, and wanted to scream his desperation to escape.

Snare stood beside the dark man, evidently cautious of him. "You deserve an explanation," he said sarcastically.

The Voidal shrugged. "For some time now I have accepted that I am not moved by chance. There is no reason for me to quit your rituals. For the moment, I am curious."

Snare frowned deeply. "You are willing to help?" It did not seem possible.

"My will has no weight. The powers that move me will force my arm."

Snare turned suspiciously to Elfloq. "Is this so?"

"Indeed," the familiar said, with a bow. "I have only to command him. And as I am utterly in your power, lord, just as he is in the power of the Dark Gods, your will is to be obeyed."

The Voidal enjoyed this odd speech from Elfloq, who was telling him — quite clearly and implicitly — what was expected of him, even though there was no truth in what he said. But why in the omniverse, thought the dark man, should I trust the little monster? In spite of the sinisterness of their situation, the dark man would like to have laughed. But who, he pondered yet again, *did* summon me?

"I ask only one thing of you," said Snare. He pointed to the gate. "When the moment is right, you must walk through that gate."

Again the Voidal shrugged. "As you wish."

Snare stared at him for a while, but then moved away. He had donned his robe and soon had started to chant something. At once the air hummed. Snare looked at the outcrops of rock behind the hollow. Somewhere out there, Shatterface would be waiting. Snare flung up his arms and stood before the gate. He looked vulnerable to Elfloq, who would love to have seen the Voidal attack him, but he dared not tamper with whatever forces were at work. He felt certain Vulparoon must be somewhere hereabouts, intent on bringing ruin to Snare and his schemes.

Around them the darkness throbbed and heaved. Out on the plain there was a rippling movement and as the chant of the priest grew in volume, earth and night sky merged as though a huge window had been opened to infinity. Elfloq gasped, for he could see through the gate, which looked out not across the Mutterings, but into the pitch darkness of deep space. A few tiny points of light dotted it. Around the gate the Mutterings had become obscured by a pink mist, and from this miasma issued far sounds, dreadful grunts and groans as of a multitude of souls in dire torment. Elfloq could also hear the rumblings from under the ground. He was trying to catch the words of Snare, but they were meaningless, as though created for a tongue that was not altogether human. Snare's body was gyrating, twisting and turning as if his bones were made of liquid, and grey bolts of light — terrible black spells — shot out from the arena formed by the hollow.

By now the appalling sounds from out on the plain had swirled close and surrounded them all. The ground shook and cracked. Up from the rocks came weaving shadows, and long sickly fronds and curling tendrils rose there, each tipped with a puckered mouth, like starving predators about to feast. The stench rose like that on a bloody field of battle when the vultures feed, and the sounds from these visitors grated on the very soul. Yet the Voidal studied this spawning of chaos calmly, apparently unmoved. He had seen far more terrible things than this. Even so it seemed to Elfloq that Snare had wrenched the Mutterings out of the dreamworld and plunged it into the void of its own universe.

Snare called out to the things in the night, his bestial face contorted by a hideous smile of triumph and lust, so that the beings he had drawn up from madness came lurching forward. In all his foul speech, Elfloq recognised one word — 'shoggoth' — and knew then that these unspeakable entities were Snare's servants, harbingers of the feared Old Ones, whom even the gods shunned. Elfloq saw also, by the light of the moon, that the mouth of the priest had become pendulous, a miniature of the frightful mouths of the things he had invoked. The shoggoths swarmed, forming a half circle, pressing forward in their scores, sickly pale and blotched like fungi, limbs wriggling at the moon as if they would tear it from the sky. Some distance from the Voidal and the mad priest, the shoggoths stopped, the sounds issuing from them disgusting and mind warping.

Snare turned to face the gate into darkness and began a new incantation. Slowly, one by one, the shoggoths gave voice to the same incantation, so that it swelled obscenely, and it seemed to Elfloq that the sounds were being eaten up by the gateway, as though it drew them to it as a hole draws water. Out into that pit rushed the chant, and as it did so, the stars beyond flickered and flared, until one of them grew and burst, showering the darkness there with red embers. Snare's incessant chanting changed pitch, forming itself into one word, long and drawn out in a stentorian voice that could not have belonged to a mere man, as if a god spoke through the priest. The word, twisted and inhuman, was 'Ybaggog'. The shoggoths added to the sound, so that the name crashed out like the weight of a world, rocking the gate and reverberating outwards into the deep vault beyond. The fabric of that darkness now rippled like a silk curtain then broke as something incomprehensibly vast drifted across it. Ybaggog had been awakened.

The priest reeled back from the sight of the approaching monster, face slippery with exertion, hands by his side. His eyes were wide, for there was no disguising his terror. What he had drawn up was possibly the most evil entity in the omniverse. He was beside the still impassive Voidal. "Ybaggog comes. You must destroy him."

"Is that why I am here?"

"Yes. Go through the gate. Destroy him before he devours everything."

The Voidal felt no divine, irresistible compunction to do this thing. He looked at Elfloq, who was gibbering with terror behind the rock on which he was supposed to be standing. Could the familiar really have imagined that the Voidal would benefit by doing this?

"I command you!" snarled the priest, his fear at its limit. Behind him the shape of the Dark Destroyer thickened and solidified, a gargantuan being, alive and thrashing in the black universe in which it bathed.

The Voidal did nothing. He stood, defying Ybaggog and defying the shoggoths, which now writhed, delirious with pleasure at seeing their lord coming. They began to press forward as if eager to kiss that awesome thing, so that Snare drew back, trapped between their squirming wall and the gate. The Voidal fought to control his own mind, for this extremity of madness in which he found himself threatened to engulf even him. Yet he must see which way the Dark Gods would move. He retained his will, knowing that had he sought it, he could have cut a way through the shoggoths and left. Who had summoned him, and why? Elfloq knew, but he and Orgoom were flat to the ground, faces buried in the dust in fear.

At that moment, the shoggoths parted to allow someone through and the figure that stepped into the arena to face the Voidal was a familiar one to the dark man. "Shatterface," he said. "But even you would not have called me, knowing the price."

"No, I did not call you. Your hand of death will not reach for me!" cried the figure, pointing to the right hand of his adversary, believing it to be the Oblivion Hand. Shatterface pulled out the weapon that had been given to him. "Through the gate!" he screamed, swinging the blade. It sang with the hate of a thousand maddened voices, and the Voidal jerked backwards, no longer unmoved. He knew the sword intuitively to be the Sword of Madness, and he had every reason to fear it. So this was the answer to these riddles — the Dark Gods wanted the blade in him, for it would rob him of everything that he had won back from them. This was the fate they had planned. He pulled his own sword out from its scabbard, but it was a mere tool, cold steel without supernatural power.

Shatterface saw this and laughed. He came forward with a cry. "Through the gate!" he shouted again. "Go to your appointed prison!"

The Sword of Madness swung down, but the Voidal was nimble and slipped past its frightful bite. Elfloq took to the air, but could not move far away from the scene of the battle, gripped as he was in the spells of the priest. Snare watched the two swordsmen nervously, knowing that Ybaggog would soon be at the very portal. Beyond it now an immense mouth had opened, an Abyss into infinity, and from it issued the most overpowering stench, as of a thousand rotting hells.

The Voidal was now no more than a few yards from the lip of the gate, and Shatterface knew that in a moment he would have his prize. He thrust forward and the Voidal's sword shattered like glass into a thousand splinters. Shatterface prepared for the critical blow and as his blade came screaming in, a blur of movement from the left of the Voidal caught them unawares. Orgoom had lunged forward and his sickle fingers caught and turned the Sword of Madness, so that shrieking sparks flew into the air. Snare cried out in fury as Orgoom was flung to the very lip of the gate. A splinter of the Sword had lodged in the Gelder's hide, and his eyes bulged as the evil in it seeped into him.

"Vermin!" screamed Snare. "Traitor. Ubeggi will punish you —"

But Orgoom was not interested in the hated Ubeggi. As he got to his knees like a drunkard, he saw beyond him the titanic maw of Ybaggog. The Voidal dragged him back from the immeasurable drop. "My thanks, Gelder, but you have chosen the wrong moment to announce your fealty."

Shatterface came on, pinning the Voidal to the very gate so that the wet blood smeared him. The shoggoths were seething forward like hounds after blood. Behind them Elfloq hovered, too afraid to help. He looked down at the rocky terrain, longing to flee across it. To his amazement he saw movement and presently figures there. Instantly he recognised Drath and the two travellers from the South, who were watching the terrible fight in horror.

Elfloq flitted down. "You must save him!" he cried. "They mean to feed him to Ybaggog —"

"You told us he would destroy the Devourer," said Umatal, face seamed with horror at what he had seen.

Drath was whispering to the shadows, and Elfloq abruptly saw to his disgust that the night was crawling with cats. All of Ulthar must have turned out, for there was a veritable tide of the creatures surrounding the hollow and the massed shoggoths. The familiar flew upwards. "What are these?"

"That gate must be closed," called Drath. "It is the shoggoths who hold it open. Whatever your master is supposed to be able to do, it is evidently no use against Ybaggog. I cannot destroy him, but the gate must be closed."

"Yes, yes!" burbled Elfloq. "An excellent idea. Excellent. How?"

Drath turned to Umatal and Ibidin. "Between us, we must command our servants." He indicated the cats.

Umatal nodded. "Yes. Our servants — whatever the cost. Begin at once."

What then followed was meaningless to Elfloq, except that he knew the men were communicating in some strange way with the ocean of cats that now lapped at the hollow. They were weird creatures, these cats, with wolf-like eyes, and lean, sleek bodies, claws sharpened and oddly gleaming, souls burning with some secret inner fire fed by a god as dark as those that slept on the dreamworld of Ulthar. A hundred of these silent predators sprang from the night upon the last line of shoggoths, and the battle began. Claws tore and slashed like small swords, and the shoggoths swung and lumbered about cumbersomely, snatching up scores of the cats as they caught them, but for each one they crushed, a hundred more melted into being, until the hollow was boiling with sound and furious activity. Wave after wave of cats poured down from the hill as if a vent into a world of cats had been opened, and the shoggoths were ripped to the ground, overrun and slashed to shreds.

Snare rushed forward, forgetting for a moment the coming of the Old One, and in a matter of minutes found himself knocked to his knees by a dozen screaming cats. They tore his cloak of flesh from his shoulders and dug into him, slashing for his eyes. His fists beat at them, but they cut at him and bit him, so that he tumbled and rolled almost to the feet of the Voidal.

So much damage had the avalanche of cats done, that Shatterface himself felt the next rush of small bodies. A score of cats were on his back, trying to tear him down, but he willed himself forward. A shoggoth, its limbs severed and hanging from it in tatters, lumbered forward and fell through the gate, exploding as it dropped through space. Snare was trying to rise, but Orgoom swung an arm at him, ripping open his chest in bloody weals. The priest tried to shield himself, but the Gelder cut at him with terrible efficiency. Snare fell, his head and shoulders jutting through the gate. There, balanced upon the edge of nightmare, he screamed. Orgoom swung down his arm with the power of madness and sliced clean through Snare's neck. The head plummeted out into the rising mouth of the Old One, and as it turned end over end, the mouth still gave vent to an extended scream.

Orgoom rose just in time to witness disaster, for Shatterface was propelled forward, smashed by the tenacity of the cats that sought to drag him down, and the Voidal could not avoid the thrust of the Sword of Madness. It tore through his flesh and ripped into and through his middle, bursting out of his back, though there was no shower of blood. Orgoom knelt there in amazement as the dark man clutched the terrible sword, and it was then that the frightful screams began. Shatterface was pulled to the ground, covered by the cats, and they began ripping at him in a blur of talons.

Elfloq flew as close to the gate as he dared and there saw the horror of what had happened. The Voidal's face twisted and pulled as he cried out in pain and madness, the Sword doing its terrible work. It would not come loose. The hand of the Voidal could not free it — the Dark Gods would have their way. Back staggered the dark man, crashing into

Orgoom, and in a moment, before Elfloq could swoop down, both had fallen outwards and were plunging far down into the maw beyond the gate. Ybaggog had claimed them.

At once the darkness beyond the gate closed down, and the stones fell, leaving only a view of the dusty Mutterings and the memory of what had raged there. Elfloq flew up and away from the body of Shatterface, leaving the cats to pull from it the still-pulsing organs.

* * * *

Orgoom felt as though all the powers in the omniverse were alternately pulling and then squeezing his entire body so that it throbbed in agony as if it would burst and scatter itself before reforming and disappearing into itself. His general direction seemed to be down, although everything about him span so much that his senses had become disjointed. Fountains of stars vomited upwards and then spread outwards, curling and winking out. Gradually this maelstrom of light confined itself to his head, sinking into it, expanding, then dissolving into darkness. All that he was aware of then was the sickening sensation of spinning, but at least he was on the ground.

Eventually he moved, discovering that the ground was spongy, a thick, brackish morass. Pale light splotched the scene around him, which was some unsightly dark plain, broken only by rounded humps of black rock, or possibly fungoid growth, he could not say which. The region stank like the worst sewers that he had ever experienced, its vapours almost tangible as they wove upwards.

He sat up, trying to scrape off some of the muck that had splattered him, and gazed about him. Either he was under some evil night sky, or he was in an enormous cavern of unprecedented proportions. There were shadows high above him, and as they seemed to be hanging, he guessed the latter, glad that he could make out no details. It was then that he recalled his fall through the gate — could he be *inside* Ybaggog? If so, then this around him was an enclosed universe. Such things existed.

Before his mind could burst at contemplating this concept, he saw something stir near him. A body floated face down in the mire and several black shapes from under the mire were worrying at it, trying to drag it under. Before they could succeed, there were submarine bursting sounds, spreading the thick muck in low waves. In a moment the body was left alone. From its back protruded the point of a sword, which moaned softly to itself. This must be the Voidal, mused Orgoom, dead at last.

The Gelder wondered if he had gone mad, for a sliver of the sword must still be lodged in him. Certainly there was nothing sane about this frightful zone. However, he had escaped the frightful Ubeggi, and had sworn to himself that he would serve Elfloq's master. He scurried over the hump of rock and reached for the body. He tugged it ashore with his sickle hands, and it moved, dragging itself to its knees, not dead at all. Slowly, like a zombie, the dark man got to his feet, eyes shut, mouth slack. The Sword of Madness gave forth a howl of glee, and the face of the Voidal came alive. Those awful green eyes seemed to be looking out on an invisible and lunatic inner universe. The man began to snigger with obscene mirth so that Orgoom drew back in revulsion. The sounds went on interminably, until at last they subsided into a sequence of monotonous chuckles, meaningless and disquieting. Orgoom had no idea how to act.

"Not stay," he said, comforted by his own voice. The eyes of the Voidal looked at him, but there was no response in them. He had been reduced by the power of the Sword to complete madness. Orgoom turned away, trying to see a way across the empty mire, not knowing where he could go. Overhead he heard the squawks of something large and vile, but there was only the hint of a shadow in this dismal misty light. Shuddering, the Gelder moved on. Mechanically, behind him, the Voidal trudged in awkward pursuit, moved by some unknown force.

Around him in the mire, Orgoom now saw a number of floating corpses, bleached white and partially overgrown with peculiar lumps that had their own strange light. They fed on the dead, for the corpses occasionally turned in the mire, mad faces glaring up at the moonless vaults above, while other corpses were not even remotely human. Yet other things swam in the black waters, keeping away from the sounds that Orgoom's feet made as he splashed loudly on. By keeping as close as he could to the outcrops of rock, the Gelder was able to avoid deep water.

Something dropped from the air and alighted on a hummock nearby. It was black and misshapen, half bird, half beast, and its curved beak opened in silence. Others flapped down, forming a half circle so that only one avenue was open to Orgoom. The Gelder looked along this, not wanting to be herded, but he could see now that the hummocks extended in a chain, like the radius of a wheel, to a point on the horizon. Something dark and ominous loomed there, embedded like a cliff or a high hill. Orgoom had no alternative but to go there — the grim visitors from the sky had made that clear.

The Gelder leapt from one slippery hummock to another, gasping as a number of them flinched under his touch: they were not rocks. Behind him the Voidal came on, tugged by a force that Orgoom did not understand, and the flapping half-birds kept well back from the dark figure, as though one touch would bring death. Ahead of him, Orgoom could see the phosphorescent mass of the huge hill more clearly. It rose up from the midst of the morass, and at once the Gelder understood its importance. It was a living organ, pulsing and throbbing with life, here at the centre of Ybaggog's vitals. Like a citadel, it towered, shimmering with eerie light, the air around it whispering like unseen life. The low rumble of its workings beat like the sound of blood through the terrain.

As Orgoom came under the shadow of those vast walls of knotted flesh, he saw that near the uppermost heights, fronds were lowering quickly, tangled and knotted like the roots of a sprawling saprophyte forest. They rushed down towards the mire, and as they did so, a great wave of filth broke beneath them and out of the murky depths came a sudden rush of elongated yellow growths, groping blindly like fleshy fingers. In moments the two great masses of wriggling life had locked in the most frightful contest of strength, so that the mire heaved and spread waves outwards, and the citadel above shook. Great chunks of tendril and yellow flesh were flung out from the entangled mass and Orgoom stood his ground with difficulty. Above him he could see more of the repulsive blotched fronds dropping down to enjoin the battle, until at last they seemed to have beaten off the terrible threat from below. Like a disjointed, smashed hand, the yellow monster sank back into the muck.

The growths from the ramparts withdrew upwards in silence, and soon all was still again. An abrupt movement beside him awakened Orgoom and he turned to see a diminutive being. It was naked, pale and shivering, its face torn by suffering and fear. Orgoom immediately brandished a sickled hand at it and it cowered so convincingly that the Gelder felt no threat from it.

"Who are you?" he hissed at the shrunken creature.

"I am No-Name. You must come with me."

"Where?"

"Up there. To the heart of Ybaggog. The City of the Screaming Eyes. I am your guide."

Orgoom looked behind him. The Voidal stood, eyes glazed, seeing nothing of this world, waiting. "Not safe," Orgoom pointed to the waters where the yellow horror had sunk.

"There is time before the next dream comes."

"What dream?"

No-Name also pointed to the waters. "From the marshes come the Sendings of the Old Ones, Dreams sent by them to attack Ybaggog's heart, for they wish to destroy him, whom they hate. Ybaggog is their master and will rule them all. He sends down powers of his own from above, the Eaters of Sleep, and they break up the Sendings. Come quickly." He darted away and Orgoom followed, not wanting to, but even less liking the prospect of staying out here in the mire with the Dreams.

No-Name found a path, a twisted and solidified artery that had once trailed out from the heart, and he and Orgoom walked along it and into an opening through a stone tangle of similar old veins. Behind them, the Voidal followed. They could hear the sword's low laughter. For a long time they climbed in the darkness, and below them dropped a bottomless well, crossed and criss-crossed of veins and stretched fibres, some hard as stone, others glowing with fluid. Orgoom had to close his mind to the stench and the echoing sibilant sounds, the cold gusts of air and the suggestive throb of movement that confirmed his presence inside a living organ.

At last they came out into the upper tiers. They gave forth a dim glow, and the Gelder saw that from the piles of living flesh yawned doorways and windows that had not been cut from it, but which had grown naturally, although they were distorted and set at strange angles. No-Name explained that the City of the Screaming Eyes was a place for the servants of the god, who went about his work here mindlessly, none knowing what purpose he served. "Ybaggog brings captives to the mire from the many universes outside himself," said No-Name. "I go down and fetch some of them in. You and the other one are fortunate, for you have been chosen to be servants, too. Those who remain in the mires and the pits are no more than fodder. Soon you will have your own secret task to perform."

Orgoom could think of nothing to say, so he sat disconsolately on an outcrop of tissue. He realised that the bizarre citadel was apparently solid here in its centre, while its outer bastions were alive with the terrible Eaters of Sleep. It disturbed him to think of them and to know that he sat upon the living god. The Voidal lurched before him, an automaton. Orgoom had thought of trying to pull the Sword of Madness from him, but nothing would induce him to touch the haft that protruded from the dark man's gut.

Instead, Orgoom watched the comings and goings of the remarkable citadel. From time to time a skulking figure would emerge from darkness and shuffle warily across the tilted plaza, always carrying some bundle. These figures all had the most frightful eyes, wide and staring as though they had looked on the ultimate vision of hell. They were mostly hybrids: some wriggled on short legs like lizards, others flopped, breathing through gills, while yet more hopped on elongated limbs and had arms like fronds. None of them retained more than a semblance of humanity, and Orgoom felt pity for them, for he had been transformed by the evilness of Ubeggi, though not so gruesomely as most of these nightmares.

They went about their mad work silently, and the objects that they carried were even more strange than they were — Orgoom was sure that he saw living things squirming in those arms, and severed members of beasts. Whatever purpose they were at, only the deformed mind of Ybaggog knew it, and Orgoom was glad that he did not have to know.

Presently a group of three beings arrived, entering the plaza from one of the twisted doorways. Their upper bodies were smooth-skinned and human, but their lower halves were segmented like the bloated bodies of huge maggots. They wriggled across the ground and came together, mouths working in silence, huge eyes staring vacantly. One of them swung something in a hand and another snatched it; in a few moments they had parted and wriggled off again on their grim errand, but in the brief minutes they had been here, Orgoom had seen enough of the object to know that it had been the head of Snare. Its eyes had been as wide and as alive as those of the others in this place.

Orgoom made to question No-Name on this, but the little figure was scrambling to its feet as if in answer to some unheard call. "It is time for us to go. You are to be given your tasks." He said no more, but went to another opening that was like the trap to a drain. Orgoom followed, the dark man plodding behind. Now they were going down a curling tunnel, where Orgoom guessed dark blood had once rushed. Set in the walls were orifices that opened and closed in silence, their function a mystery to the Gelder, though he kept well away from them. Across narrow spans the figures went, and Orgoom saw deep drops into darkness and heard the grinding and hammering of colossal organs deep below. It was like traversing the inside of a world, so vast and horizonless was its extent.

When they had come to the bottom of a steeply inclined tunnel, No-Name turned and pointed to the valve-like door ahead of them. "I go no further."

"What is beyond?" asked Orgoom, suspicious and ready to use his awful clawed hands. He had no wish to become the slave of Ybaggog and go about as those in the citadel did.

"It is a portal that looks out over the vast spaces of Ybaggog's mind. There his dreams sail past and he will choose one for you both, and in the reading of it, you will have your tasks. You and the man must go out and accept the Seeing."

Orgoom hissed and leapt back, almost colliding with the Voidal. "All this way for that? Not Orgoom!" he cried vehemently. Rather he would go back into Ubeggi's service than bow to this monstrous deity.

No-name suddenly rushed past both Gelder and the Voidal and ran back up the tunnel. He turned. "I have done my duty. Ybaggog is not to be denied. You cannot keep from him his due." With that he fled, leaving the bemused Orgoom watching. The Gelder had no idea how to act, but on no account would he go through the valve to the place beyond. He had seen quite enough of Ybaggog's revolting visions. Thus there was only one direction to take, and he began the cautious walk back up the tunnel. He had not gone far, however, when he saw movement beyond. No-Name must be returning.

But it was not him.

Something was squirming down the tunnel, clumsy and uncertain of its progress. It was a creature with an ovoid body that resembled a huge slug, with dangling limbs that were more like fins than arms. From the centre of its body rose a long neck, and upon this grew the head, like a bizarre fruit. It was human, but grown three times its normal size. Orgoom saw the staring eyes first, but as the thing came slithering down the tunnel, blocking it entirely, he recognised *the head of Snare*. It had been given a new and blasphemous life. As it saw the Gelder, it laughed evilly, its voice that of the man who had been Ubeggi's slave. "No escape, Gelder! Not here."

Orgoom readied both hands, prepared to tear this disgusting abomination to pieces, but would it be possible? Could he destroy it? He waited, shaking with terror, and the thing that Snare had become drew closer, moved only by the fires of its madness.

Behind him, Orgoom heard the valve hiss open and beyond it could sense the great void that was the dreaming mind of Ybaggog, the hell of hells. The Voidal was moving towards it. Orgoom turned, shielding his eyes, and tried to catch his sickles in the cloak of the dark man, but the fabric was like mist. The Gelder could not stop him.

Snare screamed with maniacal glee. "You cannot save him! He belongs to Ybaggog now. The Dark Gods have thrown him out — they have no power here! Only Ybaggog can command. Follow him, Gelder! Follow him and plunge into the deeps of the Dark Destroyer. Drink!" Snare flicked out a whip-like tongue and Orgoom slashed it in half with a lightning chop. But the awful mouth spat out more of them. Orgoom slashed again, but as each severed part fell, it wriggled back and was absorbed by the round bulk of Snare's body.

The Voidal was through the orifice and stood beyond, eyes facing whatever was out there. Inside his body, the Sword of Madness began an awful gush of sound, twisted and painful, a crescendo of all that was frightful. The blade turned and shivered as if it, too, endured agonies. Orgoom's ears threatened to burst as he lurched back to the tunnel wall and crouched there, almost melting into the walls. They seemed to be made of pulp, shuddering as if vibrating to the din made by the sword, as though its appalling sounds cut deep into them. Snare struggled on past Orgoom, no longer interested in the huddled Gelder.

There was a timelessness about the Voidal's encounter with the void. Ybaggog's wild dreams and nightmares floated across the pit of his mind like vast naval fleets, some drifting across to the Voidal, whose own tormented mind was closed in on itself, chained up by the madness lodged in his vitals. The first of the Sendings enveloped the dark man, and something of its power seeped through. Huge aerial monsters were tearing and ripping at each other, scattering stars in their wake and crushing whole universes as they struggled in the wildest regions of the omniverse. Gods roared their fury and burst asunder, while billions of their servants fused into rivers of molten light that poured away into the abysses of oblivion. Entire pantheons were reduced to cinders as god after god perished, and the spreading plague of horrors spawned by the lunacy of Ybaggog devoured and devoured. In the memory of the Devourer of Universes, every struggle of the gods of the omniverse still reverberated, locked into a repeated cycle of perpetualness. All was confusion, chaos, tumult and turmoil, and on this ghastly diet, Ybaggog thrived.

Yet the Sword of Madness had built its own wall of turmoil around the walls of the Voidal's seething mind, so that as the visions came, staggering in their immensity, they struck the eyes of the Voidal and shattered like ice images before the steel hammers of a madman. Ybaggog's universe shook to its roots, the entire length of it reverberating to the impact.

The Dark Gods had not allowed for such a confrontation, for the Voidal picked out from the slivers of smashed image many things that had meaning for him. Shards of memory gleamed there and he snatched them avidly, repairing them until new visions came to him. As the mad god sent more of his awesome dreams across the void, the Voidal snared at will the pieces that he wanted. As long as the Sword inside him countered the oncoming Sendings, he was in command.

The Snare creature rushed through the valve, made aware by Ybaggog of what had happened. The mad god commanded its beast. It wrapped its broken fronds around the hilt of the Sword of Madness and pulled, shrieking deafeningly as it did so. Orgoom could not watch as the sword fought like a living serpent to remain in the body of the Voidal. Snare pulled and pulled, inching the weapon out, his flesh charring, his limbs shrivelling and dropping off. Yet gradually the sword came out, until a last heave brought it free. Snare's mouth opened wide in a crazed laugh of triumph, and then that ghastly head burst in a welter of smoking gore. Within moments the body began to rupture and then it, too, burst, its leaking remains flung far out into the void of Ybaggog's dreams.

Orgoom tore free from the wall of the tunnel, which had been absorbing him like a sponge. He saw the Sword of Madness fall at the feet of the Voidal, and looked up at the dark man. The latter stood with his back to Ybaggog's lunatic void and abruptly looked down at the weapon with an intensely evil smile. In a moment he had picked it up and caressed it. He stared at Orgoom, and in that look the Gelder knew more terror than in anything he had yet lived through.

"Orgoom," said the Voidal. "The Sendings have not broken your mind."

"No, master," said the Gelder, shivering anew. Plainly the Voidal was far from mad, and no prisoner.

"Do not look at what lies behind me." The Voidal said no more. Ybaggog must have understood now that the dark man was at his mercy, for he began to send out across that black space the most terrible of his visions. The Voidal could feel it coming like a tidal wave of lunacy, but he was ready. He raised up the sword in his right hand, grinning at the hand that was his own and no longer moved by the will of his tormentors, and waited. Eagerly.

At last he span round. His eyes were closed as he flung the weapon, and it tore like a blazing sun across the interstellar vastness of that black mind, its point seeking the vision that raced to meet it.

"To your feet!" the Voidal shouted, gripping Orgoom's elbow and lifting him. They were both racing up the tunnel as the impact came. It was as if a score of universes had met and fused themselves. Soon the consequent explosion came: Ybaggog's mind writhed and tore itself apart in the chaos that followed. His body felt the rigours of an immense seizure, followed by more, greater than the first.

"What happens?" cried Orgoom, stumbling but still running.

"Ybaggog's power is disintegrating, smashed by a greater one." The Voidal laughed horribly. "I have seen it." He said no more, but laughed again. It was no longer the laughter of a madman, but laughter that spoke of some unimaginable secret, something that only the dark man knew of, for in that laughter there was confidence that a god might envy.

When they came to the plaza, they found that all of Ybaggog's servants had burst like fruit, and the heart of the god was pumping madly, turning huge parts of itself to stone and dust. These cracked and tumbled. Orgoom whimpered in terror at the thought of what must happen to him, but the Voidal gazed at the carnage with a terrible smile.

"I think this will not be the end for us, Gelder. Ybaggog will writhe and shudder for eons to come, locked away inside his own mad universe. His Sendings will torment only himself until the distant millennium when he rots at the edge of the omniverse."

"How we get out?"

"Our work is done. We have all been used, even Ubeggi. The will of the Dark Gods has triumphed here, as I guessed that it would."

The Voidal ignored the terrible sounds of destruction around them and put his hand gently on Orgoom's blue skin. "Go to sleep."

"We meet again?"

"In some other hell perhaps."

Within moments the Gelder had slumped down, eyes closed, and soon after that he was gone. For a while the Voidal was left alone to contemplate the broken riddles of his own destiny, then he, too, slipped into the great darkness until the Dark Gods would see fit to wake him again.

* * * *

The inn was silent, the cats asleep, the embers of the fire burning low. Drath nodded to himself and closed the last of the shutters. Outside there was some kind of disturbance, the air stirred as if by a distant storm, passing mercifully beyond Ulthar. The innkeeper thought of the strange company who had visited the inn, their impact on this stranger world. It was over. Tomorrow night, what stranger dreams might come?

Meanwhile, far from Ulthar, Vulparoon the Divine Asker listened with the keen ears of a bird of prey to the remote sounds, almost beyond the limits of hearing. Somewhere a mad god was falling, as mad gods did. The Asker smiled for a moment. But then he thought of the burden he carried, the knowledge that he must pay for the summoning he had made in Ulthar. Tomorrow, a week hence, ten years? Better not to know. But, as with death itself, let it be swift, he prayed.

And Elfloq, the errant familiar, popped out on to the astral realm with a grunt of mixed emotion. He was thankfully free of Ubeggi and the revolting Snare, but what of his master? Elfloq squinted into the fog. He would have to begin again. Next time they would, he hoped, meet under more auspicious circumstances. But with the Voidal, one never knew. Only the Dark Gods really knew anything. Elfloq grimaced. Even in his scheming mind, he did not have the temerity to curse them.

PART FIVE

THE SLIVER OF MADNESS

And so again to Cloudway, most enigmatic of all havens.
Fate wheels and deals and still the guests sit in as the dice roll, the cards fall. Still they play their hands, convinced that this time, they will control the flow of destiny.
Only one card matters. Everything else is simply a preparation for its revelation. One card.
The last one.
—**Salecco**, who prefers to observe and record, rather than participate.

* * * *

Eye Patch of the Smile served wine for one. Rarely had Cloudway been so empty. The warden of the astral haven indicated the silent hall and its deserted tables with a nod of his head. "Busy times outside," he noted. "Portentous events unfold, I feel."

The green-eyed man at the bar sipped the wine appreciatively. "This idlewine is faultless, host. Is this not a vintage sample?"

Eye Patch smiled with something approaching secret understanding. "Indeed it is, sir. The very best idlewine."

"I am favoured, then. I have never tasted better. Better even than your Gundroot Smoothyear or your remarkable Ascapandrian Cream-of-the-Dew."

"The very best," agreed Eye Patch, closing his good eye in a wink. "You are undoubtedly a man of great taste. I had guessed as much. Perceiving that, I chose idlewine for you."

"My thanks. Your knowledge of things generally is no less remarkable than the quality of your wine. I find it strange that you are able to judge me a man of taste. Usually I am a man without identity, fate or memory. You seem to take an alternative view."

Eye Patch merely adjusted his eye covering, which today was a regal purple, the patch one of scores that he kept in a locked casket. Rumours about the powers of these patches abounded in Cloudway, though only the host was party to the truth of the matter. "No man who knows his wine as well as you do can be bereft of memory. You have named the three best wines in the entire omniverse. Once tasted, never forgotten. Surely you cannot be an aimless man."

The other also smiled, the answer seeming to please him. "It is true. I am much travelled." As if by afterthought, he took from his dark cloak a small, sealed jar and placed it on the counter. "This will test your knowledge, though. I doubt, good host, that you have ever seen the like of the contents of this jar."

Eye Patch stared at it, his smile for a moment dissolving as he concentrated. The contents of the vessel were murky and had about them an air of unpleasantness. "I think you are right."

"Will you keep this for me?" said the traveller, pushing the jar across the counter. "It is for someone who will shortly be coming here. His name is Elfloq. He is a being you could not fail to recognise, even should Cloudway be full to bursting."

"In that you are also correct." Eye Patch took the jar and hid it away, again smiling. Then he had disappeared into the shadows as he collected used glasses from revels of earlier.

The Voidal went to one of the large fireplaces where embers glowed comfortably in its grate. Yes, he recalled those wines, and many other things besides. Not an aimless man? Yet it had been his lot since the curse of the Dark Gods had fallen on him. To have no purpose but theirs. He shook his head, bent down and lifted a handful of hot embers in his right hand. He blew upon them and flames sprang up like a torch. He licked at them, as if testing their reality, then closed his hand snuffing them out. His hand was unharmed. But he knew that the hand was his own, not the dread member he had carried for so long for his masters.

From one of the tables there came a flutter of sound. The Voidal screened himself behind a large chair back from the view of whoever had arrived. Someone had dropped from the rafters high up in the smoky roof of Cloudway. The dark man smiled to himself, recognising the squat form and unmistakable bulbous eyes of Elfloq. The familiar folded his delicate wings and went to the bar, peering about him in obvious agitation, as though, as usual, all the horrors of the omniverse were hot on his metaphorical tail.

"Host!" Elfloq called. In a moment he found himself gazing at the regal purple eye patch of that very being. The significance of the colour escaped him, but he had no mind to ask what it might be.

"Elfloq," said Eye Patch of the Smile, his features living up to his name. "Have you come to shelter here once more? Who have you offended this time? Swindled some god out of his due? Pinched the assets of an unwary sorcerer?"

"I would never be so foolish," Elfloq retorted, but he knew well enough that his host understood his nature all too well. "Bring strong wine. Nothing but the best, mind. Tutorbora Blue, if you have it."

Eye Patch snorted with amusement, Elfloq having named one of the most overrated wines known in the omniverse. "Of course. And is this luxury for one? Or are others to be privileged to share your generosity?"

Elfloq shook his head in exaggerated sadness. "For one. I fear I am alone in the omniverse once more."

"With no master? Frozen stars, Elfloq, however will you survive? You seem cursed with atrocious fortune," Eye Patch laughed, amused by the sour expression on the face of the ugly little being.

"My master is truly doomed. Locked now inside a terrible universe, himself utterly insane. I tried to enter and aid him, but alas, the gate to the evil place closed on me as I flew away — that is, as I attempted to enter it." Elfloq swigged at the proffered wine as if intent on getting intoxicated as quickly as he could.

"So the Dark Gods have locked the Voidal away, then?" mused Eye Patch. "Presumably he will remain incarcerated for all eternity and not disturb them again?"

"I fear that is their intent."

"Then who will you serve?"

Elfloq gripped the wine bottle tightly and strutted over to one of the tables. "That is a secret not fit even for your ears," he grumbled.

"Take heart. As long as your master is alive, you have life. If he is trapped, then you may roam the omniverse at will. It seems to me, Elfloq, that you are your own master now," Eye Patch added, with a chuckle. He glanced briefly at the chair where he knew the Voidal to be listening, though the familiar remained oblivious to that.

Elfloq banged the wine bottle down and turned, huge eyes alight. "Why — yes! That must be so. The dark man cannot control me. I may do as I wish."

He was about to launch into a dissertation on the possibilities of being his own master, when what threatened to be a lengthy speech was cut short by the abrupt and noisy arrival of a further party. A door had opened and slammed shut and in a blur of movement, someone had come in, practically tumbling, spinning as if tossed in by a storm or the hand of a giant. Tables crashed over and chairs toppled as the newcomer lost his balance and fell. Elfloq took to the air and hovered some ten feet from the ground, fully expecting this to be a curse upon him for the things he had said.

Eye Patch approached, rolling up the cuffs of his shirt, prepared for any difficulties. There came a garbled stream of unrelated obscenities from the fallen entrant, mingled with snarls and growls and the most perfidious muttering that any of the onlookers, hidden or otherwise, had ever heard.

Eye Patch brought a large candle and held it above the shape that snarled at him from where it had fetched up under one of the tables. It was blue, like a hound or a small animal and had long, curved claws that swished through the air in a particularly unnerving fashion. It also had the ugliest face that Eye Patch had yet seen in all his years as host of Cloudway (and that included the face of Elfloq, which was not at all pretty) and its mouth drooled and dribbled revoltingly, confirming that whatever manner of being it was, it was without doubt completely mad.

Elfloq dropped lower, but remained out of reach of those grim sickles. "Gods of the Abyss! This is none other than the Blue Gelder!"

"You know him?" said Eye Patch.

"Why, yes! It is Orgoom!"

At the sound of his name, the mad Orgoom slashed through the legs of a chair, parting the wood like hairs. He snarled anew, then subsided, muttering to himself.

"A Blue Gelder," murmured Eye Patch. "One of Ubeggi's unsavoury little servants. It is a very rare thing to have one here. They usually frequent Mindsulk, or some such warren of the night. This one is evidently not what he should be."

Elfloq's mind was racing. "Orgoom!" he cried. "What happened? Did you not fall into the belly of Ybaggog?"

Eye Patch grimaced. "Have you also lost your senses? Ybaggog — the Devourer of Universes? Must you mention such an obnoxious god in this place? You will frighten off the remainder of my guests."

Elfloq looked at him suspiciously. "What guests?"

"There are always guests here. Upstairs there are a handful, resting, or mulling over their parchments, or entertaining guests of their own. That is their affair, not yours. I will leave you to amuse your blue-skinned friend. But I will expect him to respect the furniture. If he becomes unruly, he will have to be ejected. It has been a long time since I had to call upon the muscular attributes of Vlod the Remover, but he would enjoy the exercise." Eye Patch patiently set upright the chairs and tables then returned to his bar.

Elfloq attempted to speak to Orgoom, but the Gelder was locked into his madness and in the end, the familiar was forced to give up. "Useless," he said. "Ybaggog must have spewed him out, understandably. But the Voidal must still be trapped."

Eye Patch had appeared again. "It has just occurred to me that one of my guests may be able to help you. He will be coming shortly for a meal."

"Who is he?"

"He told me earlier something of Ubeggi, master of the Gelders. All is not well with the Weaver of Wars. His latest tapestry appears to be in something of a tangle. Oh, and in the confusion, I nearly forgot to give you this." He placed the mysterious jar on the table directly below Elfloq. "A guest left it for you." Eye Patch said no more, once again at the bar.

Elfloq dropped beside the table and picked up the jar gingerly and tried to see into its black interior. He found no clues as to what it contained. Left it for him? Who would have done such a thing? But the familiar knew countless beings in the astral regions, some of whom he had traded with. Probably this revolting jar was from one of them, a gift in return for favours he had done. For the time, Elfloq set it aside and tried to content himself with watching the door to the stairs.

A short while later his vigilance was rewarded as a figure entered the hall. At sight of it, Elfloq drew back, recognising the scarlet robe of one of the Divine Askers. Yet the Asker went and sat in silence and apparent misery at a table, ignoring his surroundings. Eye Patch of the Smile gave him a simple meal. The host nodded meaningfully to Elfloq before disappearing. The familiar pondered his dilemma, for he could not bring himself to face the Asker. Instead, he prepared to leave Cloudway. However, Orgoom suddenly slashed out with his sickles, narrowly missing Elfloq, but sending him sprawling.

The Asker heard the commotion and at once had recognised the squamous familiar. "Elfloq!" he called. "Stop crawling about under the tables. Come here!"

Sheepishly the familiar obeyed and found himself for the second time before Vulparoon, the Asker who had been cast out of Hedrazee for his moderation. "Your servant," Elfloq bowed.

"Nonsense! But what are you doing here?"

"Recovering from the terrible powers you unleashed on Ybaggog."

Vulparoon nodded. "What happened?"

Elfloq's eyes narrowed very slightly. "Your pardon, majesty, but our host informs me that you have a tale to tell —"

Vulparoon looked vaguely irritated for a moment, but then grinned. "Oh, of course! I had forgotten your persistence at bartering for information. You would like to bargain with an Asker?"

"My apologies, lord, but I understood that you were no longer a member of that elite company."

"Be careful, Elfloq."

But the familiar was pointing to Orgoom. "Lord, it is my friend. My poor and luckless companion —"

"Whom you recently pronounced to me to be your hated enemy —"

"A misunderstanding —"

"Well, what of him?"

"He is mad."

Vulparoon stood up and walked over to where the Gelder gibbered on his belly, his wrigglings not unlike those of a large worm. "Perceptive of you. Mad indeed."

"I wish to help him. He is too lowly to deserve this."

"Then tell me what happened to the dark man and to Ybaggog."

Still Elfloq hesitated and Vulparoon sighed impatiently. "Oh, very well, very well. I am far too weary to haggle. What do you want to know? What is this tale I must tell you?"

The familiar was both amazed and suspicious that the Asker, albeit a former one, had accepted the challenge so easily. "Merely what you told Eye Patch of the Smile. About Ubeggi's tapestry."

Vulparoon sat. "Hardly relevant."

"To myself, powerful one, everything is. And to poor Orgoom, who serves him."

"None of the Gelders serve the Weaver now."

"He has released them?"

"There has been — an upheaval. Tyrandire, once a fabulous organ of power, has been scattered to the very ends of the omniverse."

Elfloq's eyes bulged hugely and he found it impossible to contain his stupefaction. "*Scattered?*"

"Just so. I met a traveller on my way here. Ubeggi's powers turned upon himself. He sought to control and direct a thousand wars and more. They twisted back on him and his Palace of Pain. Once his powers collapsed under the unendurable pressure, the Blue Gelders rushed upon him and used those ghastly sickles to telling effect. They cut him into as many pieces as there are stars, or so my informant told me."

"How could this have happened?" gasped Elfloq. "Not that I am anything but relieved. Was it the Dark Gods?"

"Ubeggi offended them more than once, and quite openly. A foolish course. Doubtless they grew tired of his insubordination. So, you need fear him no more. They have punished him. It would seem, however, that Orgoom here has been caught in the ripples of this debacle. His own punishment, perhaps."

Elfloq nodded, wondering.

"And the Voidal?" said Vulparoon, gently pulling Elfloq to him. "What of him?"

"You are safe. Though you invoked him, you will not have to pay the price. He is trapped inside Ybaggog, trapped and as insane as Orgoom, for Shatterface plunged the Sword of Madness into him. Ironically Ubeggi's wishes were realised, for they were also the wishes of the Dark Gods. I am certain that you have earned the reward of freedom."

Vulparoon sagged back. "Then I am absolved. I have done my part. I can go my way in peace. You, too, have your freedom. Orgoom, it seems, is not so lucky, though there is a kind of freedom in madness. Perhaps it would be best to kill him. That, to be honest, would be a kindness."

Elfloq demurred, knowing that Orgoom had not been made mad by the fall of the Weaver. Vulparoon did not know that Orgoom had fallen into the maw of Ybaggog. There must be knowledge inside that mad brain, if only Elfloq could prize it open. "No," he said. "At least, not here in Cloudway. No one kills here. Besides, let us not bring upon ourselves the terrible ire of Vlod the Remover."

Vulparoon laughed. He had thrown off his mantle of sadness. "*I* would not kill Orgoom! That is for you. When you leave, take him to some remote astral place and kill him gently and swiftly. It is for the best, I am sure."

Elfloq nodded solemnly, pretending that he would do this. In fact he would be glad to have Orgoom to himself.

"But for now," cried Vulparoon, "a toast! Host! More wine! And if you have other guests, why, bring them to us to join our celebrations."

"Celebrations?" echoed a deep voice behind him. He turned to see a short, but hugely fat fellow waddling into the candlelight. "Join you? Kind sirs, I would love to accept your offer."

"By all means join us," laughed Vulparoon, a little drunk. "Sit with us and drink. Your only fee will be your name."

The gross man struggled on to a chair, which succeeded in accommodating no more than half of his great behind, and set down a large trunk that he had been lugging over his shoulder. Dust rose from it in clouds. He wiped his sweating brow and jowls, catching his breath. "I am Humble Jeddo. I bear gifts."

"From whom? And what have we done to deserve gifts?" said the Asker suspiciously but politely.

"You misunderstand me, sir. The gifts I carry are rare treasures. I do not give them away — that is, not for nothing. I am a barterer, sir. A prince among them. And such marvels as I carry in my trunk are not freely given."

Vulparoon was too pleased with the news that Elfloq had recently given him to regret having asked the pedlar to join them. "Well, perhaps I will look at your wares later. First, some more food and wine. Or would you prefer to enjoy some of the more potent pleasures our host can offer? The fumes of the forbidden addleroot are said to be particularly conducive to delight."

"Indeed they are," Humble Jeddo nodded. "As my own simple experiences will testify."

Eye Patch appeared at once. "I have plenty of everything," he told them. "No other guests are down, save one, who seems to be asleep and is best left undisturbed."

"Well," said Vulparoon. "I am sure that Jeddo here will entertain us."

"Humble Jeddo, sir. Humble Jeddo."

Elfloq had dropped on to a chair and sat himself now upon a second table, gracing it like a bizarre ornament. This fat merchant, he felt sure, could be very useful. *A most fortunate meeting*, he mused, not remembering that meetings in Cloudway are not arranged by chance. "You must have a fine range of treasures, Humble Jeddo," he observed.

"I have, small sir. Anything you desire, it is my humble promise to provide. For a price, of course, though a modest one."

"It is not for myself that I ask," replied Elfloq.

Humble Jeddo sipped thoughtfully at wine. He had waved aside the dubious pleasures of the addleroot and other intoxicating inhalants of the house and now allowed his eyes to feast on the food set before him in quantities that would have made even a robust warrior grimace in alarm. He began to put his thoughts into deeds, and fed. Here was an area in which his modesty deserted him. "I am open to bargains of any kind."

"It is my colleague," Elfloq said, pointing to Orgoom, who appeared to have fallen asleep under the table. "He is cursed with madness. Do you have a cure for such a thing?"

Humble Jeddo's attention was focussed principally on the assault of the food mountain before him, his eyes clouded in ecstasy as he masticated. "There are many kinds of madness. How long has your friend been like this?"

"But a short time."

"How did this occur? A curse? An accident? Nightmares? Did he eat something that poisoned his mind? Has he been in the company of wild animals, or demons?"

Both Elfloq and Vulparoon exchanged baffled looks at this last comment, but let it pass. "No," said Elfloq. "I fear he has been involved in a war with certain gods. They perished and in the consequences of their demise, Orgoom lost his reason."

Humble Jeddo nodded thoughtfully. He slipped a book from the many folds of his robe and held it up. "*The Variants of Disjoint,*" he stated. "An anonymous little pamphlet, but attributed to the wise scholar-god, Psytrobus. I had it from a Master of Inner Serenity, who took in its place the *Seventy Nine Parables* of Ork Yun Dodical." Humble Jeddo went on with his eating, referring to his book as he chewed. Vulparoon, who had been steadily sipping his wine, sat back comfortably in his chair, yawning. If Orgoom could be cured, so much the better. It did not seem that important, though.

"Certainly I could cure him," announced the fat merchant at last. He opened his trunk, rummaging and then put a number of items on the table while he searched deeper among his collection. There were several bottles, jars and manuscripts, all calculated to attract the eye. Elfloq stared into the coloured depths of one such jar, which seemed extraordinarily deep, as if he were gazing through a window out into a vast sea.

"What are these?"

"Beautiful are they not? They are universes."

Vulparoon opened one of his drooping eyes and fixed it on the jar. "Of what? Seaweed?"

"I have traded these with the gods themselves. That one is the bottled universe of Shiverdeep, while there you have the Universe of Golden Noise. Here you have the Ever Changing Waters of Olypse and there —"

"Gods? Which gods?" said Vulparoon, curious.

"Well, sir, the gods are many and diffuse, as you know. I have trafficked mostly with minor deities, such as Adang the Reasonable, Sunderbant, Glaucoster and then again with the servants of higher beings, such as —"

"Quite, quite," nodded Vulparoon, bored already.

"They enjoy these bottled universes as gewgaws. When they tire of them, as a noble lady might tire of a pair of earrings, they trade them for new ones. I am told, though I have no proof, that some of them enter the universe and amuse themselves therein. The universes are closed, shut up by great powers that can hardly be guessed at, but even so, they are open to the gods. They are generally pretty to gaze upon, but you and I could have little time for them."

Elfloq drew back. A swapper of universes? It was not something to dwell too long upon.

"Should I cure your companion," said Humble Jeddo, "what would you give me?"

"Well," replied Elfloq, "I, too, have travelled. I have some extremely potent spells, a number of truly frightful curses and the means to entering certain shunned places that any decent warlock would give a limb for."

Humble Jeddo looked disappointed. "How dull."

"Is the curing of madness," said Elfloq, "a large undertaking?"

Humble Jeddo began a renewed offensive on his meal. "In some cases, it is. Can you be more specific about your friend's madness?"

Vulparoon interrupted. "It was in a war. Recently the Weaver of Wars, whom you can scarcely have failed to hear about, was brought to his downfall. In the resultant confusion we must assume that the Gelder received some awful blow, or perhaps even the wrath of the dying Ubeggi himself fell about him as a curse. We will only know by curing him and asking him."

That, thought Elfloq, will do nicely, though it is hardly the truth.

Humble Jeddo nodded. "The curse of Ubeggi the Deceitful, eh? Not easy to remove something as weighty as that. I fear this will be an onerous task."

"And thus expensive," muttered Elfloq testily.

"All things must be balanced," agreed Humble Jeddo. "However, as Ubeggi is no more, I can do this thing. What will you give me?"

Elfloq looked to Vulparoon for assistance, but the Asker shrugged. "I have nothing of value, save my freedom, and I will not give that away for a godship."

"And what of you, little familiar?" said Humble Jeddo, a fresh hunger unmasked.

"I am not free. I have a master."

"What is he?"

"He is — far away on business."

"What would he give me?"

Vulparoon chuckled. "His curse, no doubt! Come, come, Elfloq! You have seen this man's valuables. You have nothing to give him that he would appreciate. Admit it!"

"There must be something," Elfloq growled, turning away.

Humble Jeddo was not at all nonplussed. "I will enjoy my meal. Please take as long as you wish to consider this matter. I have time in abundance. Do not hesitate to make suggestions, no matter how meek.

The strangest things fascinate me and those with whom I trade. Why, I recall an irascible satyr, Fulderhorn his name was —"

While Humble Jeddo regaled the partially sleeping Vulparoon with this bawdy anecdote, Eye Patch of the Smile returned to the table with a tray. He was collecting empty wine bottles. But leaning over the thoughtful Elfloq's shoulder, he nodded at a lone jar standing in shadow on an adjacent table. "Shall I clear away the jar that was left for you?"

Elfloq jumped, snatching up the jar at once. Again he studied the murky and unpleasant contents. "Who left this?"

"He did not say. Only that it was for you."

"But — what is it?"

Eye Patch shrugged. "I have no idea. But I could venture a suggestion."

"Yes?" said the familiar, eagerly.

"Don't drink it." Eye Patch chuckled and went off again.

In a moment, Humble Jeddo had finished his enormous meal. The dimensions of his interior were clearly as flexible as those of the jars that contained their universes. He reached for wine and sat back with a stentorian belch. "An excellent repast. Well, familiar, have you thought of anything?"

Elfloq stared at the jar in his hands and then at the other jars and bottles that the merchant had set down on the table. Apart from the unwholesome colour of the contents of Elfloq's jar and its odd shape, there was a marked similarity between it and those on the table. "I have very little to offer, it is true. By pure chance, however, I do have this jar, although I am exceedingly reluctant to part with it."

Humble Jeddo eyed the jar without any apparent interest. "Oh?"

"It was given to me by an illustrious but dying god, Neandak the Killer. You have heard of him and his appalling reputation?"

Humble Jeddo unleashed yet another loud belch. "Should I have?"

"He was the envy of his fellow gods. Handsome, indomitable, beloved of all the most desirable goddesses in the omniverse. I am not surprised that you have not heard of him, for the jealous gods have not only destroyed him, but they have purged his memory from the entire omniverse."

"Strange then," said Humble Jeddo, "that *you* recall him."

Elfloq thought swiftly. "Into my unworthy hands was given the task of keeping his remains. *In this very jar*. Until now, only I have known of his existence."

Humble Jeddo neither smiled nor scowled. "An interesting story. Show me the jar."

Elfloq made a passable display of being reluctant to part with his estimable prize, but did so and the pedlar took the jar and studied its dark contents. After a few moments he gasped and set the jar down hard upon the table, which rocked under the impact. He sat back, eyes boggling with fear.

"What have you seen?" said Elfloq, wondering what in all the omniverse was really in the jar.

"You lied," hissed Humble Jeddo.

Vulparoon had opened his sleepy eyes again and was looking at the jar, though he retained his indifference to it.

"I did?"

"That is not Neandak the Killer, if such a one exists. It is a bottled universe."

"It is? I mean — yes, it is. I lied. You have seen through my bluff."

"I did not ask so great a price for the restoration of the Gelder's mind," said Humble Jeddo, shaking visibly. "It is too much."

"Whatever is it?" said Vulparoon, turning to Elfloq for the answer.

"I know very little," said Elfloq defensively. "Perhaps the pedlar has the full tale."

"Well?" insisted Vulparoon.

"I did not think such a thing possible. Some universes can be bottled, as you have seen. But most of my samples are simple, uncomplicated things, containing no more than basic, placid universes. But *this*!"

Vulparoon snatched up the jar impatiently and stared into it. But almost at once he put it down, his face suddenly ashen. "No!" he breathed. "I did not see —"

"What did you see?" said Elfloq, bursting with curiosity.

"Such a universe could not be put inside a mere *jar*," gasped Vulparoon. "If so, then only by powers beyond imagination."

"Precisely," affirmed Humble Jeddo, who had never looked more humble. He stared at Elfloq with a new respect. "Can it be possible that you serve the powers who have done this?"

Elfloq said nothing, still wondering what in all the hells they had seen.

"The Dark Gods have done this," said Vulparoon. The statement appeared to have afforded him some relief. Then his face clouded once more. "But why have they given the jar to you?" he asked Elfloq.

"Well," mumbled Elfloq, for once quite lost. "I am their servant. I have always said so. I swore to Darquementi himself — here in Cloudway — just that."

"Do you know what is in the jar?" said Humble Jeddo. "No, you could not, else you would not have offered it to me in exchange for the sanity of the Gelder."

Elfloq could restrain himself no longer. "Very well, very well! I do not know what is in there!"

Vulparoon sighed and sat back. He did not understand what was happening, but he now questioned the security of his freedom.

Humble Jeddo pointed to the offending glass container. "Unless I am much mistaken, that jar contains no less a deity than Ybaggog himself. The Devourer of Universes."

Elfloq shuddered. He stared. He gasped. He staggered backwards. "Pardon?"

"The Dark Destroyer. Confined to that very jar."

Elfloq fought to restrain a titter of nervous amusement, but failed. This was ludicrous. "I — I must find our host. I must discover who left the jar here." He turned to do just that but the shadows moved.

"Allow me to answer that for you. It was I."

Elfloq fluttered back, almost into the vast lap of the pedlar. Out of the wavering light stepped the lean figure of the Voidal, an unfamiliar smile upon his face. "Well met," he said.

Vulparoon choked and shrank into his seat, incapable of further movement as if smitten by a spell, while the pedlar testily thrust Elfloq from him. He stared nervously at the newcomer, his shirt of nightweb, his tall leather boots, his embodiment of shadow.

"Good evening," the pedlar said. "If you have come with an explanation, please render it at once. I am in a hurry and must leave soon."

"With the jar?" said the Voidal.

"I —"

"No power in the omniverse can open it, save that which locked it in there. It is harmless. Take it. But first, the trade."

Humble Jeddo stared at the still sleeping Orgoom. "Restore him?"

"Why not? You have the jar."

Elfloq, who had been gaping in open amazement at the dark man, could no longer contain himself. "Master, if Ybaggog is in the jar, why are you not inside the jar also?"

The Voidal laughed and lifted his arm. Everyone shrank back, but the dark man was simply holding a glass of wine, from which he now sipped. "Why should I confine myself? It was I who put Ybaggog in there."

Elfloq bravely attempted to look as though he were not about to have a series of violent convulsions. The Asker had become as immobile as marble, face a carving in sheer terror. Humble Jeddo quivered, his mass unstable. Was this stranger who he thought he was?

"But where," gurgled Elfloq, "is the Sword of Madness?" He looked fearfully at the ebon haft protruding from the Voidal's scabbard.

"No longer embedded in my vitals, as you can see," the Voidal smiled. "But a sliver of it is lodged in the unfortunate Gelder. It served him well in the hellish universe of Ybaggog, paradoxically preserving his reason there. But here it makes him mad. We must have it out. I have a use for it. Well, pedlar, where is your art? Do we have a bargain?"

Humble Jeddo hurriedly scooped up the jar and placed it in his trunk with all the others. He was not about to argue with the Voidal, for he had no doubt now that it was the very Fatecaster that stood before him. And he could be rid of the jar as soon as he quit Cloudway. He brought out a phial of bright green dust and a long, sharp instrument. "As your eminence commands. Though, permit me to say in my humble way, you have cheated yourself. I owe you much more than the restoration of the Gelder's mind."

"I think not," said the Voidal. "Be content."

At once the pedlar went to Orgoom and having removed the table from over him and pushed aside the chairs, he sprinkled the green dust over his chest, so that the Gelder breathed some of it in. "Now he will not wake until afterwards." Humble Jeddo worked on, using the instrument to probe the blue skin and mumbling an odd incantation to himself. After a while he had located the embedded sliver of the Sword and he worked at it, perspiring profusely. It was like trying to remove a live worm that wriggled to avoid capture.

Vulparoon looked on as one in a dream, immobilised by terror. A reckoning, he knew, was coming. It hovered over him like a thick, oily cloud.

Elfloq was guardedly watching his master, who seemed to him to be changed. His manner, his sense of purpose, was more direct. Usually the stuff of his nightmares clung to him in waking life, hampering and confusing him. But here he appeared very direct, certain of himself. He turned his gaze upon the familiar, who flinched.

"So, little fellow, you are free of me?"

"Master, I meant only to do your will, as always —"

"By *fleeing* from the fight at the gate to Ybaggog?"

"I could not reach you —"

"As it happens, it is as well that you fled. Orgoom fell with me. I need you both now."

"For what, master?"

"You will learn soon enough. But you can begin by telling me what has happened since last we met. Since before the inn at Ulthar, where you were so careful to explain absolutely nothing."

"I acted then under the will of the foul Weaver —"

A gasp from Humble Jeddo interrupted them and they turned. "I have it," said the sweat-soaked pedlar and in a moment there came the tinkle of something metallic dropping on to the floor. Using the instrument with which he had extracted the sliver, Humble Jeddo delicately lifted it and placed it in the middle of the table. It gleamed fiercely, red as fire, ominous as thunder. Everyone studied it, but no one moved to touch it. There came a groan from the floor and seconds later Orgoom was sitting up, looking very vague and as dazed as one in the grip of a powerful soporific.

"He looks no saner than he was," muttered Elfloq, but the Voidal lifted the Gelder and sat him on the table.

"Well, Gelder?"

Orgoom peered about him as if emerging from a thick mist. He shook his head. "Dreams," he said. "Bad, bad dreams."

"No longer," said the Voidal. "You are in Cloudway."

"What happened?" said Elfloq impetuously.

Orgoom's face then did something that it had never done before. It broke into a ghastly smile and then the most unusual of sounds broke from the twisted mouth: he was laughing.

The Voidal was amused by the extraordinary show of mirth. "It is over, little fellow. For a time."

Elfloq was hopping from one foot to another in impatience. "What is over? What happened?"

Orgoom saw him and scowled, but was soon laughing again. "Free! Free! Ubeggi no more!" he cried.

The Voidal smiled. "Not entirely free, Gelder. Free of the Weaver, but not of me. You serve me yet."

Orgoom bowed. "Your slave," he said, as though quite content.

"What has happened?" repeated Elfloq.

Orgoom pointed to the Voidal. "Destroyed Ubeggi. In Tyrandire. Called up all the wars of the Weaver. Welded them and flung them back, each by each. Too much evil. Too much pitch black power. Too many dead. Ubeggi weak. I called all Gelders. We saw Ubeggi on his belly." He held up his sickles. "We cut and cut — and cut, until pieces too small." He finished with a long sniff and spat with a surprising degree of venom.

Elfloq wrinkled up his face in a grimace of disgust, but even so was pleased to hear confirmation of the demise of the Weaver. "And what of Ybaggog? You were his prisoners? Did the Dark Gods destroy him also?"

The Voidal was shaking his head. "I have said. It was I who bottled him in his glass prison. The Dark Gods sought to imprison me, fearing that I would win again my forbidden powers. They made an error at last, so they are not infallible. They had the Sword of Madness lodged in me to secure me, but instead of enhancing the mad visions of Ybaggog, it broke them apart!"

"You — *defied* the Dark Gods?" Elfloq said incredulously. "You actually performed an act of your own will? Are you sure they are not behind it?"

The Voidal's face clouded in the old anger and frustration. "I am not free of them yet. But in the mind of the Devourer I saw many visions that have been forbidden to me and I recovered many of the secrets that have been kept from me. I am no longer weak. Soon, I will be stronger still."

Elfloq knew instinctively that his dark master was not exaggerating. There was a new steel about his mien, a strength of purpose that had not been present before. Fresh power clung to him, personal power that made the familiar uneasy. "Ybaggog imprisoned," he murmured. "So the awesome darkness that was gathering itself has been dispersed."

The Voidal turned on him, that growing power nowhere more evident than in the depth of his gaze. "What did you say? What darkness?"

Elfloq then spoke of the Council of Gossipers that he and Orgoom had attended and of the concern of that Council about the grim force that had been gathering itself for the potential annihilation of the omniverse. "The Council concluded," said Elfloq, "in the light of much evidence (the best of which was provided by Orgoom and myself) that the Dark Gods were busy working against this nameless force, knowing that the gods of Light could never agree to combine their powers effectively against it. You, yourself, master, were being used as a means of thwarting this evil. But it seems that Ybaggog's plan to swallow up the omniverse itself has failed."

The Voidal thought for a moment, then shook his head. "Intriguing, Elfloq. But I fear you have created riddles, not solved them. As always, you bring priceless knowledge, though your reasoning is faulty."

Elfloq looked pained, while Orgoom smirked.

"Consider," went on the Voidal. "Ybaggog sought to devour the omniverse and bind it. Had the Dark Gods sought to use me to destroy Ybaggog, they would not have had him devour and imprison me. Insane and without power, I would have been useless to them trapped inside Ybaggog. And the Dark Gods must have wanted him alive, in order to contain me. But alive, he would have been able to continue his own mad destruction. So was he this evil power so feared by all the gods? I think not."

Vulparoon broke his statuesque silence to speak softly. "Your own reasoning is at fault, dark man."

The Voidal's jade eyes fixed him icily. "How so?"

"You claim to have destroyed Ybaggog yourself. Perhaps the Dark Gods knew that the Sword of Madness would not contain you. Perhaps they knew it would turn against Ybaggog in your hands. Did they not have it fashioned by Thunderhammer? Have they not, after all, used you again?"

The Voidal studied him coldly, but remained calm. "Perhaps. They are devious."

"And Ubeggi," went on Vulparoon, his own confidence slowly returning like blood to cramped muscles as he tried to unravel the riddles. "The Dark Gods did not love him. You have destroyed him for them. By your will, you say. Possibly. But the Dark Gods certainly benefit from the passing of these vile beings. It suits them well. You are free of Ybaggog's trap, but better that than his being loose."

Elfloq and Orgoom looked horrified by the words of the Asker, for they prodded raw nerves. For a while no one said a word. Yet the Voidal's frown disappeared as he lifted a bottle of wine and studied its red contents. "Well said, Asker. So you think I am yet a pawn?"

Vulparoon shrugged.

Humble Jeddo, who had been attempting during this last conversation to make himself as inconspicuous as possible (a hopeless task) coughed gently. "Kind sirs, if you have no further use for me —"

"One moment," said the Voidal and the gross pedlar shrank a little further into his seat.

The Voidal sat across the table from Vulparoon. "Now, my scarlet friend, it is your turn to speak."

Vulparoon's colour drained from him and tears of fear oozed on to his cheeks. "I am absolved. I did my duty. I am free."

The Voidal shook his head. "I may yet be a pawn, but you also obey the will of the Dark Gods. You are bound by their rules, their desires."

"I did not summon you in Ulthar at my will! I was forced —"

"He lies!" snapped Elfloq. "He thought you would be trapped and that he would escape the penalty. He believed that Ybaggog would imprison you. He wanted that."

"If I am yet the pawn of the Dark Gods," said the Voidal quietly, "then I will be powerless to stop the course of events, a course that includes the payment of the fee for invoking me. You invoked me, Asker. You must pay."

Vulparoon was incapable of speech or movement. Elfloq did not relish the thought of what might happen. Orgoom watched more in curiosity than anything else. Humble Jeddo found himself shivering, as if in an icy blast from his own private hell.

"However," went on the Voidal, "I will make a bargain with you. Give me what I want and I will not seek to extract the penalty."

For a moment Vulparoon did not understand. "You will spare me?"

"Give me what I want. I do not seek to harm you. Nor shall I."

"But the Dark Gods decide —"

"So you say. But I say otherwise. This will be the test. If you are not punished for invoking me, it will be proof that I have wrested much power from the Dark Gods. In this I will not serve them."

Vulparoon shook uncontrollably. "What do you want of me?"

"Knowledge. I have learned more about the things I seek. But you must tell me all that you know."

"I dare not speak."

Elfloq flitted to the table and tugged at his master's cloak. "Master! I recall something he said in Ulthar. I have a question for him."

The Voidal scowled, but then nodded for the familiar to go on.

"Who is it that the Dark Gods answer to? Who do *they* serve?"

Vulparoon shook is if he had been slapped. "That mystery has not been revealed to me. I did not attain such heights within the Askers. But others know."

"I think he lies, master."

The Voidal glared at the Asker. "Is that true?"

"I cannot say."

"You must answer."

Some inner conflict worked at the Asker like fire and the veins stood out on his brow. Abruptly his hand shot out and reached for the metal splinter on the table. His fingers closed around it, but before they could press the metal into his flesh, Orgoom had flung himself forward. With a hiss of air, the Gelder brought down his sickle hand, as if to sever that of the Asker at the wrist. But the Voidal was faster. His own right hand shot out in a blur and Orgoom's sickles were deflected by it. Vulparoon was flung back with a shriek of horror, the metal splinter again falling to the table. The sliver of madness had not had time to do its work.

The Voidal smiled grimly. Orgoom had jumped back, nonplussed. The dark man held up his black-gloved right hand. "Interesting. This is not the Oblivion Hand. I no longer bear that burden. This is my hand. It carries out *my* will. And it was my will that your own hand remained intact. More importantly I did not want to see you turned insane by the sliver of madness. That, of course, would have suited the Dark Gods. I could have let Orgoom try to cut off your hand to thwart them, but I fear that his blow would not have succeeded. His own hand would have disintegrated."

Orgoom gaped.

"Oh, yes," said the Voidal softly. "The Dark Gods want this Asker to keep his secrets. The blow would have failed. And this Asker would have succumbed to madness, just as you did, Gelder."

Vulparoon's nerve broke. He passed out, slumping to the floor.

Elfloq looked even more appalled. The Voidal, seeing the familiar's amazement, removed his glove calmly and held up his hand. "Flesh and blood, Elfloq. I recovered this from Krogarth and the Dark Gods have allowed me to keep it. What has happened here was not their work. My intervention was truly an act of defiance."

"You hand is restored?"

"Yes," said the dark man coolly. "Pass me the wine." He took an open bottle from Elfloq and poured the contents over Vulparoon's face. In a moment the Asker had spluttered awake.

"So you punish me after all!" he gasped.

"You torment yourself. You prefer madness to my questions. But I say again, who do the Dark Gods serve?"

Again Vulparoon demurred.

"Perhaps, if you truly desire madness, you would like to join Ybaggog in his bottled universe? I can arrange that for you."

Vulparoon shook his head. "No! I will speak. I know only a small piece of the greater mysteries. The Dark Gods number Thirteen, as with their Seneschals. They have a Prime, an Ultimate. His will is their will, which is the will of the Seneschals and in turn, that of the Divine Askers." He shrank back in the pool of spilled wine. His face had aged by a score of years.

The Voidal turned to Elfloq and Orgoom with a grim smile. "Then this Ultimate god is my true nemesis. His power against mine, when I have restored it all."

For a moment Cloudway fell very silent, chilled by the words of the dark man, the terrible confidence that seemed to well up in him now.

The vacuum was at last filled by the quaking voice of Humble Jeddo, who had been momentarily forgotten. "An interesting revelation, masters. I have heard such things whispered in remote parts, but never thought it truth. An Ultimate god? No god could take upon himself such a mantle. Or so it seems to a meek creature such as myself. Well, enough of this. I must be leaving. I have to see a minor god (a very minor god, I now perceive) on Creeping Hagula." He rose, with unusual ease, and the Voidal nodded to him.

"Keep that jar safely. Trade it for some worthwhile item. But leave the sliver of madness." He indicated the metal that gleamed on the tabletop, which had evidently become yet another object of the pedlar's desires.

Humble Jeddo pretended to be repulsed by it. Instead he bowed awkwardly and left them.

"What now, master?" said Elfloq at the Voidal's side. "There must be other things the Asker can teach you."

The Voidal shook his head. "No, Elfloq. He knows less than I. There were strange visions open to me in Ybaggog's black universe. My memory retains them. The Dark Gods watch over the Asker. I will call him again when I have need of him. But we have other work."

Elfloq masked his surprise at this newfound confidence in his master. It was more than a little unnerving. "What must I do?"

"There is a woman you must seek for me."

Elfloq was clearly nonplussed. "Not — not —"

"She that we found among the lamias of Nyctath? No, I will not enter her life again," said the dark man heavily. "She has suffered enough. There is another. You must find Scyllarza. I think she may hold the key to some of the things I now seek."

Elfloq dropped his voice to a low whisper. "Your soul, master? The Sword of Shadows?"

The Voidal stared at him in mild amusement. "Possibly. Find her, Elfloq. Look on Alendar. I think she has powers that will strengthen me."

"Are you truly your own master?"

"It would be foolish to assume it. You know that the Dark Gods are dangerous enemies. Vulparoon has sewn more than a few doubts in my mind with his interpretation of the fall of Ybaggog and the Weaver of Wars. But it is time for me to move against those who have cursed me for so long."

Orgoom came forward. "I serve, master."

"Yes, Orgoom. See Elfloq, the Gelder is faithful to our cause. You must help one another. Scour the astral for knowledge. Find Scyllarza. But you must both be wary. She has a servant named the Babbler. He will serve you foul."

Orgoom instantly flashed his sickles. "I cut."

The Voidal laughed. "No. Just be cautious. Find them! When you have done so, tell Scyllarza to invoke me. There will be no price."

Neither familiar nor Gelder needed time to ponder this. They were glad to have a task to perform. With no more than brief glances at one another, they went out on to the astral.

The Voidal looked down at Vulparoon, still slumped on the floor, then beckoned Eye Patch to him.

"See that he does not leave here until I send for him."

Eye Patch shrugged. "I cannot force him to remain."

The Voidal retrieved the sliver of madness and slipped it inside his shirt. "A little of the madness that hovered about us here has seeped into him, I fear. But he will be safe in Cloudway. If you let him leave, he will fall prey to gods who will show him no mercy. They have never been kind to him. Spare him. Keep him here."

Eye Patch nodded. "Until you send for him, then."

Shortly after this exchange, the Voidal had departed.

Eye Patch began clearing away the last of the plates and wine bottles, cleaning down the tables. He saw the Asker get up and sit at a table, staring vacantly into space and heard snatches of his mutterings. "Darkness gathers," the man in scarlet seemed to be repeating, over and over. Eye Patch would ask Vlod the Remover to see that no one harmed the Asker.

Other guests were already arriving.

PART SIX

AMONG THE BONES OF GIANTS

In matters of conflict, whether issues are resolved through debate, individual battle between two protagonists armed with swords or an all-out war between men or gods, the application of tactics and strategy plays a vital part.

And in the employment of these, honesty and openness do not necessarily bear the ripest fruit. Duplicity, deceit, mendacity — ah, these are more trustworthy devices. For example, in a fight between two swordsmen, it is not simply a case of one warrior hacking through the defence of the other. There are such ploys as feints and bluffs: one man may pretend to be wounded or exhausted.

The Dark Gods are as skilled in such methods as any other. Those who would deal with them are well advised to scrutinise each play of the cards, metaphorically speaking. Black may not be black at all, just as white may be purple.

Or blood red.

—**Salecco**, whose aversion to contests is based on the sound principles of self-preservation.

* * * *

High up in the mountains, the Monastery of Tranquil Resolve perched precariously above treacherous crags and scree, a sea of cloud lapping at its walls and spilling over its windowless towers, the air thick with vapour, damp and chill. The tallest of the decaying turrets leaned precipitously out over the eon-scarred walls of the monastery; within it a bell tolled dolorously, disturbing the black-feathered birds that flapped around the intrusive buildings, voicing their raucous protest. Across the weeds of the central court, two figures hurried, eager to be out of the perpetual drizzling mist. The first was swathed in the dull grey robes and deep cowls of a Peace Monk, the second in the hooded cloak of an outsider from the lands below the mountains. They passed through a doorway and went down torchlit steps to where a small gathering of the Brotherhood awaited them. All eyes turned up to face the men, each face pasty with distress and fear.

One of them pointed to a bare table and whispered to the first man descending. "It is Brother Jeroba."

"Dead?"

"Soon."

The leading Peace Monk dismissed all the others with a wave of his white hand and in a moment was left alone with his companion and the stricken other. They dropped their cowls and went to the bare table on which the body was lying. "Bring a torch," said the first monk and in a moment he took it and held it up to see the face of the man called Jeroba. He leaned over the inert form, whose pained face was like carved wax. "Brother Jeroba — what is it?"

For a moment nothing happened, but then the eyes opened, burning and dazzling with the radiance of some strange inner madness. Strong hands snatched at the robes of the Peace Monk as Jeroba tried to drag himself upright. "The dawn of darkness is coming! Let the omniverse tremble!" gasped the strangled voice. The man sank down once more.

The Peace Monk shook him without apparent sympathy. "Jeroba!"

Again the eyes opened. "It is here. It is now. Evil Time. The Crimson Gate...*must not open*..." The voice trailed off in a last gasp, air being sucked out of the body, which now shrivelled. The eyes died, their light frozen to glass. Hell danced behind them.

"Is he dead?" said the second man.

"Yes." As they watched, the body began to shake wildly as if a wolf had hold of it. It began to contort itself horribly. The watchers both stepped back.

"Quickly," said the first. "We must get out. Whatever has him may attack us." They left the chamber and slammed its door, bolting it firmly. Behind them they could hear many voices, vile and tormenting, as if a pack of demons feasted.

"Brother Torruvas, what does this mean?" asked the second of the men, making no attempt to hide his deep shock.

"It is just as I feared. There have been signs for some time now. This is the last and strongest of them. There will be no more warnings. Seven Peace Monks have died, just as Jeroba has died. The plague that has taken them is over. Now the horror truly begins." They were climbing another narrow stairway and in a moment had entered a frugal chamber where more torches flickered. Torruvas sat and waved the other to a bench opposite him.

"I brought you here for a purpose, Renegorn. I am calling in your family's debt to the Peace Monks. We sheltered and fed them once, and healed their sick."

"I understand my obligation. My father told me that one day I might be needed here. What horror is it that begins? What did Brother Jeroba mean? I could make no sense of his ranting. For three nights and days he has spewed forth such gibberish. Curses and damnations. Can you read anything into these ravings? I have travelled far to come here, just to listen to the delirium of a madman, or so it seems."

"All this was promised," sighed Torruvas. "Many years ago. Have your people not heard of the Evil Time?"

"In legends. Is it real?"

"When our world was a beautiful garden, long in her past, it was foretold that she would be visited by evil. This was so, for our masters took immense powers upon themselves and warred, bringing upon themselves evil such as had never been known before. The results of that blasphemous devastation surround us, a perpetual reminder of its magnitude. Its relics cover the world, monuments to the past. Yet there is a teaching preserved that tells of a second time of darkness, a true Evil Time. Evil will come again to our world and all worlds, folding the very omniverse in its coils. We of the Monastery of Tranquil Resolve have been watching for centuries. We know very little of the nature of this Evil Time, yet there have been signs. Brother Jeroba and the others are forerunners, all of them. They have looked upon the future and seen the Evil Time."

"So what is to be done?"

"We are the last of our world's protectors —"

Renegorn snorted. "Protectors! A few score Peace Monks? What powers do you have?"

Torruvas refused to be stung by the warrior's outburst. "We have certain duties to perform. So do you and other men like you, whose families were once fed and nurtured by our ancestors and whose debt to us is now due."

Renegorn shrugged. "I have no magical powers, nor do other men."

"You are one of the Homeless, a wanderer from the Open Lands. But you have your codes, your laws. You must speak to the men of the empty places. If we are to stand against what comes, man cannot remain disparate."

"What would you have me do?"

"You must guide me out in the Open Lands."

"To where? There is nothing out there! Bare as your mountains are, it is no more frugal than the Open. Mankind is scattered like sand in the wind." Renegorn laughed, but without humour.

"There is an oracle, which I must consult. From it I may learn something of the Evil Time and what must be done. You must guide me deep into the Steel Graveyard."

"To what end?"

"To find a legend. Have you heard of the Bone Burrower?"

Renegorn smiled. "Yes, but he is not real, Brother! He is a story, an idea, a ghost invented to amuse. He is the spirit of the Steel Graveyard. But surely you know this."

"Perhaps. But I must seek him. He is the oracle."

Renegorn could see by the Peace Monk's face that he was perfectly serious. "Cross the Steel Graveyard? It could take a lifetime! No one knows how far it spreads. It may cover a continent. Some say it ruptures other realms and is the tomb of other worlds besides this one. And I do know that it is almost impassable."

"Nevertheless, we must try. This is how your debt must be paid."

Renegorn scowled, but nodded. He was a man of honour, bound by duty. Among his scattered people, such things carried vast weight.

* * * *

They carried the broken corpse of Brother Jeroba to the walls of the monastery and gave it up to the night, for the rules of the Brotherhood were strict. None of the dead Peace Monks could remain within the walls. The last of them prayed as Jeroba's wrapped body tumbled down into infinity. Soon afterwards, Brother Torruvas and Renegorn went deep down into the bowels of the rock on which the monastery stood and entered a chamber where horses were groomed. Everything had been prepared. The two men mounted and rode out on to a ledge that spanned the night, beginning the long ride down out of the mountains to the Open Lands and the interminable plain that was the start of the Steel Graveyard.

This infinite expanse of tangled metal was silent as the horses came down the last narrow canyon to its edge. Dawn began to unravel individual curves of metal from the mass, emphasising the features of those immense suits of armour, weapons and war machines that bloody chaos and then time had blended into this nightmare fusion. Huge steel gauntlets jabbed fingers up at the sun, hung from splintered bone accusingly, like mad towers. Early rays splashed like blood on the buckled sheets of steel, or daubed curved bones, some encased, others piled high in parody of statues. It was a landscape of fallen giants, incredible warriors who had clashed in their thousands and dashed themselves to oblivion against each other, waves breaking on a pitiless shore. It was a domain of death, as derelict as a city scourged by fire. Shattered skulls stared with hollow sockets in frozen agony as light began to seep down like a stranger into the tangle of knotted bone and armour. The shells of corpses clung together like mountains, heaped higher and higher as the men wove inwards.

Rust clouds filled the air as the breeze shifted and the men pulled tighter their scarves around their mouths and noses. Within the silent wreckage there yet seemed to hover a suggestion of fading energy, as though the innumerable corpses dreamed of the carnage that had been wrought here. But time was reducing this steel cemetery to compost, the blackened earth dragging into it every last bone, no matter how vast.

"You wish to cross *this*?" said Renegorn. "These were more than giants. Surely they were *gods*. I swear you could carve a city in some of these bones! Man does not belong here."

"We must find its heart," said Torruvas stoically.

"How? Death is all around us. A million bones and skulls testify to that. Nothing could live within this place. There is nothing to sustain life. The very earth is blighted, charred and blasted by whatever sorceries these armies flung at each other. There are no birds above us. They would fall with exhaustion before reaching the other side."

"Yet you have travelled within it, have you not?"

Renegorn darted Torruvas a suspicious look. "As a boy, yes. We all did. But I was warned of its dangers. Collapsing bones, steel weapons that could rip you open if you as much as brush against them."

"I think that you, of all men, know something of the Steel Graveyard's labyrinth. There are men of the Open Lands who yet worship its fallen gods. I have no wish to intrude on their sacred ground, nor mock them. I seek only the oracle."

Renegorn did not comment, leading them onwards and the two horses passed under a low arch of corroded steel, an immense javelin, its one end rammed deep into a forest of bones that had once been a chest. Occasionally they could hear the creak of settling steel or the twisted shriek of metal as it collapsed under the weight of what was piled above it. They had to let the horses go back after a while and the beasts were glad to return to the Open. Torruvas and his guide threaded their way upward, hands gloved as a precaution against the dangers of poison. It was midday before they had climbed high enough to get above the contorted tunnels that interlaced the heaped steel like the workings of maggots.

They walked along the ribbed spine of a titanic steel skeleton, levelled and now like a vast ship, emptied by unimaginable forces. Even up here it was difficult to move forward, for many of the bones and fragments of armour that clung like cerements were rotten, turning to powder at a touch. They hopped like fleas, while on all sides the bones piled ever higher, ranging like hills to the horizon, their curves broken only by jagged bone, lance or swords like denuded trees.

Renegorn called a halt and slumped, pulling his water bottle from his belt. "Have you much food? We will find nothing to kill in this place."

"There will be food," Torruvas smiled.

"You seem certain." *Or mad*, thought Renegorn. "Food in this place?"

"You would not have come this far if you had not expected food."

Renegorn nodded. "You are wise, Brother."

"There are caches? Those who visit the secret shrines to the Fallen Gods would secrete food, I think."

There was no point in deceit. "There are such places. You would eat the food of those you view as blasphemers?"

"When the Evil Time is upon us, all men must stand together, regardless of what gods they worship. I do not judge them."

"Those who come here are scavengers. Bands of wanderers who have organised themselves like hunters. They seek out artefacts, relics of the war that they can handle. There is trading of a sort beyond the Steel Graveyard. Some men harbour foolish notions about restoring the old powers. The scavengers scoff, but they earn their food from such dreams."

"And do they talk of the Bone Burrower?"

"In their sleep, perhaps," said Renegorn guardedly.

"After food, where then?"

"If we must persist, I think we must go to the Tower of Windows. It rises up far out in the Graveyard, near its heart, although I should warn you that neither the boundaries nor the dimensions of this place seem to be fixed. However, if there is a such a being as the Bone Burrower, he may be in the Tower."

It was not long afterwards that Renegorn found a food cache left by the scavengers and he pulled up a thick skin, which contained carefully wrapped bread, some meat and a little brackish water. He slipped some metal discs into the sack as payment when he replaced it. "They will know I passed here," he told the Peace Monk.

"Will they be offended?"

"No. I have their trust. But if they knew a Peace Monk had been here, they would hunt us and offer us both to the dead gods."

Torruvas regarded the warrior for a moment, but did not comment. He knew that the man's honour came before his respect for the scavengers and their gods. The Peace Monk was glad of that, for this would be a terrible place to die.

As they struggled once more over the bizarre tangled landscape, the sun slipped downwards, as if succumbing to the clutch of a thousand metal fingers. For many days they traversed the canyons and spines of the Steel Graveyard, more than once coming perilously close to death on its sharp metal claws. Yet Torruvas found reserves of fortitude from somewhere within himself. It seemed also that they were sometimes heading in strange directions, almost as if clinging to the underside of a fallen giant, with the sky beneath them like a sea. It became more and more like the meandering voyage of a dream.

But on the twentieth evening, with dusk drawing a blanket over the smashed terrain, Renegorn pointed to a towering pile of metal on the lopsided horizon that had speared the early moon. It was as though a lone god had raised itself up, only to be pierced and half flung back, impaled on the weapon of its undoing. Propped high up, it slumped like a lone sentinel, watching over the massed husks of the Graveyard. "The Tower of Windows."

"What noise is that?" said the Peace Monk, for to their ears there now came a weird and persistent shrieking, as if a thousand tortured souls had fused their mad voices into a chorus. The sounds came from the Tower of Windows, that huge, groping pile that held sway over the fallen giants. They could see that sections of its armour plates had fallen away to reveal areas of pitch darkness, open orifices in its sides, chest and high up on the massive moon-like helm. From these black, unfathomable openings, the sounds gusted forth like storm winds, clashing against each other, merging into a solid wall, a concerto from chaos itself.

It was another night before they reached the base of the titanic metal colossus, this shell of a fallen god from beyond time. There were innumerable ways into its base, which covered an area of countless square miles and Renegorn selected one that was partly lit by slanting light and had relatively few sharp spars protruding from its curved walls.

"We should begin the climb at once," he suggested. "The scavengers worship this monstrous tower. It is better that they do not know we are here. There are tales of living machines deep under the mounds of armour and bone, to which the scavengers offer sacrifices. We will be safer if we climb."

Throughout the last of the day and deep into the night they climbed, until at last Renegorn said that it was safe to rest. They had to stop up their ears with dampened pieces of cloth in an attempt to keep out the howling of the wind and the screaming of the countless windows. Brother Torruvas, exhausted, fell asleep, although his dreams were fitful and terrifying. When dawn came, he found Renegorn leaning over him, his eyes attesting to the fact that he had not slept.

"We must climb," he said. After a little food and water, they began again, worming their way up through the calcified vitals of the tower. Three days later they were still climbing and the whine from the windows had grown in intensity, threatening to cuff them into madness. They no longer knew whether they were still on their own world, or if they had crossed to some other lunatic realm. That night they rested on a wide, twisted curve of metal, drained of energy.

Renegorn woke in the middle of the night to find their makeshift platform bathed in an eerie light, as though the stars outside the nearest window were on fire. Torruvas was beside him, evidently wanting to know what was happening. Renegorn pointed to the windows, great gashes in the steel sides of the tower. The two men crawled across the cold floor and stared out from a gaping opening. It was indeed not their world that they saw beyond.

It was an undulating landscape, white and blotched like the skin of a cadaver: as they looked it rippled and stirred like a faintly moving sea. The alien sky above it was filled with scarlet stars and great round whorls of purple and green that resembled huge spores. Quickly the men turned away, their attention at once caught by a smaller window. They looked out from it and saw yet another world where immense jagged spires of rock rose up in endless avenues against an orange sky. In the black crevices between them, shadowy forms jerked into life. Again the men averted their eyes.

By signs, Torruvas tried to ask Renegorn what these awful places were, but his companion only shook his head in amazement. Behind them they sensed movement and turned. Something like a huge beetle was scuttling between the gnarled bones beyond the platform. In a moment it had come out into a pool of green moonlight filtering in from yet another torn window. The creature appeared to have a steel carapace, fashioned from the materials in the tower. It hopped forward like a great flea. Abruptly it stood upright and light washed over the face of a man, his breastplate cut from bone.

"What manner of monster is this?" said Torruvas, his voice clear for the moaning windows suddenly lowered their din to a whisper.

"This must be the legendary Bone Burrower," said Renegorn.

The beetle that was a man came forward, hopping on both feet. He stopped before them and bowed, the curve of his shell gleaming. "The god welcomes you," he said cheerfully.

"Then you are real," said Torruvas.

"Indeed I am. And what brings such intrepid warriors up into my home? Men do not dare these regions as a rule. Plunder? I think not, Brother Torruvas."

The Peace Monk shuddered. "You know me?"

"Of course!" laughed the odd creature, hopping from one foot to another. "I have been watching you for many days. And your redoubtable companion, Renegorn. Finally plucked up the courage to climb the Tower of Windows, eh? You've contemplated such a quest many a time."

"You have been watching us?" said Renegorn, face clouded.

"Yes, yes. From here I can scrutinise every inch of the Steel Graveyard. At night I have the power to study the entire omniverse and its many dimensions."

"Are you — a god?" said Renegorn dubiously.

Torruvas was unnerved by such open blasphemy, but the Bone Burrower simply chuckled. "Not at all, no, no! Human, like you. But the powers in this place, twisted and broken though they are, stemmed from the War of the Falling Gods."

"There is only one god," said Torruvas, as if warding off the clutch of evil.

The Bone Burrower simply sniggered. "Indeed? Who am I to argue? There are a thousand thousand dead gods outside."

"Do you know why we are here?" said Renegorn.

"Yes, for I have listened to all that you have said as you crossed the Steel Graveyard. You are looking for me!"

"You are the Oracle?"

"If you wish. You have come to question me. Well, well, I am at your disposal. What do you seek to know? I am not a jealous person, nor greedy. I will gladly share with you the visions of the omniverse. But have a care! Some things are more than mortal eyes can bear to see." He sat down and rubbed his hands, another beetle-like movement. The howling of the windows had stopped altogether now, to be replaced by an unnatural silence that immersed them all, as if the worlds outside were looking in, listening.

"It was said by my ancestors," began Brother Torruvas, "that the Evil Time would come. I believe it will soon be upon the world."

"As it threatens all worlds," the Bone Burrower nodded.

"*All worlds?*" said Torruvas, appalled.

"Indeed. There is a terrible darkness fomenting throughout the omniverse. This shattered world, where space and time have become so deformed, will be a focus for the madness that threatens all existence."

Torruvas shuddered. "What must be done?"

The man-beetle stood up and began pacing, his steel carapace creaking. "I have studied the windows each night. This world, your world, is but a speck of dust, like all the other worlds in the many dimensions. The return of evil is known and feared through countless myths and legends. Even the gods tremble as the darkness bands itself into a thickening cloud. Soon it will be whole again. This Power has risen before. Look through the windows and you will see certain signs, confirmation that the deep darkness gathers."

Afraid to do so, but compelled, the two men went to the first window and gazed out from it. They saw not the madness of some remote, hell-blasted world, but their own, beyond the Steel Graveyard, far out in the Open Lands. There sunlight played on a bare but not entirely desert land, flecked with pale grass. Someone rode across the terrain, a woman on a powerful horse such as were not known here. Behind her, on a smaller steed, a smaller figure hunched forward, chattering to itself like a monkey.

The Bone Burrower pointed to the figure of the woman, whose hair streamed out behind her and whose proud face studied the land eagerly, apparently searching. "She is called Scyllarza," said the Bone Burrower. "Terrible are the demons that she can call upon to aid her."

"*Demons!*" cried Torruvas in horror.

"Oh, yes, yes. There are far worse things in Hell. Scyllarza bows to very few of them. With good reason has she been called their scourge."

They moved on to another window, which showed yet another part of their own world. "Here," said their guide, pointing to clouds of curling mist, "are others who seek. Mark them well." Both Torruvas and Renegorn drew back in shock at the two grotesque figures they saw alighting on a rock outcrop. These, they felt sure, must themselves be demons. One was squat and scaled, with thin wings and a face like a frog, while the other was blue-skinned with fingers like tiny sickles. The creatures appeared to be arguing.

"Is this Hell itself that you show us?" said Torruvas.

"Not at all, no, no. Even now they are out there, in the Open Lands. But none of these compare to the other who comes. Him I will not reveal to you. But you will know him when he arrives. Oh yes. He has the power to save or damn you. Can you guess his name?"

Renegorn scowled, but Torruvas felt suddenly cold.

"Out there in the limitless omniverse," the Bone Burrower went on, "he is known as the Voidal."

The windows flickered and in a moment all that could be seen from any of them were the stars of the world of men. All the wonderful and terrifying visions of the omniverse were gone. The wind had come back, this time laughing even more maniacally than before.

"Voidal," breathed Torruvas. The word sounded like a curse.

"When he comes," said the Bone Burrower, "Evil Time will have begun."

"We ask again," said Renegorn, "what must be done?"

The man-beetle looked very thoughtful for some time before he spoke again. "Your ancestors spoke of a great war, the war to come in Evil Time. And yes, it will be soon. The Voidal will come. He is opposed by the Dark Gods, who seek to control him, while he seeks to wrench himself free of their hold. You men must go out into your world and rally the remnants of humanity. This war is not against them, but all things are drawn into it. They must choose, for in their choosing lies a key."

"Rally humanity?" cried Torruvas. "To oppose this Voidal?"

"Or fight with him."

"*With him?* You said he was evil —"

"No, no. You must decide. Either he is evil, or he opposes it."

"You speak in riddles!" snapped Renegorn.

"It is the way of darkness to obfuscate," smiled the Bone Burrower. "You have a little time to decide. Use it well." He beckoned them to yet another window, but all they could see through it were stars. However, after a moment they noticed something drifting across the heavens there, like an island of earth, its roots trailing brokenly behind it.

Torruvas muttered a prayer, sensing the evil in this thing. "What cursed thing is this?"

"Cursed, ah, yes, yes," nodded the Bone Burrower. "Listen to the wind, Brother Torruvas. This island is but a crippled fragment of the dispersed demi-god, Dreamwarp. Listen to its whispers."

Through the window came a low grumbling, apparently invective, then words directed at the listeners. "The man who is immortal, yet not so. The Voidal." The name was spoken with acidic hatred.

"What does it mean?" said Renegorn. "One cannot be mortal and immortal."

"*Who speaks?*" came a roar like a storm from the island, a voice full of both anger and suffering.

"Those who will be visited by the dark man," said the Bone Burrower.

"Friends to Dreamwarp if you destroy him! Listen, the dark man cannot be destroyed, but he can be *revoked*. There is a way to send him back to the void from which he comes. It is a secret that drifts about the omniverse and which some hear in dreams and pass on."

"Will you reveal it to us?" said Torruvas, overcoming his terror of the island.

But already Dreamwarp was drifting far out toward the stars and with the shrinking mass went the whispers.

"More riddles!" snapped Renegorn. "You tell us nothing!"

The Bone Burrower merely chuckled. "I never pretend to understand the workings of the omniverse, nor the schemes of its gods. I merely watch and listen and sometimes I pass on what I learn. Perhaps I serve them by doing so. If there is but one god, perhaps all these other manifestations are his thoughts. Who can tell? But I can promise you this — there is one who will come to you with what you wish to know."

"The exorcism?"

"Just so. One who has performed it once before upon the dark man. When you have drawn together the last of humanity on this world, he will come."

* * * *

Scyllarza dismounted at the top of the bare knoll and looked southwards to where sunlight gleamed on an expanse of dark water. She waited, certain that she had seen movement on the slope far below her and equally certain that it would be the Babbler, returning to her with a report. She had seen no other living thing on this wasted, sterile world. There had been several ruins and most of the hills were topped by monoliths or rings of stone, as if the people who had once lived here had gone in dread of straying far from such hallowed places.

Soon the little figure came riding up the hill. "What have you found?" she asked him.

"More proof that we should quit this evil place!" said the Babbler. "A dead world, long since abandoned by gods as well as men! That is no ordinary sea or lake, but a vast expanse of marsh, thick with sludge and noxious deposits. In it lie the broken carcasses of giants, bones muddied, arms rotten. Like fallen gods smothered in their own excrement. The whole world is a tomb."

"Nothing lives?"

"How could it? On a plain to the east I saw what I took to be mountains, but when I reached the lower slopes, I discovered to my horror that it was a titanic flying vessel that had burned out in some holocaust, leaving only a shell, littered with huge skulls and broken weapons. Gods must have built such a thing. And gods felled it."

"I think we have slipped into some long forgotten dimension that has nothing at all to do with the omniverse that we know, if that is possible. The war here was so destructive that it warped every known horizon, every boundary. Its twisted powers must have drawn us in."

"All is death, mistress. I fear that your own powers will succumb if we remain."

Scyllarza smiled at his concern. "You would not like to lose the gift I have bestowed upon you, the gift of being able to cross the astral. You are a good and loyal servant, Babbler. And you are right. This is no place to linger. We will rest a short while and then search on another world." She turned away, hiding the sadness that she felt. But the Babbler knew it and bit his lip. He only prayed that she would not find what she sought.

They rode to the west and were abruptly surprised by a spring that trickled out of the hillside. The elemental horses sniffed at the water, testing its safety and then drank it. Scyllarza also drank, urging her servant to do so. Afterwards they travelled down the stream, which debouched into a narrow valley. Below them they could see a green tangle of wood. The Babbler spurred his horse on to investigate.

At the same moment, from the cover of the emerald leaves of the wood, high in the uppermost of its branches, two figures watched the arrivals.

"A strange little man," said the more squamous of the two. "And my eyes, which rarely lie, tell me that the woman is she whom we seek. These must be the two we were told of on the astral by Grudfax the familiar. See, these chargers are elemental beasts if ever I saw any!" Elfloq, for it was indeed he, grinned, certain that this particular search was over.

Orgoom gripped a bough with his sharp hands. "Think you're right. What next?"

"Wait," said Elfloq and they did so. It was not long before the Babbler had discovered the fresh pool in the heart of the wood and sped back to his mistress. The two watchers allowed the woman and her hunched squire to ride into the trees and dismount by the pool. There was fruit growing nearby that was not poisonous and the woman rested on the lush grass, relaxed.

"So, Babbler, an oasis in a miserable land. The fruit is good and the water remarkably clear. I detect no sorcery here. Let us sleep until we leave."

"I will not sleep until we are gone," replied the Babbler, his eyes suspiciously scanning the trees. It was at this point that Elfloq made his appearance. He stood on a bough some distance above the Babbler and waved a cheery greeting.

At once the squire had drawn a narrow sword. Scyllarza was evidently on her guard, though she seemed more amused than concerned. "The creatures of this world appear to be as misshapen as the wretched lands," she commented.

Elfloq ignored the insult. "Would you be the lady Scyllarza?" he asked. "I am an astral traveller and recently my companion and I met a certain elemental on the world of Tartennian, Phunatast by name. He said that he had seen you collecting two fine elemental steeds from a smith he knew. Their trail has led me to this bleak world."

Scyllarza nodded, grimacing at the blue figure of Orgoom, who looked as fierce as any demon. "And who would you be?"

Elfloq introduced himself and the Blue Gelder. "Our master seeks you, just as, we believe, you seek our master."

Scyllarza's eyes flared. "And who would he be?"

The Babbler rushed across to his mistress, hissing like an angered cat. "Do not heed them, mistress! This is a trap!"

But she silenced him and asked again whom the figures served.

"He is known by some as Fatecaster and by others as the Voidal."

Scyllarza gasped. "He seeks me? For what purpose?"

"We are simply his servants, my lady. He asked us to find you."

"And then?"

"Deliver his message."

"Which is?"

"You must, uh, well, you must *invoke* him."

Again the Babbler interrupted, waving his sword in fury. "Kill them! They seek to destroy you, mistress! You dare not invoke the dark man. Did he not desert you? On Alendar, did he not slink away from you, leaving you at the mercy of its rulers? Call him now and he will destroy you. You know the laws that bind him."

She silenced him yet again. Since quitting Alendar, she had spoken to a number of sorcerers and sages. In Cold Yvar, the world of Sleeping Secrets, she had been warned by a seer of the dangers of seeking the Voidal. "Why must I invoke your master? Why does he seek me? Why does he not come to me?"

"You know that his powers are incomplete, my lady," said Elfloq. "He seeks to repair them and believes that you would help him. He cannot control his destiny alone. You must call him to you. You will not be harmed. You are protected."

"Lies!" snarled the Babbler and Elfloq was about to spit out a retort, when they all heard the unmistakable rumble of many hooves. Elfloq at once took to the air and, drifting up over the wood, discovered to his amazement that a very large party of horsemen was approaching it. The familiar returned promptly to the glade.

"Warriors! I think it would be well to flee them."

Scyllarza called the horses to her at once. "Where shall I go to make this invocation?"

"You will summon my master?" said Elfloq.

"I have been searching for him for a long time."

"When these warriors have passed on, you can invoke him here, on this very world."

Scyllarza nodded. "The Babbler knows a place. Babbler, that sea. I doubt that we would be disturbed on one of the huge corpses you described."

Her squire protested, not eager to meet again the dark man that he had so treacherously revoked on Alendar. But he knew his mistress had made up her mind and would not be gainsaid.

"Time is short," she said. "Use the astral. You in the trees! Go with my servant across the astral to the sea. Wait for me there."

"Mistress, I —"

"Take them!"

"What of you?" called Elfloq, one ear on the horsemen.

"Leave the horses with me. I will use them to outwit these warriors. But I wish to see these men first. Hurry!"

Elfloq and Orgoom dropped down beside the Babbler, wary of him, and he of them, but Orgoom's awful hands were enough to keep the sour-faced squire at bay. Scyllarza waved them all away and they slipped on to the astral at once. She whispered something to the two horses and they raced away through the trees. Upon their backs were two shadowy figures that looked human, the workings of Scyllarza's illusion.

* * * *

When the steeds broke from the trees and raced up the hillside, the scouts of the warrior party saw them and at once cried out. The entire party of horsemen gave chase, certain that they had discovered something of importance, for they were Renegorn's men, seeking the creatures of their master's troubled visions. Scyllarza watched them all disappear over the hill, knowing that it would be some time before they realised they were chasing shadows. The elemental steeds would return to the astral, awaiting her summons. She turned back to the empty glade. Nothing now was likely to disturb its garden-like peace. Cautiously she set spells about its perimeters, to warn her of any unexpected and unwelcome intruders.

Beside the pool she began to murmur a soft incantation; as she recited the strange lines, she set aside her armour and weapons and stood bathed in the sunlight that filtered through the foliage overhead. She walked around the glade, treading its mossy carpet as softly as a cat, touching each tree gently, speaking to the spirit within it. In a moment there were whisperings out in the wood and then movement as the first of the spirits she had called upon gathered. Faceless beings, little more than wisps, ghost-like, they ringed the wood at her command, isolating it from the outside world, making of it an enclosed universe. The flowers that bloomed within it seemed to draw something from Scyllarza's workings and their colours flushed the glade, scenting it with a deep, rich fragrance.

Scyllarza plunged into the icy pool, her powers quickened by its embrace. She swam below its surface to the far side and came up on to the bank, sleek as an otter. Water droplets sprayed from her as she shook herself and raised her arms, eyes closed in concentration. She could feel the power in this place focussing on her, coagulating, rich in magic.

"Voidal," she whispered. "Voidal, come to me. I invoke you. I invoke you and summon you to me. Voidal." The words went out into a deepening silence and she watched the air stiffen, anticipating.

A brief darkness flickered across the glade, but then was gone. The spirit guardians never moved, unable to interfere with the powers that had been set in motion. Then, as easily as a breeze, the dark man himself stepped into the glade, answering the invocation, as he always must. He stood on the other side of the pool, his green eyes immediately fixing on Scyllarza.

"Scyllarza!" he called, with a smile. "So you did answer me."

She would have dived again into the pool and swum to him, but he was already in the water, arms propelling him across it in moments. She helped him out of the water as he laughed. It was a rare sound. He took her in his arms and kissed her gently.

"Why did you leave me on Alendar?" she breathed.

His smile faded, replaced by a familiar expression of frustration, anger held in check. "I had no power to prevent it. I thought the Dark Gods would at least allow me a little time there, but they were as impatient as ever. I believe they feared our alliance. Yes, feared it. What we felt between us on Alendar was a power they need to suppress. But I will deny them. I am no longer powerless."

She kissed him again. "Tell me of this later," she said softly and they felt the ground gather them up, as if it were alive and protective of them. As they became one in their act of love, it was as it had been on Alendar, when they had first shared themselves and given the power of their lovemaking its release. The Voidal knew again that this was a vital key to the things he sought. He felt once more the rising of some inexplicable tide.

It surged up in a wave and burst over him, and with its breaking there came a new understanding, as though he had crossed one of the barriers that had imprisoned him for so long. Locked together with Scyllarza, he had become fused with her into one mind, one essence. The doors to many hitherto secret chambers stood ajar. Their passionate union had become a voyage of the mind.

On that voyage, the dark man began to see further how the Dark Gods had tricked him and how they had used deceit as their principal weapon in binding him to their will. He knew that he had once loved a woman and that she had shared his great, unspoken crime with him. Yet the Dark Gods had always prevented further communion between them. And for reasons they dared not reveal. But here, pulling away the thick curtains of falsehood, the Voidal began to understand. As the powers flooded through him in this enclosed world of Scyllarza's working, light played across truths that stunned him.

The mendacity of the Dark Gods became clear. For they had led him to believe that with the loss of his love, irretrievable after the horrors she had undergone in Ludang, he had also lost powers that would also remain unattainable. Love had been maimed, set aside, to be no more than a memory. To share it with another, to raise up again the power set free by its working, would be denied him, just as the Dark Gods denied him so many other things. *Yet they were lying.*

Here, in this glade, Scyllarza had taught him that. Her own past was riddled with grim secrets, the torment of guilt, forbidden pacts. She, like him, had been cursed, for on Alendar she had been snatched from her mother and flung down into the deeps of the castle, left for the elements and although she had survived, it was to be as half woman, half demon. The Dark Gods had cursed her, and set her wandering, as they had the Voidal. *They must have known*, he mused, *that we would seek to meet again. They must know that between us, we create a key. We must tread with great care. The Dark Gods could have prevented this union. Somehow, it must serve them!*

The Voidal stood up, in shadow now, beneath the curve of a thick bough. The magic had extended its powers fully: Scyllarza had disappeared as if she did not exist. Already she had gone on ahead, across the astral. But something of her remained, for she had become a part of him. He had drawn her back into himself for the moment, aware of her power, as he was aware of thought, emotion, the pulsing of blood through his veins. It brought another rare smile to his lips. *This much is in defiance of the Dark Gods.*

"And who am I?" he said to the pool, as he strapped on his sword. But the water was as motionless as a sheet of glass. He would know, he swore it. Out in the wood, he heard the soft whispers of the spirits as they dissolved back into their own secret places. This place was open to the world once more. The Voidal prepared to leave, to take the short step to the place where the others were waiting.

* * * *

Elfloq, Orgoom and the Babbler stood upon the curved chest plate of a huge, rotting corpse in the heart of the sea that was a vast morass, hung with vapours that bore the appearance of endless cerements strewn across yet more fallen giants. The carcass on which the beings stood was now no more than a metal husk, the armour that had clothed the warrior, its innards held together with bones eroded and gnarled by the mire. The figures walked about nervously, like fleas on a massive cadaver, none sure of their next move, all fearing the worst. The Babbler held tight his short sword, determined in his own mind to destroy these two demons at the first opportunity. Orgoom would already have slit the Babbler open from crotch to chin had he not been ordered by his master not to do so. Elfloq was eager to be away from this disgusting world, the very surface of which seemed to bleed endlessly with the wounds of its history.

At last the air trembled and someone arrived. Scyllarza walked out from the darkness, an enigmatic smile upon her face. "I expected you all to be squabbling," she laughed.

Elfloq shuffled forward. "Call my master, quickly! We cannot remain."

"Why not?" she said. "Worlds are worlds. The omniverse is full of them."

"Invoke my master," persisted Elfloq. "He means you no harm."

"I have already met him," she said, pointing to the shadows behind her. As if in answer, the Voidal stepped forward.

"It is done," he said. "You have served me well," he told Elfloq and Orgoom. He frowned at the Babbler. "But you I am not so sure of. The hate that smoulders in your heart is as clear as fire on a hillside."

Scyllarza put an arm around the little man warmly. "It is only his love for me that makes him thus. Is it not so, Babbler? But you must understand — the dark man and I are united in our cause. You must serve him as you do me. If you do not do so — should you seek to harm or defy him — you harm me. We go on together from now on."

"To seek what?" said the Babbler.

The Voidal looked out over the mire, a grim smile of confidence on his features. "Certain things have been stolen from me. I want them. My memory, my identity, my soul. Your mistress has shown me how I may win them back."

"How, master?" said Elfloq with bounding eagerness.

The Voidal laughed and gripped the familiar, tossing him up into the air like a child, and Elfloq fluttered his wings, hanging there, jaws agape.

"How?" said the dark man for him. "I require the Sword of Shadows. In fact, I require all of the thirteen swords. Each one is in the keeping of the Seneschals of the Dark Gods. The Thirteen."

"But how will you wrest the swords from them?"

"I will summon each of them."

"*Summon* them?" gasped Elfloq, almost with a shriek. "As well summon the Dark Gods themselves!"

"Nevertheless, I will summon them. And then I will take the swords from them."

Elfloq dropped to the steel ground, eyes popping in stupefaction. Orgoom also looked uncomfortable. The Babbler did not understand and only Scyllarza looked unconcerned.

"It will mean a struggle, Elfloq," said the Voidal. "But what will it matter on this dead husk of a world? I will raise up the Thirteen and face their terrible powers. Let it be my challenge to the Dark Gods."

"But…but…if you…I mean, we…*fail*?"

The Voidal, amazingly, laughed out loud. "Fail? Why then this time it will mean true oblivion. The Dark Gods have bent me to their will for too long. I spit upon their machinations! If I fail, they will have to make nothing of me. Perhaps it will suit me. However," he said, turning to the three little figures. "You have all served us well. Better that you go. Find new masters and mistresses. If you wish your freedom, take it now."

Elfloq was astounded. His master had never been so sure of himself. What was it that had made him thus? Love? For he shared something with Scyllarza, that was evident. Yet, if he *should* triumph, the power he would gain would be — but the implications were far too staggering to think of.

Orgoom merely grunted. "I stay," was all he said.

The Babbler was thoughtful as he approached his mistress. "Must you be part of this? It is madness."

"It is my fate, Babbler."

"Then let it be mine."

"Well, Elfloq?" said the Voidal.

"You seem sure of victory, master."

"Nothing can be certain in this turbulent omniverse. Who knows?"

"You can overwhelm these Seneschals?"

"Possibly."

"Well, I —"

"Well?"

Elfloq muttered on for some little while, not actually stating that he would remain, but it was assumed that he would.

"Then it begins," said the Voidal.

* * * *

On his cold stone throne sat Shatterface, morose and thoughtful. There seemed to be no end to his lonely exile and fate appeared to have decreed that he would never break the chains imposed upon him. Twice he had sought to win his freedom and twice he had failed. Even though he had thrust the Sword of Madness into the Voidal, just as the Dark Gods had commanded, somehow it had been to no avail. The face of the brooding man was still masked.

"Melancholy thoughts," purred a voice from the shadows at the walls of his tower.

He looked up like one drugged to see a dim figure wavering in the glow of a solitary candle. "Have you come to mock, Asker?" he said, recognising the scarlet robe of the servant of the Dark Gods.

"Not at all." The Divine Asker approached him. "I would commiserate, though this would be of no comfort to you. But the Dark Gods know you have tried to serve them well."

"The accursed Voidal must be strangely empowered to have escaped the magic of the Swords. Did I not perform my task? Did I not undergo the rigours of death outside Ulthar, only to be woken up in this prison once more?"

"Indeed. You have earned a reward for that."

Shatterface stood up, eyes shining behind his mask. "But the Voidal still roams the omniverse — even here the whisperings reach me."

"That is true. He is not without power. It is time, therefore, to make your last assault on those powers."

"And if I fail?"

"It will be easier this time. But first, your reward. Do you have a mirror in this place?"

Shatterface almost snarled with derision. "Mirror! To look upon the vile havoc your masters have wrought upon my face! Have you no pity?"

The Asker ignored him and calmly drew from his scarlet robe a hand mirror. "Take this. Remove your mask and look at the left side of your face."

Shatterface made no move for a long time, but then clutched at the mirror. His mask gaped back at him. Then he retired to a dark corner. The Asker heard the gasps as Shatterface saw what had been done to him. In a while he came back to his visitor, proffering the mirror. He had put back the mask.

"Half my face has been restored, just as was promised."

"The Dark Gods are just. Now — the remainder of your face. Doubtless you would have that restored?"

"What must I do?"

The Asker pointed to a bare slab that served as a table. On it rested a sword in a black scabbard. "Once more the Dark Gods give into your keeping the Sword of Oblivion."

"To plunge into the Voidal —"

"No. The game has become more complex. There is another that you must thrust it into. No god, nor demi-god, or wizard. A mortal. So your task should be a simple one."

Shatterface laughed hollowly. "Is this a trick to torment me?"

"No. Ask no more. Take up the sword and I will tell you what must be done."

Cautiously Shatterface lifted the weapon. "Nothing mortal can withstand me," he told it, as if it were a living thing.

* * * *

The Babbler could not sleep, even though his beloved mistress had insisted that he should do so. He kept himself apart from the Gelder and that cunning familiar, neither of whom he could other than loathe. The dark man he yet hated keenly, for the intensity of his jealousy was boundless, though his mistress must be obeyed, for his love for her was equally as intense. He had always honoured Scyllarza. Ah, but she was besotted with this evil, black-clad monster. What powers did he tap? What evils did he seek to unleash? The Babbler could not settle. He crept about the rusting metal reaches of the fallen god like a wraith. He heard then the gentle laughter of his mistress and the soft voice of her lover. Silently he drew closer to where they had hidden themselves and he looked upon them, unseen.

They were locked in each other's arms as one, speaking very low. As the Babbler watched, unable to tear himself away, he gasped at the transformation that was taking place. *This must be an illusion!* He told himself. For the Voidal was drawing the woman into himself, *absorbing* her. Like some vampiric demon, he was making Scyllarza one with himself. For a second, the image shifted and it was as if the man had been drawn into the woman. But slowly the shapes blurred until only the dark man remained. Aghast, the Babbler fled. In another moment he had taken to the astral, the limitless unknown of its expanse.

For a long time he let its grey light enfold him, aimless and bewildered. My mistress is overpowered and destroyed! he kept telling himself. This is how the Voidal has tricked us both! Scyllarza is already dead! All we have seen here is an image of her! But what is to be done? I could flee, but that would not be enough. She must be avenged. The Voidal must be destroyed, wiped away.

At last he smiled. He remembered Alendar. It was there that he had first thwarted the Voidal. He had learned the secret of the exorcism from the dying Crimson Priest, Eordred, and he had used it, cutting into the dark man the fatal rune and sending him back to the void. It could be done again. The Voidal would be wary of him. There was a better way. The warriors! There had been many of them. If the Babbler could find them, he could teach them the revocation and they could work it upon the dark man, perhaps even destroy him in the process.

At once the Babbler left the astral and came back to the decaying world, this time far from the stultifying carnage in the sea of mud. In the landscape that opened up around him now, there would be lights.

* * * *

Out of his dreams the dark man came like a swimmer struggling up a beach from the clutches of a heavy surf. There had been deep visions, fragments, all dislodged by the powers that were swirling within him, though more of the mysteries were taking on distinct hues, better focussed. The power was shifting, no longer as elusive as it had been.

Scyllarza stood beside him once more, gazing at the grey dawn. She pulled him closer to her. "We begin today?"

"It has to be. Out there in that wilderness, there are incalculably ancient shrines, places where Light is worshipped and has been since then dawn of this world, or whatever worlds have been fused to create it. It is in such places that evil is banished, so residues of power remain there, to be used. I will go to one of them. There I will call up the Thirteen."

She was frowning: he saw this. "Your logic," she breathed, in answer to his questioning look, "may be at fault. The Dark Gods have proclaimed you as the evil power. It may be that in these ancient shrines the powers will work against you and strengthen the Thirteen."

The Voidal nodded. "Perhaps. But in my dreams I saw a certain hill, which I must find. They tried to obscure it from me, as if afraid I would reach it. I am certain they will defend it against my coming there. Why? What are they afraid of? They are gathering the scattered armies of this world, puny as they are, and have sent them to this place. I believe that if I win the hill, it will be a defeat for the Dark Gods."

"Then let us find it. How will we know it?"

"Under its skin of grass and broken menhirs, it is comprised of a million skulls."

* * * *

The Babbler climbed up into the coming dawn, muttering to himself, engorging his mind on the hate that seethed inside him. He was upon the warriors before he realised it: the hands that seized him and pinned him tore a shriek of terror from him.

"What vermin is this?" a man grunted, shaking the Babbler like a rat.

"Spare me! I bring you power! Power to destroy the evil that comes to your world!"

"Well, a prophet, is it?" one of the warriors laughed, his companions joining him.

"He stinks of the mire! Toss him back!"

"Wait!" cried the Babbler. "Kill me and you will all perish. I hold the key to your salvation."

From out of the armed ranks came a cowled Peace Monk. He motioned the warriors to release their squirming captive and stood before him. "Who are you? What is this gibberish?"

"The dark man is coming," said the Babbler and at once a curtain of silence came down.

The Peace Monk shuddered, crossing himself. "His name?"

"Voidal."

"Then you are indeed a prophet." He nodded at the men. "We must take him to Brother Torruvas. He has been expecting this." The monk turned again to the Babbler. "You know how to revoke this creature?"

The Babbler cackled, nodding furiously. Warriors parted for him as horses were brought. He mounted up and the escort gathered, the Peace Monk leading. Quickly they raced over the hill and out of sight.

As they galloped down into a valley, preparing to cross a ford, a single figure stepped from the low trees ahead of them. Those leading the party were forced to reign in tightly.

"Stand aside!" called the monk. "We are on urgent business."

For answer the tall figure swung a huge blade that sheared clean through the front legs of the monk's horse, toppling the rider into the stream. Another chop from the sword near split the man in two. At once the dumbfounded warriors were leaping off their horses and all became chaos in the churned stream. The intruder swung his heavy weapon as if it were as light as a twig and began hewing a bloody path through men and beasts alike. The warriors rushed upon him in force. There were a dozen of them, but those that drove their own blades at the man's body seemed to have no effect. The slaughter that followed was brief but terrible.

The Babbler, who had been unseated by his own panic-stricken steed, sprawled dazedly beside the stream, unable to comprehend what was happening. At last, with the remaining horses dashing away from the carnage at the ford, all became still. The Babbler found himself staring up in horror at the intruding warrior, whose head was encased in a terrible helm that obscured all of his face but the eyes. The warrior tossed away the blood-smeared sword: the Babbler thought that he must have been spared.

Shatterface drew from a black scabbard another blade, the Sword of Oblivion. The Babbler instinctively drew back in terror.

"What do you want of me?"

"Your secret, little man."

"I will give it to you gladly! I will teach you how to revoke the Voidal. It is a simple thing —"

But the Sword of Oblivion ripped down and up, its point tearing free of the Babbler's back. A single scream broke the restored silence and the eyes of the Babbler stared, huge orbs, seeing nothing, his mind wiped as clean as polished stone. Shatterface satisfied himself that the work was done and then turned away, sparing no more than a brief glance at the corpses strewn about him. He walked up the river a little and in the brightening hues of dawn, removed his grim helm. When he at last bent to look at his reflection in the water, tears coursed down his remoulded cheeks, for staring back at him was the face he had once possessed, forgotten for millennia. He was restored.

Slipping into the trees, he hid himself, for there were riders coming. He watched as they inspected the dead warriors and heard their cries of alarm. Then they had wheeled away, ignoring the madman that sat by the river, babbling nonsense to himself and plucking uselessly at the hilt of the weapon protruding from his chest. Shatterface prepared to leave this world. He was content, but puzzled. Why had the Dark Gods denied the men of this world the power to revoke the Voidal? Why should they want the dark man to summon the Thirteen? But it was not for him to know. He was free, made whole, and the omniverse would reopen for him. Joyfully he went out into its infinity.

* * * *

"They come!" was the cry that reached the ears of Torruvas and Renegorn where they stood high on the walls of the crumbling temple that stood atop the holy place. Here, at this ancient shrine of power, they had assembled the army that had taken them months to gather, awaiting the arrival of the creature that the Bone Burrower had foretold would come.

"How many of them are there?" said Torruvas. "Are they legion?"

Renegorn shook his head. "I don't understand. Reports say that there are only the four. The dark man, his familiars, and the woman. Her companion is not with her."

They waited apprehensively, the army about them tensed for war. Soon, crossing the brow of one of the lower hills, they saw two horses and flying above them a diminutive figure. Below the walls, the massed warriors prepared to defend the temple, whatever the cost. Torruvas's face paled. "Where is the one who is to help us? We do not have the secret of revocation, the means of sending this black crusader back to the darkness from which he came."

Renegorn spat angrily. "Then we must fight. The blood of the gods of Light is in this hill. Its powers will give us strength."

Torruvas did not respond, instead closing his eyes and praying.

Down in the valley, the Voidal reigned in his horse. Orgoom sat behind him, muttering about the discomforts of riding. Elfloq fluttered down from the sky, face twisted with anxiety. "I see a great host, master. Armed for war. We have arrived at a bad time. I fear we may be crushed between two forces."

Scyllarza had drawn her sword. "Is this not the ancient hill you spoke of?"

The Voidal nodded. "I know that I have to stand on its crest and summon the Thirteen Seneschals from there. The temple means nothing to me. But that host is there for one reason, Elfloq. To defend the hill from me."

"From, from *you*, master?" Elfloq gasped, appalled by the numbers surrounding the hill. There were several thousand warriors there.

"They seem to know that I want to climb the hill."

"How are we to overcome them?" Scyllarza asked.

"I have no quarrel with them. I mean their world no harm. I will speak to their leaders," said the dark man. He said it without fear, but clearly something troubled him. "Wait for me here."

Orgoom dismounted and at once the Voidal was galloping up the steep incline towards the forces of Torruvas and Renegorn.

The Peace Monk saw the dark figure coming and drew back. This was no man that threatened them, he was certain. "Does he come to mock us?"

Renegorn grunted. "This waiting gnaws at me. I will go out and speak to this creature, demon or not." Before he could be stopped, he had gone down into the temple and out to his men. He called together a few of his best warriors and they rode out with him to meet the Voidal, though they all writhed inwardly with fear. Moments later the dark man had pulled up no more than a few yards from the warriors.

"What army is this?" he called to them. "Why is it here?"

"You know that, I think," replied Renegorn.

"Am I the one you are waiting for?"

"Why are you here?"

"It is given to me to perform an ancient ritual. Great evil threatens not only your world, but the entire omniverse. It gathers itself, coiling like a great serpent about its boundaries. I cannot leave here until I have fought with it. I must stand at the crest of that hill. I have no quarrel with your people. Let them stand aside and they will suffer no harm from me."

"What is this ritual?" said Renegorn suspiciously.

"It will disperse the evil I have spoken of."

"This hill is blessed by the powers of Light," insisted Renegorn. "Do you serve them?"

The Voidal laughed softly. "I have been cast out into darkness, but I will return to the light. My quarrel is with gods, not men, warrior. Quickly, take your mortal troops away before hell breaks loose."

Renegorn stood his ground. "My army draws upon the ancient powers locked in the hill. Do not underestimate that power."

The Voidal sighed. "I assure you, I do not. I have no wish to harm your men, but they mean nothing to me, or the gods. I will show you." He pointed to the uppermost tower of the temple and said something quietly. In a moment the upper bricks of the tower began to tilt, heating up and *melting* until they ran in great globules of molten stone, slithering down into the temple courtyard, congealing like wax. Half the tower sagged in this way, clotted like mud in a matter of moments. Within the temple there were shouts of horror.

"I ask you again," said the Voidal. "Will you leave? I will wipe away your men if I have to. Don't make me do this."

Renegorn was visibly shaken. What could he do against this horrific power? Even the Peace Monks could do nothing and whatever forces the hill possessed seemed to have been powerless against the destruction of the tower.

"There is another way to resolve this," said the dark man.

"How?"

"The forces of evil will try to destroy me. Your armies and the power of the hill combined with my own power would aid me to destroy them."

Renegorn grimaced. "Help *you*? This is a trick!"

He heard hoofbeats behind him and in a moment turned to see Brother Torruvas reigning in. "Do not listen to him!" the Peace Monk called. "He is our enemy."

The Voidal rode closer and drew back the shirt of nightweb from his chest. "Here — plunge your weapons into me. Strike me. Do what you will. I cannot die. I have been cursed with immortality."

Torruvas steadied his horse, which seemed unnerved by the presence of the dark man. "You can be revoked." He could see that his words had puzzled the Voidal. "Yes, it is so. You fear something. And I have that power, dark man. I can send you back to your darkness."

A deep silence fell over them all like a cloud. There was a mystery here that the Voidal did not understand. His dreams had not revealed it to him, though part of it shone through the veil. Something else broke into the thoughts of all the gathered company, for they heard strange mutterings and mumblings and saw movement on the slopes below them. It was the hunched figure of the Babbler, staggering along with the blade still in him. The Voidal watched the little man as he disappeared from view, baffled by him. In his mind he saw again his first meeting with the Babbler, on Alendar, recalling at last that it had been he who had betrayed him, cutting the rune into his flesh and sending him back to the void. And now he had given the secret to these monks! But — who had plunged that blade into him? The Babbler was dying, but by who's hand?

No one moved towards the fallen figure. The Voidal pointed again to the temple. "You must choose. Either I destroy your temple, or we use it against what comes."

"Why are you opposed to the coming evil?" said Torruvas. "Why do you not seek to rule it, or at least, serve it?"

Before the Voidal could speak, there was a rush of darkness and a boiling of the skies. Something of their unnatural gloom pressed down towards the earth. A great shape had formed itself on the hillside, as though the dark man had already begun his invocation of the powers of night. He, however, recognised the pulsing spectre that reared up, clothed in shadows. He urged his elemental steed towards it before anyone else had moved, shouting defiance at it. There followed a deafening clap of thunder and the darkness funnelled upwards at unnatural speed, something flashing in its nebulous embrace as it went. On the dry grass of the hill, the broken body of the Babbler lay, wrapped in sunlight as the premature night retracted its clouds.

Behind the dark man, the mounted warriors edged forward, though none of them understood what had happened. Perhaps, they thought, the spirit of the broken man had ascended. Some had seen the gleaming of something as it rose. The Voidal, however, knew instinctively who had appeared. It had been Xatrovul. One of the Thirteen Seneschals, he who had charge of the Sword of Oblivion. What could he have wanted with the Babbler?

"Who is this man?" demanded Torruvas, pointing to the Babbler's corpse.

"One of your servants?" Renegorn asked the dark man.

"He was," nodded the Voidal. "Did you not see the darkness claim him? Already that evil seeks to bring me down, through my servants." *And with him,* deduced the Voidal, *went the secret of my revocation! Then the Dark Gods want me here.* He turned to the Peace Monk. "Again I say, you must choose. Either take all your people far away to safety, or stay and aid me. There will be terrible things seen here. Some will bring madness upon you. I do not want that."

"We are here to oppose evil," said Torruvas. *How am I to decide?* He asked himself. The Bone Burrower said this dark man had the power to save us or damn us. Yet the mad island god, Dreamwarp, had wanted him revoked. Had Dreamwarp been one of the evil powers that wanted the Voidal destroyed? It was true that the coming of the dark man heralded the Evil Time, but was he here to stand against it? Did he intend to open the Crimson Gate that the legends referred to?

"If you think that I am the vessel of this evil you so fear," the Voidal told Torruvas, "then revoke me now."

The warriors were watching the Peace Monk, expecting him to perform this miracle. But the dark man had guessed correctly: Torruvas did not possess the secret. Without it, he was impotent. The monk could not speak. He could not meet this challenge.

"To the hill, then," said the Voidal, not waiting for an answer. "Have your men bring the body of the little man." He rode through the confused ranks of the warriors and on up the hill towards the temple. As he rode, he shouted to the skies. "Elfloq! I know you are there. Bring Scyllarza and Orgoom. We go to the temple."

No one dared to prevent the Voidal's entry into the temple. He felt the dormant power of the place quivering as he dismounted and his feet touched the earth floor of the inner court. The weight of centuries hung from the walls, an antiquity beyond imagining. There had been a battle here, millennia gone by, but he could smell the blood from its excesses as if freshly spilled. In the cool shadows of the walls he waited for Torruvas and Renegorn to join him. One of their warriors, eyes filled with fear, had brought the Babbler's corpse. The Voidal nodded for him to put it down beside him.

"None of my other companions are to be harmed. I know that two of them are not pretty to look upon," he added with a grim smile. "But they are not the demons you fear."

Even so, Orgoom and Elfloq's arrival caused near panic among the gathered warriors, but they held back from them. Elfloq was relieved to be able to perch near his master, himself clearly terrified by the hostile glances of the army. Scyllarza attracted almost as much unease, for as she dismounted her eyes fell upon the fallen Babbler and her snarl was more demon than woman. The men of the temple drew back, their faith wavering.

"The Dark Gods have done this," the Voidal told her as she bent down and gently touched the cold brow of her squire. "The Sword of Oblivion was in him."

She frowned. "But why? What did he know? He shared everything with me."

The Voidal took her hand and pulled her to her feet. "There will be an accounting," he assured her. "Bury him here. Time harries us." He could feel her fury vying with sorrow, welling like a storm.

Brother Torruvas was studying the creatures that had invaded the temple. *What have we done?* He asked himself. *Can they be our salvation? Are they to battle evil with us?*

Renegorn was at his shoulder, echoing his thoughts. "If we are wrong about these demons, Brother, it is the end for us and this world."

"Aye. But he gave us the chance to flee. Should we? I have spent a lifetime preparing for this hour, but I fear for our world. Humanity may have seen its last dawn."

Renegorn stood in silence for a long while, watching the woman opening the earth to receive the body of the fallen half-man. Then, as if something had snapped within him at such heresy, he strode forward, hand on his sword hilt. With a swift blur of movement, the Voidal turned to him and put his hand over the warrior's. Renegorn could not move, the grip of the dark man impossibly strong.

"No," said the Voidal softly. "Save your killing blows for what is coming. The Babbler would not have harmed you. Let the earth have him. We are none of us diminished by his burial here." He released Renegorn and turned away from him, and with an arm about Scyllarza, began the climb up the stairs of what remained of the tower. Orgoom, glowering at the warriors, sickles open, followed Elfloq.

Torruvas was again beside Renegorn. "I am certain that he could wipe us all away in a stroke. That he has not done so suggests we are powerless against him. And he is immune to the powers of this temple. We are in his hands."

Renegorn nodded. "Very well. I will prepare the men for battle. The gods know, they are utterly confused."

Above them, the Voidal spoke to Scyllarza. "The Dark Gods desire this battle. It is why they snatched the Babbler from these people, who would have used him to revoke me. He did this once before, on Alendar."

She was taken aback by his words. "The Babbler —?"

He nodded. "I would not have told you. But he had the secret from the Crimson Priest. The Dark Gods would have had a hand in that. Feed your anger on them. The little man served you alone. And with his passing, the Dark Gods bring on this battle. They must be sure of victory."

"Then must you do this?"

"I will never be stronger, unless I win back the last of my powers. I can only attain them through the Sword of Shadows. I am sick of wandering through lost dreams! Yes, I must do this. I will begin it!" He stepped to the edge of the wall and flung open his arms to the sky. He closed his eyes and from his lips there came a stream of strange incantations as he invoked the first of the Thirteen Seneschals of the Dark Gods, the keepers of the swords. Spells sang and burst, while unseen beings sped across the back of the unfurling winds, hissing and cursing, the clouds forming mouths that hurled obscenities down upon the terrified warriors below.

At last the Voidal shouted a name aloud. "Come from your dismal lair, Khadwhaan, bearer of the Sword of Light, maker of suns! Rouse yourself and face me!" No sooner had he cried this than the skies grew bright and fiery as though a dozen new suns burned there. Great clouds of shimmering gold burst like surf across the hills, reforming themselves into a tall figure. It held up a sword that shone like fire, the Sword of Light: as the figure raised it, brilliant light streamed from it so that the warriors in the army were forced to turn away, hiding their faces. Those who were not quick enough to avert their eyes were instantly made blind. But the Voidal laughed and held up his open palms, receiving the streams of light. They sank into the black gloves as if into deep wells and were lost in their darkness.

Khadwhaan stood like a statue made of burning gold, faceless and volcanic, but the Voidal was not deterred. He felt the powers in the earth beneath him running up into him as light met light and he turned the rivers of fire back upon the blazing figure. For long moments the struggle endured, until Khadwhaan wavered and then burst into a million fragments, a scintillating cloud of embers tossed to the skies, blotting out the sun as a false twilight spread across the world. The Sword of Light fell to the hillside and struck point first, quivering for a time until it fell still, its light subdued.

The Voidal called to Scyllarza, who had shielded her eyes from the glare. "The Thirteen are now twelve. Khadwhaan is dispersed. I was right to test myself here." He looked out at the distant sword, which seemed to mark the Seneschal's grave. "Elfloq! Fly out and retrieve the Sword of Light! Fear it not. Only I can empower it now."

The familiar muttered and grumbled, certain that he would be in serious danger, but nevertheless he flew over the hillside and tugged at the buried sword. It came away easily and he took it to his master. Then began the next invocations as the Voidal pursued his war against the Thirteen.

Within moments the second of the Seneschals had burst up from the earth like a pillar of livid anger, for this was Envargoth, wielder of the Sword of Dispersal, and he smote into the army, pulping a score of men at a stroke, squashing men and steeds like flies, tearing huge chunks of stone from the temple. The claws of this furious Seneschal reached out and dislocated everything they touched, but the Voidal used his power to draw the strength of Envargoth's weapon upon himself. At first all the power in that awesome blade raced for the very heart of the dark man. It struck there in a concentrated beam of screaming madness, but it was as water pouring into a canyon. In moments it had spewed back, fountaining in a spray that thrust Envargoth backwards. As the Seneschal crashed to the earth, the ground opened and curling fingers of darkness reached up and pulled him down into his grave, smothering him and leaving only the Sword of Dispersal on the waterlogged grass above. Elfloq retrieved it nervously, but its power seemed spent.

After this came silence as the elements drew back. The Voidal, weakened by his efforts, went down from the tower to survey the havoc that had been wrought amongst the men. Many had been torn apart and the sounds of the wounded were terrible to hear. Renegorn confronted the dark man angrily.

"This is *insane*! What use are mortals against the legions of hell?"

The Voidal drew breath. "Forgive me. But your people have not died without purpose. This hill contains the powers of the ages. But even those powers are not limitless. Tell your men and the Peace Monks to pray. Each and every incantation against these Seneschals gives me strength to oppose them. This war is not for your world alone, it is for the omniverse itself."

"This terrible darkness that is gathering," said Scyllarza. "These Seneschals are a part of it?"

The Voidal glanced up at the curdling skies. He had no answer.

Instead he went back up to the top of the fallen tower, to begin anew. Moments later there were shouts and screams down among the warriors and Elfloq fluttered above their ranks in amazement, for they were fighting themselves. Several dozen of the men had gone berserk and were hacking wildly at each other in the press. This sudden madness spread so that the mass of soldiery began heaving and shrieking. It was the work of Azlomec, who held the Sword of Madness that had once been buried in the Voidal's vitals. Now the Seneschal was churning up the warriors, reaping through their chaos, a crimson harvest. Hundreds of them fled from the inner temple, screaming, eyes bulging, while outside there were scores of slithering horrors coming up from the valley, monstrosities conjured up by Azlomec to shatter the sanity of all who looked upon them.

The Voidal searched the stone stairways of the temple and saw a laughing phantom, a ravening monster that was vomiting out spells and curses. The dark man rushed around the inner walls to confront it. Azlomec turned upon him the vilest of countenances, seeking to rip out his mind with his most hideous aspect, but the Voidal's hands reached out inexorably and closed on the frightful head. They squeezed and heaved, crushing its screaming form and ripping it from the neck, dashing it against a wall, where it burst in a last sizzle of sparks. The noise from the warriors below ceased as many of them collapsed. Few of them rose again, either dead or mindless.

Torruvas came to the Voidal's side, face white with horror. "We should have left! We should have done what you asked! For months we have culled the Open Lands to bring this army together, and for what? To have them wiped out to a man? How does that serve us?"

The Voidal breathed heavily, the conflict exhausting him. "Go if you must. But there is no protection outside. The Seneschals will break your world into pieces. All that can save you now is the power within the hill, and what powers I have."

"But...what of those outside? The families —"

The Voidal looked away, saying nothing.

Fresh cries of horror up on the battlements snared his attention and together with a group of warriors, he went up to see what had transpired. They looked across the slopes to discern a seething army of demons cavorting and leaping towards the temple, unleashing fire arrows and handfuls of scalding embers at the regrouping defenders. "This is the work of Yssussquot," said the Voidal. "Keeper of the Bane of Demons. Every one of them that he has ever chained up with the sword, he has unleashed."

"They are countless!" cried Elfloq and Orgoom grunted in shock. The Voidal called to his familiars and Scyllarza and went down the slopes to meet the capering army. Scyllarza, who had wrought havoc among these creatures on Alendar, drew her sword eagerly. Orgoom opened his sickle fingers in readiness, while Elfloq flew overhead, uncertain how to aid in the defence. Between them, this small company formed a circle, drawing the demon assault, but none of the monsters was able to penetrate the mesh of death that awaited it. As he fought, the Voidal laughed,

Scyllarza too, and from the temple and its grounds the last of the monks and warriors watched as the incredible carnage began. As each demon was smashed down, it rose again, but only to turn upon its fellows and rend them.

Not until there were tall heaps of demon slain did the battle end. Then the Voidal dragged from the ranks of the enemy one huge and bloated demon, Yssussquot himself. Orgoom sliced this vile hell-beast into a dozen pieces, tossing the chunks of flesh out into the last of the demon horde, where they burst, dispersing the demons for a final time.

After this, Cerudis, bearer of the Sword of Winds, smote the temple in a storm that pulled down two of its walls, crushing scores of warriors, the damage awesome before the vent of the Voidal's anger wrapped itself around the Seneschal and negated his power. Zerrizzan, holder of the Sword of Fire, attacked, flinging his flaming bolts, making a great pyre of both living and dead, until he, too, was engulfed in his own flames as the Voidal reversed the flow of his power. As Zerrizzan turned to ash, Elfloq brought his sword to his master. There were now six of them, bundled up like tinder on the battlements. The Voidal called a rest for the night, collapsing into Scyllarza's arms. But he could not contain the flow of powers he had loosed. They would appear when it suited them now.

In the night there came a new attack. By the scarlet moonlight, the warriors saw a grim frost forming rapidly, hardening and becoming a sheet of white ice. Men shivered and wrapped themselves tightly in their pelts, until at last the cold became so oppressive that bones were heard to snap and crack. "Umecal is here!" cried the Voidal. "Keeper of the Sword of Ice."

His own sword became like a torch and he raised it aloft, searing away the great spears of icicles that had sprung up everywhere in the temple. As he drew upon yet more power from the hill, he ran outside to see a tall steed, seemingly carved from ice and upon its back the laughing figure of Umecal, pointing down at him with a glass trident. The Voidal rushed under the trampling hooves and smote upwards with his molten blade. Umecal shrieked in agony as the blow shattered both his horse and him. The ice became water, sluicing away into the earth, only a few wisps of steam trailing up into the night sky to mark his passing.

In the dawn that followed, there was another attack, one of terrible noiselessness, for this was the work of Maakadur. Men could neither speak nor hear, for the Sword of Silence tipped them once more towards madness. There were less than a thousand survivors from the hell-frosts of the night, the walls of the temple now split apart and fallen. The Voidal knew that the power in the hill was being sucked away, its reservoir emptied. Yet he would use it all, and the lives of these people, to win the

Thirteen swords and his soul. He was committed, and the Dark Gods were wavering.

He let forth a great cry that rocked the very heavens, like thunder across a world, splitting apart the wall of silence that Maakadur had set up. The noise ruptured the ears of numerous warriors, but when reverberations died down, the Seneschal had broken apart.

There was little time to recover, for soon afterwards Taliphor, keeper of the Sword of Stone, began his assault upon the temple. The earth split and opened, swallowing great pieces of the shrine and raining huge boulders down from the sky. Again the Voidal redirected the power of the Seneschal, turning Taliphor into clouds of dust that swirled like a sandstorm before settling back into the cracked earth. The dark man sagged down on to a rock, weariness threatening him. He realised just how much he had taken upon himself. He had triumphed this far, but would he have enough reserves of power left to complete the task? The temple was almost flattened, its tower no more and there were but a handful of the warriors left alive. Scyllarza looked spent and the two small figures of Elfloq and Orgoom were huddled up like birds sheltering from a rainstorm.

Renegorn lived yet, though he was covered in his own blood, his sword broken. "The world is dying, dark man. Have you not done enough? Must the last of us perish here?"

The Voidal stared moodily at the shattered earth. "There are four Seneschals left."

"There is a small amount of power left in this hill. Do you know that Brother Torruvas and his Peace Monks are all slain. Can you not leave us to rebuild? It was foretold that you would either be our saviour or our destroyer. Look about you! All is death and destruction! We are destroyed! Can't you understand that?"

The Voidal stood up. "I need the last of the power. To give up now would mean defeat for all worlds. *You* must understand *that*. This conflict is not simply about your cinder of a world. Victory here frees countless others. Men die here, but mankind survives."

Renegorn could not contain his frustration and fury any longer. "Then may the darkness claim you!" he snarled, lifting his blade. But before he could use it, something gripped him and shook him, a dark, unseen force. The dark man realised that another of the Seneschals had joined the fray. Renegorn dropped his weapon and began to tear and claw at himself, ripping with his fingers, pulling strips of flesh from himself. The screams brought Elfloq and Orgoom, who saw madness loose again among the warriors.

"Xengoye," the Voidal told them. "The Sword of Pain."

The remaining warriors were crying out, defenceless against the invisible shafts of pain. Renegorn fell to the ground, his body broken, shaken like a straw doll, his bones twisted. Something leapt upon the back of the watching Voidal and flung him to the earth, but the dark man rolled over and put the Seneschal between himself and the floor of the temple. The shadow-shape that was Xengoye tried to break free, but the power under the earth rose up into him like heat from a sun, charring and searing, so that his own pain was beyond all that he had meted out. When he was no more than a husk, the Voidal stood up and tossed the Sword of Pain to Elfloq.

Now no more than a few score of the warriors remained alive, too dazed to look up, ignoring the bodies of Renegorn and the monks and all the other countless fallen. Scyllarza gazed at the carnage with a sorrowful shake of her head. "We are seeing the death of this world," she breathed.

"You see the handiwork of the Dark Gods," the Voidal told her coldly. "They wanted this. You know well enough how they use me."

"But you sought this confrontation —" She stopped, seeing the look of anger on his face, the confusion.

Elfloq, who had gathered up the swords, interrupted them. "Master, have we not done enough? Can we not leave now?"

"There are three swords left. I will have my soul, Elfloq. I have not come this far to be frustrated again. And besides, I cannot put an end to this. It is inexorable. Already it begins anew."

He was right, for in the devastated temple, the last of the men were stirring. Something had visited them and was working its poison. They were writhing upon the floor, trying to bury themselves like worms into the very earth, as if it could save them. In their midst sat an old woman, wheezing and cackling to herself, as if her mind had collapsed under the strain of the horrors about her. But the Voidal knew her and nodded.

"So you are here, Kubashte. You have used the Sword of Plague."

"Yes, creature of darkness. I will sew my ills among your closest followers, for no one survives the crawling death I spread!"

The Voidal walked through the carpet of dead and dying warriors to the hideous crone, holding out a hand to her. "If you are so powerful, put your plague into me."

Kubashte looked about her and chuckled gruesomely as she saw Elfloq and Orgoom gasp in horror, for great blotches had broken out on their bodies. Scyllarza, too, had become riddled with the plague. The Voidal ignored the moans of the dying. Instead he snatched the fingers of the hag and gripped them fast. At once the awful being shuddered, scores of boils breaking out on her body like living things as the Voidal poured back into her the diseases she had spread. When at last he released her, she was no more than a sack. She fell to the ground and burst into flames.

The Voidal motioned his companions away and they saw to their infinite relief that they had been cleansed. Not so the warriors, though, none of who were spared. The fire quickly spread across the ruins, eventually muffling the screams of the last survivors.

Elfloq hugged the swords, but they were cold, seemingly lifeless, their size diminished so that they had become as light as daggers.

"The power of the hill is no more," said the Voidal. "All that we have left to draw upon is our own resolve. Two Seneschals remain. I sense that Germunden is near."

Scyllarza drew herself up with difficulty. "Which sword?"

"The Sword of Illusion," said the Voidal. "The most dangerous."

They did not have long to wait. The Seneschal swooped down from the skies and alighted not far from them, a huge winged being, reptilian and ferocious, his outline wavering and changing constantly. At once he began to pour forth its repulsive visions, but the Voidal closed his mind to them and strode toward Germunden purposefully. He directed his right hand at the Seneschal, and to the utter amazement of Elfloq, the hand *parted itself* from the Voidal's arm, dropped to the floor and began to crawl across to Germunden.

"How can this be?" Elfloq whispered, knowing that his master had won back from the Dark Gods his own hand.

Germunden's blazing eyes gazed at the awful member and he took to the air with a shrill scream of fear. But the hand leapt upwards, grew in size and smashed the Seneschal down as if swatting a huge insect. Behind the maimed Seneschal, shimmering in the grass, was the Sword of Illusion. The Voidal walked to it and picked it up, thrusting it deftly into the writhing body. Germunden dissipated like mist.

"Illusion against illusion," the dark man laughed. "Mine was the stronger."

"The hand —" Elfloq began.

The Voidal held out both of his hands. "Mine are as they are. What you saw was an illusion."

Scyllarza was frowning. "This was the easiest victory."

The Voidal frowned thoughtfully. "Yes, it is strange. But we have twelve of the swords. Elfloq, bring the others here."

At once the familiar obeyed. In a moment the swords were here, thrust into the hillside like grave markers. The Voidal surveyed the lands about them. "I still lack the Sword of Oblivion. But I have already seen Xatrovul. He took the sword after he had felled the Babbler with it." He called out an angry challenge to the brooding skies.

To the surprise of the others, they discerned a hunched figure toiling lamely towards them across one of the sloping hills. It was garbed in shadow, apparently weak, barely able to move.

"A trap!" hissed Scyllarza, sword raised to strike.

"Spare me, master," came a tired voice, which seemed heavy with the weight of years.

"Give me the Sword of Oblivion," said the Voidal, himself wary of any trick. He was so close to his goal. The Dark Gods would be at their most dangerous now. They would gain so much pleasure at thwarting him when he was a blade's width from victory.

"I do not have the sword," breathed Xatrovul. "It was taken from me. The Dark Gods have it."

The Voidal nodded slowly. "As I thought. But they fear me. Do they not? Well, is it so?" He made ready to destroy the last Seneschal.

The figure slumped back pitifully. "Yes, yes! It is so. They fear you. Spare me, master. I served you well once."

The Voidal's eyes burned into him, trying to see through the opaque glass of memory. "You served *me*?"

"We were all your servants. Until the Dark Gods banished you and enslaved us. But I will serve you again. I will help you to recover the Sword of Oblivion."

"Kill him!" hissed a voice, that of Elfloq, who was standing beside the dark man, hopping from one leg to another. "He's the last. Kill him, master!"

But the dark man was deeply puzzled by the Seneschal's words. He gathered up the twelve swords and said something to them. In the blink of an eye, a shadow wrapped around them and they had become a single blade. "I need the last one," the Voidal said again.

"Your soul, master," Elfloq nodded. "But, what of the Sword of Shadows?"

"When the Thirteen are one, they become the Sword of Shadows," came the faltering voice of Xatrovul.

Elfloq groaned. Gods of the Abyss, would this never be over?

"Where is the missing sword?" grunted Orgoom, himself eager to be far from any further conflict.

The Voidal smiled. "The Dark Gods do fear me. There will be a last journey, friends of the man who was to have none! To claim all that we are owed. I *shall* be restored."

Scyllarza put an arm about him. "So be it, but will we not rest first?"

The Voidal held her, immediately strengthened by her. "For a while. Elfloq! You must visit Cloudway again. Bring me the fallen Asker, Vulparoon. I will need his guidance on our voyage."

"But, will his mind stand up to such a voyage?"

"Just fetch him!"

"At once, master," said the familiar and took to the air. But he lingered for a moment, remembering a certain Vlod the Remover, who was sure to be watching over Vulparoon on behalf of Eye Patch of the Smile. As Elfloq pondered this queasily, he overheard a further conversation below. It was one which filled him with more dread than he could remember.

"A voyage," said Scyllarza. "And where will it take us?"

"To Holy Hedrazee," said the Voidal, leading the way down from the smouldering hill. "To the very sanctuary of the Divine Askers. To the halls of the Dark Gods. There they will render up all that is mine."

As they went from the grim place of death, the shambling figure of Xatrovul followed, like a tired dog following its master after an exhausting hunt. The Voidal did not look back at him, but the riddle that had been set him nagged at his mind. The Seneschals had once served *him*. What did this mean?

PART SEVEN

GATE AT THE EDGE OF REASON

Wars beget wars beget wars.
Where does one war end and another begin? One could ask the same question of life, of the omniverse, of the gods. Some things are perpetual. There is only change. Change defines everything, even time.
One war may justify another. Its end may justify its means. And in the case of war, the means are always sacrifices, invariably vast ones.
—**Salecco**, who reserves the right to decide what sacrifices he would make to serve any cause

* * * *

The world was dying in the embers of sunset, a funeral pyre to the army that had perished. Scyllarza, Orgoom and the Voidal had been travelling away from the hill of the slain for most of the day, saying very little, their energies still sapped by the conflict. Around them the landscape seemed withered, as if already the last of its juices had been drained from it by the clashing of those dark powers on the hill. Now, high above a cracked plain, the three survivors could see emptiness stretching away, a limitless expanse of settled dust, riddled with fissures. From out of it poked an occasional lump of eon-old armour, or a metal arm, frozen in a last impotent defiance of fate.

"What do you seek?" said Scyllarza beside the dark man. His bleak mood troubled her, for he seemed to have withdrawn into himself, closing her out.

"There will be a ship," he murmured, as if trying to interpret a dream.

"From where?"

He shook his head. "It will take us to Holy Hedrazee and our destiny." He said no more, holding her to him, sensing her anxiety. Their elemental steeds grew restless: they could feel the earth vibrating as though huge engines were locked away deep below it. Spurts of dust like miniature storms gathered out on the plain. The cracks there groaned like mouths and widened, the sound of splitting rock echoing across the land as chunks of it slid into the emptiness. A widening gash, canyon-like, ran for miles to the horizon, and as it grew wider and darker, huge clouds billowed up from its depths as if a monstrous beast was about to rupture the confines of its grave.

Something speared up from the ground, followed by two more of these tall spines. When the black smoke thinned, the watchers could see that these resembled the masts of some immense ship. It was breaking through the crust of the shattered land, a black hulk from which the dust and earth spilled in colossal cataracts. The earth shook and burst, like a giant pod releasing its fruit. Around it the world was disintegrating.

"Come," called the Voidal and they rode down towards the chaotic plain. Above them reared the awesome shape of the ship, or beast, whatever it might be. It reeked of decay, as if alive but partially rotted. If it were a ship, there were no sails, no oars and nothing living aboard it. Yet something moved, for out of its endless length there came a wriggling snake, a narrow, limb-like bridge that flicked down to where the party stood. They dismounted, allowing the elemental steeds to disappear on to the astral. The Voidal stepped on to the grotesque bridge and indicated the dark opening from which it had emerged.

"We must board," he said, moved by a dubious instinct, and began the climb up the precarious strand. Scyllarza followed him, with a scowling Orgoom bringing up the rear. Out of the dust behind him came the drooped figure of Xatrovul, shuffling along as if on the point of collapse, face hidden. A weight seemed to burden him, as around him the world began to break up like surf upon waiting fangs of rock. The broken Seneschal lurched up the bridge as emptiness groped for him, dust fingers that he ignored in his reverie.

Into the gut of the mighty ship the party went: once inside they climbed a stairway of web, woven by an invisible spider they were relieved not to see. Eventually they came up into the fading evening light on what must be the upper deck, where they could hear the doom of the world as the ship dragged itself from the last rocks and earth that had been its sepulchre for so long. The debris still poured from it like water flowing out of a mighty sieve. Now that they could see the world spread out below them, they understood the truth of its bizarre nature.

"The War of the Falling Gods," said the Voidal, "wrought utter chaos to many worlds, ripping apart the very dimensions. A kind of order restored parts of them and settled them here, on this world, but it perches like a stone on the lip of an even vaster chaos. The conflict I unleashed has torn asunder the last fabric of stability. Only this ship can steer through it."

"But what manner of creature is it?" said Scyllarza. "For it is alive, is it not?"

"It is," he nodded vaguely. "I cannot be sure yet. I only know that it waited here for me. That knowledge was locked inside me."

"By the Dark Gods?"

"Perhaps. But it may be that once it served me. We will know soon enough."

Orgoom was pointing excitedly out at the shifting sands of the world. "Master! World is filled with creatures! Not dead!"

There were cries and ululations, mingled with an unnerving dirge rising from the crumbling plain and the Voidal leaned over the side of the ship to see what caused the sounds. To his disgust he saw thousands of shapes crawling across the landscape, massed like maggots over rank meat. In places the surface could not be seen for the sheer numbers. Each of the wretched creatures seemed to be staring up at the ship, as if in torment, reaching out, eyes pleading, mouths emitting the frightful wails and shrieks that made up the dirge. When they saw the Voidal, their fingers pointed him out in unified accusation, their curses flung at invisible powers, calling for his damnation.

He drew away, appalled, almost cuffed back by the weight of their bitterness. He was trying to unravel this mystery when he saw two figures on the deck below him. He knew them at once, relieved to see them.

The first of them flew up to him, ugly face riddled with anxiety. "Master!" It was Elfloq, newly returned from Cloudway.

"You have brought Vulparoon?"

"Indeed. It was not easy. I had to persuade Eye Patch to dismiss Vlod the Remover, and he would only do so after I had regaled him with every detail of our exploits here. And Vulparoon is not himself, as you will see. He insists that the fiends of Hell are intent on tormenting him. But in coming to this ghastly place, I wonder if he is correct in his assumption, for what are those horrors below us?"

The Voidal scowled at the reference to the innumerable masses below. But he strode past the hovering familiar and climbed down to where Vulparoon waited, bemused and quivering, though not mad.

"You are under my protection," he told the Asker. "No matter what befalls us, serve me and you will be shielded."

Vulparoon's expression changed, as if he had been released from a nightmare dream that gnawed at his very reason. He drew back from the dark man, still afraid of him.

"I have not brought you here to torture you," said the Voidal. "Others may judge you. I cannot help that."

"What is that *sound*? Is this Hell itself?"

"For those outside, doubtless. They are the souls of the people of this world, and perhaps many others besides, who have come back to curse me. But we will not remain here. The ship needs piloting to Holy Hedrazee. We need your guidance."

Vulparoon shook his head in amazement. "*You* wish to go there? Has the sliver of madness that was in Orgoom now lodged in you?"

The Voidal involuntarily touched his shirt where the sliver was secreted. "No, I am not mad. But I will confront the Askers. And those they serve."

"Confront them?"

"I did not bring you here to discuss it! Simply do as I command. Or would you prefer to join those out on the plains?"

It was not necessary to repeat the question. Vulparoon sagged, his resistance shattered. "As you wish. I can guide the ship to Holy Hedrazee. But not until Evergreed has been appeased."

The Voidal frowned. "I should know that name. It has a ring: who is he?"

"We stand upon his deck. This ship is Evergreed. You do not recall him?"

"In time I will. How is he to be appeased?"

Vulparoon barely masked his horror. "You must speak to him. He will tell you what he desires."

The Voidal controlled his mounting anger, knowing that Vulparoon could do nothing but obey him. He motioned for the Asker to lead the way down into the hold of the ship and Vulparoon did so. Scyllarza followed, and with her was Elfloq, his own curiosity bristling, as ever. Orgoom elected to remain on the deck, though the dreadful sounds from beyond the ship made even his skin crawl. He watched the lone figure of Xatrovul, slumped down near the base of a mast, but the Seneschal's strength appeared to be ebbing fatally away.

The Voidal and the others went deep into the clammy hold of the ship in almost total darkness, the stench that rose from below almost unbearable. At length they stood on a rubbery expanse that overlooked a huge, empty place, a cavernous hold that resembled the innards of a beast rather than a construction. In that huge, curved vault there was movement as something shifted in its oily bed. It was hard to discern what shape it took, for it became a writhing mass, as if gigantic serpents had knotted together in their thousands. The poor light played upon organs that seemed to grow externally on the body of whatever leviathan it was that lived here. A membrane flickered and a huge eye opened, staring like a blotched moon at the figures. Incredibly, light shone from *within* the eye, bathing part of the monster's body in a sickly green radiance. Vulparoon drew back from the awesome being. It appeared to the Voidal to be a hellish fusion of organs and limbs and convoluted serpents, the extremities linked into the sides of the ship, themselves forming a carapace. This creature was the living heart of the ship, which itself formed a shell around it.

"Who comes before Evergreed?" called a thick voice that rasped and gurgled from some unseen orifice below.

"What manner of creature are you?" said the Voidal.

There was a long pause, the strange eye narrowing. "I know *you*, dark lord," said the voice. "Only power such as you once possessed could wake me from my grave. I smell its odour upon you yet. They could not suppress you forever."

The Voidal's memory shifted, partially focussing. "You served me—"

"And will again. My body is weak. I have been entombed for countless ages, as you must know. But I will give you passage. My price is as it always was."

"Name it," snapped the Voidal, unmoved by the unthinkable size of this ship-creature. Elfloq had hidden himself behind Scyllarza, eager not to be singled out by that baleful eye. He could feel the woman's unease, and a quick glance at Vulparoon told him that he was the most afraid of them all.

"Such impatience," came the sorrowful voice of the monster.

"I have waited lifetimes for what I want," the dark man told it.

"No longer than I have spent in my tomb. Have you no wish to learn how I came here, since your memory is so vague?"

"Is this an outpouring I must hear as part of the payment for your service?"

"No, it is not. But have you no pity?"

"Should I display it, who am shown none?"

THE SWORD OF SHADOWS | 155

Scyllarza came forward, in spite of her revulsion. She touched the Voidal gently. "Beloved, perhaps you are too hard. This creature suffers for some great sin, just as you do. You seek justice for yourself. Perhaps it is the same for Evergreed."

The Voidal's scowl softened and he nodded. "You are right. Impatience is not an ally on this quest. Very well, Evergreed. Give us your history. Then earn your release."

Evergreed emitted a deep sigh that made his entire superstructure shake. "Would that I could. Well, to begin. It is my zealous appetite that has been the cause of my downfall. Once I had a place among deities, although I had no ambition to be a mighty leader, nor all-powerful. I had enough companions to suit me and was too insignificant to have enemies, or any of consequence. Alas, I loved only my stomach. It became my shrine, my place of worship, for there was nothing I would not offer it to appease its endless craving."

The listeners heard this with more than a little dismay, not the least Elfloq, who scowled at his surroundings with an even more heart-felt squeamishness.

"In the omniverse," Evergreed continued, "there were many choices of things to devour and for a long time I fed on all manner of them, ever more voraciously: men, beasts, demons, sweet and bitter alike. Then one day — by pure accident, you understand — I devoured a minor deity. Such a trivial, hardly worshipped deity! And yet, for all his worthlessness, such a delicious victual! From that moment I had become addicted, enslaved. In no time at all I had eaten other small gods, until at last the time came when I swallowed quite a large god. Ah, succulent Octopang! My sins then came to the attention of far greater gods than I.

"From that time, I was undone. Such a demanding stomach, said the gods, must be put to use, for an engine like that must surely produce remarkable energy. This should not be wasted, they said. Hence they trapped me, all too easily, and caused to grow around me this ship, which itself feeds from me and has become both my prison and my external body. All that you see is Evergreed, and neither one can be separated from the other. I cannot move, only by satisfying my craving for food, but dependant upon what I eat, I can travel anywhere in the omniverse. But I can never see the places I visit, trapped as I am within myself. So you see, there is no release for me. I doubt that you could destroy me, for the gods are not likely to permit such a thing."

The Voidal had been considering all this in silence. He could feel the hunger seeping from the creature as it spoke. "You said you served me once. How did you come to be buried in this world?"

Evergreed did not answer at once. "I am not certain I remember. It was long, long ago. I have been dreaming, as I do after any meal of reasonable proportion. I am unable to recall who it was that last fed me so that I could carry him on his journey. Nor can I recall what it was that I ate. There was some rather vile wine that did not mix at all well with the food. Yes, I recall that. It quite upset my system and I can assure you, that is something most rare. Perhaps I was poisoned."

The Voidal looked uneasily at Scyllarza. "I do not like mysteries. It is too convenient that the ship is here."

"You knew that it was. You sought it."

The dark man scowled. "Yes, somehow I knew that."

"The ship claims to have served you once before —"

"Tell me," said the Voidal to the ship, "how you know me. How did you serve me? Do the Dark Gods command you now?"

"Your memory is blighted. So is mine. I know that, before my fall from grace, I was one of a number of subordinates to you, but I cannot recall what it was you did. You had power, great power. Many were jealous of it. Yes, and it was taken from you, for you were banished! I remember that much. And, and it was then that my own gastric cravings began! Yes, yes, self-pity, self-torment, all followed. Your servants were cursed, just as you were. Cursed and scattered."

The Voidal was nodding. "Then you have no love for the Dark Gods. Like me, you would strike at them. Repay them for their so-called justice."

Evergreed gave another deep sigh. "I fear them, I admit. But you, dark lord, have recovered much of your powers. That much I can sense."

Elfloq edged forward. "Will Evergreed take us to Hedrazee, master? Or would it not be prudent to avoid that place? It may well be a trap for you."

"All that I desire is there. Within me are powers that cannot be chained forever. The Dark Gods fear them. Tell me, Evergreed, what is the price of travel?"

"It is determined by the place to which you wish to travel. There is nowhere in the omniverse that I cannot reach. Even now, it is so."

"Indeed? Then take me to Holy Hedrazee, where the Divine Askers hide themselves from my vengeance."

Evergreed again fell silent, though only for a moment. "Hedrazee, you say? Yes, I can deliver you to that place. But I will need to consume a monumental repast. To get there will require much energy." The hunger in the voice was a palpable force.

"What will you have?"

Elfloq had again slipped back into shadow, not at all certain what his master would be prepared to sacrifice to win Hedrazee's halls. Since the goal had come in sight, the Voidal had become fixed and determined, far more cold and ruthless than Elfloq had known him before. There was a new darkness in him now. But perhaps there was no other way to oppose his enemies.

During the silence that ensued, while all of them considered their possible futures, the frightful din from without breached the very walls of the ship's hull. Evergreed gasped volubly. "What sounds are those?"

"A world sinks into final oblivion," said the Voidal. "You hear the cries of its damned souls, slipping down into eternity. As they recede, they curse me, for in *my* hunger, I have brought their world to its doom."

"There must be — many of them," said Evergreed softly.

"Others have joined them, down through the fog of time. As many as there are pebbles on a beach."

Evergreed's hull shuddered. "That many? How deliciously timely! Give them to me."

The Voidal's face clouded. "To you?"

"Let it be the price. Give them to me."

"How?"

"You have only to command it and they will come into me."

Scyllarza and Elfloq drew back at the horrifying suggestion, understanding at once what the huge ship intended.

But the Voidal did not hesitate for long, shrugging. "Very well. If that is to be the fee, I will give you what you ask."

The ship shivered in ghastly anticipation. The Voidal turned, about to return to the deck, but a last question reached him from the pit.

"You have a pilot? I need eyes."

"I have a fallen Divine Asker," the dark man said, indicating Vulparoon, whose silent horror at the conversation was etched across his white features.

"Then let him steer. My time on this trip will be occupied with two simple functions, sleep and digestion. Once I have feasted, it is all that I am able to do. Your pilot will steer me easily enough, provided he chooses his course with skill. Go! I will open ways for those outside to enter me. My appetite is truly whetted."

The Voidal and his companions wasted no time in quitting Evergreed's presence. Up on deck an anxious Orgoom joined them, eager to know what was to happen.

"You will go through with this sacrifice?" Scyllarza asked the dark man, her own face filled with doubts.

"I have no choice now. I stand against the evil powers that they feared, this Evil Time as they call it. It spreads throughout the omniverse, not just here, as I told Renegorn. It will take more than the men of this world to overcome it."

From beyond the ship there now came an unnatural silence. Vulparoon rushed to the side to gaze over at the plains. He saw at once the long files of beings as they ascended the sinewy, tongue-like pathways into the orifices of the ship's hull that Evergreed had opened to them. The Asker pulled away, utterly appalled.

"What have you done!" he cried.

"Get to the helm!" the Voidal snarled.

"But — the souls! Are they to have no rest? Is it not enough that you have destroyed their worlds?"

"This does not concern you."

"Darkness has tried to conquer this world before. But Light triumphed here and the Peace Monks have tended the remnants, ensuring survival. But in this act, you have not served the Light —"

"You saw evil fall! You saw the Seneschals broken. Look at Xatrovul! He serves *me* now. We have driven back the darkness. We must pursue this to the end!"

"I cannot do this," Vulparoon murmured. "I cannot obey you."

The Voidal spoke more softly. "Go to the helm. Be ready to pilot this ship."

Still Vulparoon refused. The Voidal drew out the sliver of madness and held it up for the Asker to see. It was scarlet with livid fire. "Must I lodge this in your heart?"

Vulparoon shuddered, but knew he was beaten, his resistance collapsing. Silently he went up to the helm as commanded.

The Voidal fixed his cold stare upon the endless ranks of souls as they fed into the ship. "This is the work of the Dark Gods," he said to Scyllarza. "They knew I would have a choice. Perhaps they did not think I would do this. Perhaps they thought they were safe in their retreat. Again they are wrong."

She nodded, but there was more than sorrow in her eyes.

His hand reached out and closed on hers. "I do not expect you to love me for what I have to do. But have faith in me. There will be a reckoning for this and for all that has been meted out to us. The others, too."

She smiled uneasily, nodding. He left her and went to where the Seneschal sat in the prow of the great ship, hunched up and gazing out into an invisible void.

"When we reach our destination, will you find the last sword for me?" the Voidal asked him.

Xatrovul turned: to the Voidal's dismay, he saw that the creature was slowly decomposing, his body like earth, drying out and crumbling.

"How long?" the dark man asked him.

"I cannot say. But long enough, I think, to help you find what you seek. The Sword of Oblivion will be yours before I join my brothers in the last emptiness."

The Voidal merely nodded, moving away again to be with Scyllarza.

Xatrovul watched him, eyes filled with a secret worship. "I serve you faithfully yet, master," he said.

* * * *

Time passed slowly, its currents dragging day into pitch night, until the endless processions ceased their march into the belly of the great ship. When it was over, there came a deep silence. After this the craft shuddered into life. Soon it was moving, the reluctant Vulparoon standing at its helm, studying the heavens where stars guided him. Evergreed seemed to slide over the surface of the world: from his sides there now protruded banks of fin-like shapes that beat in slow sweeps against the air, drawing the ship on like some immense aerial fish. From the rails, the companions looked down and saw the world beneath them as it changed.

Now it became more clear that it was part of a gigantic collision of worlds and dimensions, warping the very fabric of reason, twisting natural laws, giving vent to all manner of confusions. The desert plains dropped down in a rapid succession of canyon walls, like a stairway of gods, to the edge of an ocean. Huge waves tore in maliciously at the disintegrating coastline, where clouds of spume salted the air for hundreds of feet. Evergreed glided easily down to the water, his hull skimming across it, the fins settling the craft, making the transition from air to sea effortlessly.

Beside Vulparoon, the Voidal studied the vast seas ahead. "This seems a singularly physical voyage. Surely Evergreed can sail the astral with ease."

"Indeed," nodded the Asker, who seemed resolved to his plight. "But we have to pass through the Crimson Gate. And it is here, somewhere in this mangled tapestry of dimensions. Once through it, the path to Holy Hedrazee will be open to us, though there will be dangers beyond imagining."

"No more than I would expect," said the Voidal coolly.

"The Crimson Gate will be defended," Vulparoon went on and in his eyes all the old terrors returned. But he watched the sea, the endless rise and fall of its deeps. Beneath him he could feel the sleep of the ship, and tried not to think of what he had seen in the hold.

Dawn found them crossing the turgid ocean and the Voidal's impatience grew with every passing minute. He was about to urge Vulparoon to greater efforts, but the Asker pointed directly ahead. "Can you hear that?" he asked.

The dark man listened, nodding. A distant roar came from the flat horizon, where thickening fog clouds rose to blot out the otherwise cloudless sky. As Evergreed surged through the waters, the roar grew disturbingly louder, apparently along the length of the horizon ahead, no matter which part of it the company listened to.

"Elfloq!" the Voidal called.

The familiar hovered near at hand, knowing full well what his master was going to ask him. "I know, I know! You want me to fly ahead and find out what it is."

Scyllarza laughed softly. Beside her, the Voidal could not help but smile, though he was uneasy about what might lie ahead. He waved Elfloq away and, muttering to himself, the familiar flew up into a thermal and let it swing him way ahead of the ship, high over the sea. He could sense the thickening of the fogs and the growing roar from beyond.

Gods of the Abyss, he thought. If this were not an ocean, I would swear that that was a — no, no! That's not possible! Even here —. But his worst fears were realised and he swung round and flew back to the ship as fast as he could, which was slower than he would have liked, for the very air now seemed to be trying to drive him back towards what he had glimpsed. But he reached the ship and dropped down to the observers below.

"Well?" said the Voidal.

"I think we should turn the ship around," Elfloq blurted.

"For what reason?"

"For a very good reason —"

"Elfloq!" said Scyllarza, though she could see that the little familiar was terrified. "Tell us what you've seen."

"It's a...well, it's a waterfall," he said, voice trailing off.

"A *waterfall?*" echoed the Voidal.

"It would have to be huge beyond imagining," said Scyllarza.

Elfloq's eyes bulged. "Ah, yes, mistress. It is."

The Voidal swung round to where Vulparoon stood at the helm. "This world's twisted dimensions permit this paradox. Evergreed's course remains a straight one. Pilot, does the craft know what is ahead?"

The Asker nodded. "We will pass Worldfall. It is nothing to what waits us beyond. But if we are to reach the Crimson Gate, we must go on." He spoke mechanically, as if he had shut his own emotions deep away inside him, protection and against the nightmares to come. "But the ship will negotiate Worldfall without mishap."

They could do little more than watch the oncoming fog banks and listen to the increasing volume of the roaring waters, which had soon become deafening. The seas around them swirled, waves rising as if stirred by invisible forces, surging forward towards the waterfall where the ocean dropped into an unfathomable abyss. Before the ship got close to the drop, the fogs, mountainous clouds composed of the rising spray, enveloped them in a cold, grey shadow. Elfloq took to the air, while Orgoom stood close by his master and Scyllarza. Vulparoon had closed his eyes, hands white at the wheel, but he did not waver.

Before they were aware of it, the ship had reached the very lip of the colossal falls. Millions upon millions of tons of water plunged over the drop into an abyss like the vault between worlds. There was a moment of supreme apprehension as Evergreed's prow thrust out into the air beyond the falls and his crew held on grimly to the rails. But the immense ship slid out into the emptiness like an oversize bird, fins beating now like wings. The fogs swirled around it, cuffing it but lifting it. From overhead, Elfloq gaped at the transition from water to air. The ship was *gliding*, effortlessly, slowly dropping down through the fogs, lower than the ocean already.

The familiar swooped down to the deck, where his companions were gasping, still stunned by the sensation. Elfloq let out a croak that was meant to be a laugh. "It flies!"

Orgoom glowered at him. "If it had not, what would you have done then? Fled?"

The others ignored the brief argument that followed. Instead they concentrated on the seemingly endless fogs that swirled up from below, the noise of the falls behind them almost drowning out their thoughts. Down, ever down the ship dropped, moving forward as it did so, away from Worldfall until at last its noise subsided into the background. They went to the stern of the ship to try and see below them, but there seemed no bottom to the plummeting falls, the grey mists like a landscape miles under them.

Ahead of them, the fogs became light mist, which eventually parted. Overhead the sky was again cloudless, but bronzed, the sun beating down powerfully, its heat intense. Evergreed was still dropping, easing down towards what could now be perceived as another landscape. As he approached it, the crew saw that it was like yet another desert expanse, flat and featureless, except for barren outcrops of bleached rock and flat, cracked expanses of stone and dust.

"A sea bottom," Scyllarza said to the Voidal, pointing to strange rock formations that might once have been banks of coral. "It's as though this world collided with the one we left above the falls. But it's own seas have leaked away."

Beyond the vivid yellows and oranges of the dried up sea, they saw the sunlight gleaming. Elfloq flew ahead to investigate once more and he came back with his usual sour face. "A small sea, or huge lake," he told them. "Stagnant. Evergreed would do well to keep to the sky."

The Voidal could see why Elfloq was concerned as the waters came into view. They were indeed stagnant, oily with rotting weed, thick like the mires on the world they had left, but emptier, as if toxic. Apart from a clump of black weed, nothing broke the surface. Mercifully Evergreed glided some distance above those foetid waters. Vulparoon confirmed that there was no need to drop down on to them, but the ship kept a direct course, rather than make a lengthy detour. They could see the shores of the sea, miles away on either side, barren, blackened and utterly desolate.

Ahead of them was only a heat haze of distance, impenetrable. Elfloq flew on but came back some time later, exhausted. "Need rest," he muttered. "This filthy sea goes on and on." Within moments he was asleep.

The day passed monotonously into afternoon, the crew lulled into torpor. Even the Voidal felt himself drifting close to the edge of sleep, though he was unwilling to succumb. He felt a tug at his arm. It was Orgoom, who had taken a spell at the prow and who had now come back, agitated by something.

"Master. The waters ahead are alive."

At once the Voidal went to the prow himself. Orgoom was right, for there was a disturbance in the waters some distance ahead, the dark surface churning, thick bubbles breaking surface as if gases were being emitted from below. Evergreed must have sensed the change, for the ship began to rise.

"What is it?" the Voidal asked Vulparoon.

"I don't know. But there is danger here."

Hardly had he spoken, than the waters burst upward in a shower of filth as something came up from under the sea. All that could be seen through the murky spray at first was a gaping mouth and row upon row of teeth. Evergreed rose sharply, swerving aside as the sea monster wriggled on to the surface, itself like a huge craft, though half the size of Evergreed. Twin eyes blazed, focussing on the ship above it with feral intensity. Its enormous fins slapped at the waters around it, its stiff tail whipping from side to side, an elastic rudder.

Evergreed surged past the monster, but as the Voidal looked back, he saw the thing turn and *lift* itself out of the water. Just as Evergreed could glide, so could this creature. In moments it was in the air, long fins flapping, tendrils streaming out behind it like pennants. The bloated body of the creature puffed out, sickly green shot through with purple. The wide mouth opened wider.

Others were breaking surface, like hounds gathering to the scent, and soon there were a dozen of the gaping aerial fish snapping at Evergreed, trying to keep pace and drive him down to the black waters below. But he increased his speed, managing to stay ahead of the rapacious pack. The Voidal and Scyllarza had drawn their swords, but the monster fish seemed intent on attacking the hull and the fins of their craft. Evergreed had only his speed and manoeuvrability with which to outwit them. Or so they thought.

One of the fish monsters positioned itself for a head-on attack. The Voidal was in the prow, but drew back as he realised what was happening, knowing that the impact would be tremendous. He felt a movement under the deck, but could not see what Evergreed had done. But the ship made no attempt to swerve aside, as if welcoming the suicidal onslaught of the fish monster.

The Voidal had reached Vulparoon, who even now held on to the helm. "What is happening?"

"These nightmares have shown their teeth. Now Evergreed shows his."

"Teeth?" the Voidal repeated. There was no further time to deliberate, for Evergreed met the oncoming monster, lifting his prow and ramming it. The whole ship shuddered violently, throwing its crew to the deck, but they scrambled up in moments. The Voidal could see beyond the prow to where the huge fish monster was writhing and shaking frantically as if it had been speared on an invisible length of steel. But, looking over the prow, the Voidal realised that Vulparoon had not exaggerated, for Evergreed had opened a hitherto unseen mouth of his own and fixed long fangs in the head of his assailant. The ship shook the beast as a dog shakes a rat, flesh and scales flying in all directions in a mist of blood.

Evergreed released his victim and the Voidal watched the mangled creature toppling toward the murky waters below. But long before it could hit, a group of the aerial fish swooped down, fastening their jaws on to their stricken companion and the most ferocious struggle ensued as half a dozen of them sought to tear it apart. The dark man and his companions craned their necks to watch the frightful affray, but Vulparoon called their attention to a new danger ahead of them.

Gliding down out of the clouds, high above, other shapes had appeared, and at first the Voidal took them to be more aerial predators, though unlike the fish monsters. The latter had broken off their attack, as Evergreed had proved too fast for them and had moved up beyond a height at which they would follow. These newcomers were not, the dark man now saw, living creatures, but flying craft, their huge sails billowing in the wind as they dropped ever lower. Their decks were lined with armoured archers and as soon as they came within striking distance, the first of them unleashed a rain of arrows at Evergreed's crew.

"Shelter below!" called Vulparoon. "The ship will deal with them." He still gripped the helm, ducking down, shielding himself as the first arrows zipped by.

The Voidal called his companions to him, including the slow-moving form of Xatrovul, and they did as the Asker had bidden them. As they went below, the dark man realised that Evergreed had dropped down towards the sea once more, within range of the fish monsters. But his purpose was clear, for in coming this low again, he had brought the new assailants into range of the aerial horrors.

While the crew sheltered belowdecks, Vulparoon watched the battle around him, which quickly became a furore. There were a dozen of the sky ships, trying to circle Evergreed, but their formation was broken up by the ferocious attack of the fish monsters. There seemed to be scores of them and they had no regard for danger, hurtling themselves into the sides of the ships, smashing through sail and rigging, crashing on to the decks and snapping at anything within range. Three ships had been brought down in minutes, their crews spilling from them as they plummeted. Again the fish monsters dived, jaws clamping on victims before the sea could claim them.

Evergreed powered his way through the ships, his sides smashing through the smaller craft on either side, himself impervious to their own teeth, for like him, they had mouths at the prow, filled with teeth. Those that tried to tear at him found his hide impenetrable. Once he was through their barrier, they had far too much to do to contend with the fish monsters to be able to delay him. Vulparoon kept his course, rising once more, leaving the mayhem and carnage of the frightful conflict raging below.

The Voidal returned to the deck. "What are those ships?" he asked Vulparoon.

"Cannibal Ships. They are from the Crimson Gate. There will be more of them and other guardians there, too. The Dark Gods know you have twelve of the swords. They would recover them."

"Further evidence of their fear."

Vulparoon said nothing of his own deepening fears.

"Those who have freed themselves from the fish creatures are pursuing us," the Voidal told him.

"We will outdistance them," said Vulparoon. "But I warn you, worse is to come."

The Voidal ignored him and went again to the prow, watching the misted horizon beyond. The sea was falling away below them, but they had almost reached its far shores, which rose up steeply in banks of tangled, dark weed, bank upon bank. Through the seeping mists, which rose like poisonous vapours from the weed, vast clumps of vegetation towered, massing like piled clouds, becoming an impregnable green wall. Evergreed slowed his forward progress, stopping altogether and instead beginning to rise like a leaf on a thermal current. Ahead of him the sky became a wall of white mist.

As the ship rose and rose, the climb seemingly endless, the Voidal got glimpses through the mist of a dark mass. This eventually revealed itself as a cliff wall of monstrous proportions. It stretched as far to the left and right as the eye could see and reached up endlessly to the sky as if it would topple over like a mountainous tidal wave. It seemed like a mirror of the awesome Worldfall at the other extreme of the seabed. But the nature of the wall was even more stunning. For it was alive with vegetation. The Voidal estimated that the ship must be several score miles from the cliff's surface, but even from this distance, he could see the bizarre nature of its make-up.

Up from the abysmal depths, incalculable large growths reached ever skywards, tangling together, vines and tendrils of unimaginable magnitude clinging to the wall's surface, interwoven like countless nests of gargantuan serpents. Their clustered leaves shook, though not with the winds, but with the sheer energy that flooded through the plants. Their growth rate had accelerated abnormally, their burgeoning tendrils writhing like tentacles.

As the Voidal watched, he saw high up towards the crest of the cliffs, countless miles above, other growths there, as thickly matted and tangled as those below, spilled over the wall and trailed their own fronds and tendrils downward. These, too, were rampant with life, their thriving growths matching the groping horrors of the lower ones. Where the upper growths met the lower ones, an insane conflict raged. The two masses of growth were attacking each other on a front that stretched all along the mid-section of the wall. Slowly, as Evergreed nosed forward, the dimensions of this perpetual war became clearer and the Voidal was forced to step back in utter amazement. The largest of the tendrils was *miles* in girth.

Beside him, he could feel Scyllarza's astonishment as she leaned against him. "Are we to fly over this lunacy?" she said softly. "It seems as if Evergreed quickens his movement forward."

They could hear the astounding sounds of the plant war now, for the ship was indeed moving ever closer to the wall, deeper into its shadow. Ahead, they could pick out more details of the face of the wall itself, for there were some bare areas between the upper and lower plant fronts, though the whipping and lashing of the tendrils and roots blurred them. Where the two forces tangled together, colossal powers pulled and tugged, each trying to rip the other free of its grip on the wall, and where one triumphed over the other, huge chunks of rock crumbled, tumbling down into the green abyss.

"Vulparoon!" the Voidal called back to the pilot. "If you take us in to the wall, we will be caught up in this hellish plant war! Get us up to the rim!"

Whatever the Asker shouted back in reply was lost in the growing noise from the cliff face, though it was still miles ahead of them. But the Voidal was looking beyond the pilot, to the stern of the ship. Out of the mists behind it came the remnants of the ships that had attacked. They had formed a line and had been joined by others, prows opening, revealing shark-like mouths: they meant to drive Evergreed forward to the very cliff face. The Voidal pulled out the sword wherein the twelve had combined. If the dark Gods mean to wrest it back from him, he would sell it dearly.

"Master," said Elfloq, bracing himself unsteadily on the deck. "Unless the ship goes up instead of forward, we will strike that wall."

The Voidal nodded. "You and Orgoom, take to the astral if that becomes inevitable. Scyllarza, you, too. Xatrovul stays with me. As does Vulparoon. He pilots this ship, to Hell itself, if he must."

Scyllarza had pulled out her own blade, her eyes flashing with demon fire. "I stand with you. The Dark Gods will have to deal with both of us." She laughed at his scowl.

He was about to reply, but a shout from Vulparoon made him spin to face the wall.

"The Crimson Gate!" cried the Asker. "Tell me now, do you still desire to enter?" He was indicating an area of the wall that was not obscured by the thrashing tendrils of the immense plants. A gigantic carving had been etched deeply into the stone surface, miles across. It was partly a face, partly a mass of sigils, woven together in patterns that shifted and changed, suggestive of many things, constantly altering their dimensions as though the stone breathed. At the lower part of the carving was an opening, a long, wide gash, and on the lower lip of this a city had been cut from the bare rock.

As Evergreed drew ever nearer, a fleet of sky ships rose up from this city, distance making them as small as flies, but they grew as they came on. Behind them, the black orifice that was the mouth of the carving opened, the stone elastic as flesh. In the carving, eyes like moons stared, their baleful gaze fixed upon the incoming ship.

"The Crimson Gate," Vulparoon said again. "Beyond the city and down into that vortex. If you dare enter."

The Voidal could see beyond the city on the lip of the huge gate and in the restless darkness there, huge shapes writhed, a dozen tongues, flicking from side to side, lashing the inner walls of the mouth, eager to draw their prey into them.

"Master!" cried Elfloq, hopping from one foot to the other in terror. "There can be no more terrible a place in all of the omniverse! Nightmares scream at us from every side! And they say, *leave this domain*!"

The Voidal nodded slowly, sensing the incoming Cannibal Ships as they closed their circle, the horrors of the Gate, the lunatic struggles of the monstrous vegetation above and below them. "The Dark Gods protect their haven in desperation. Madness and abomination have dogged my footsteps through every awakening I have suffered. Get below, all of you. Evergreed has been paid! He is chartered to take us to Holy Hedrazee, and he must do so. Get below!"

Elfloq decided that it would not be diplomatic to remind his master that a short while ago he had told him to take Orgoom and get on to the astral. He also decided that it might not be the best of moves to go there now. In this place, the astral would likely spawn horrors even more ghastly than those around the ship. So with no more ado, Elfloq hopped away, Orgoom a few paces behind him.

"I must speak with Evergreed," the Voidal told Scyllarza and they, too went down to the hold.

They again stood before the strange being that was the heart of the ship, sensing at first that he was dormant, unreachable as he continued to digest the meal that had fuelled his trip to this forbidden region. But after a while, the huge eye opened lazily and observed them.

"Ah, Voidal. You have interrupted my sleep prematurely. Holy Hedrazee is a long way off yet."

"We are approaching the Crimson Gate."

"Yes. Have you changed your mind? Do you wish to go to some other destination? I can change course, though there will be a reckoning when we get there."

"We are beset on all sides —"

"The Cannibal Ships? *I'm* not bothered by them. They may test the sanity of your companions, but they are no barrier to me."

"What lies within the Crimson Gate?"

"Ah, you have seen its many tongues? Particularly horrible experience, negotiating them. But let Vulparoon worry about that. I simply need to sleep on. I'll get you to Holy Hedrazee, if you still wish to go there."

"Then do so."

"Very well. Please excuse me. I would rather be dormant as we pass through the gate. If I were you, I'd stay below decks."

Above them, Vulparoon's eyes widened as the city drew closer, its strange architecture bathed in the unnatural glow from behind it. Cannibal Ships swarmed in from all sides, snapping and battering at Evergreed, but the ship was unharmed, a shark swimming through a shoal of sprats. The Crimson Gate grew wider, ever wider, the things within it belching forth clouds of foul gas in which smaller things flitted and flapped.

They know, the Asker told himself. The Dark Gods know that he is coming to them. They cannot prevent him. Nor do they wish to.

He felt the shadows closing around the ship as it flew above the city. The Crimson Gate was aptly named, for all within it was daubed in a crimson radiance, as though its walls and the writhing tongues were engorged with blood. The grotesque buildings below seemed bathed in fire and such shapes as slithered about within them or on their angled battlements bore no resemblance to anything human. If eyes watched from below, they watched from hidden recesses, deep down in the leaning canyons.

Vulparoon closed his mind to the hideous things ahead of him as the gate yawned. He had been a Divine Asker. He knew this Gate and why it had been set here and made so monstrous. He knew also that Evergreed was meant to pass through it. As if he had shouted aloud this thought, the Cannibal Ships that swarmed about the ship now pulled away, as if they, at least, feared the horrors within the Gate. The tongues parted to reveal an inner mouth, an enormous entry to the maw of a deep dwelling creature, but Evergreed flew on, never diverging for a moment. Deeper reds suffused the air as the ship went into the inner gate.

The darkness of infinity closed around it. Below, in the hold, the crew waited like creatures entombed, as though doomed to walk the vaults of the dead thereafter.

PART EIGHT

IN HOLY HEDRAZEE

> *There are those, among gods as well as men, who insist that some secrets should not be disturbed. Some truths, they aver, are best not known, or faced.*
> *Others stop at nothing to reveal all. They insist that there should be no darkness.*
> *It is an intriguing theory. After all, how does one define Light without reference to Darkness?*
> —**Salecco**, upon whom Light rarely shines in his isolation.

* * * *

Across new wastes of time and space Evergreed journeyed, the huge creature yet somnolent as he dreamed his private dreams, digesting his outrageous repast. His unique crew had come up on deck, watching the emptiness around them with more than a degree of trepidation.

Vulparoon remained at the helm, silent and filled now with despair, for he had resigned himself to the madness that would come at this voyage's end, in which he saw nothing but pain for himself. He had transgressed and he would be made to pay. But he had nothing with which to contest this law. Elfloq and Orgoom huddled together like children, their fears obvious, knowing that their own chances of escaping the wrath of whatever gods they were about to offend were slender. Yet they were committed to their master, who alone seemed confident of success.

Elfloq had shared this belief until this last voyage had begun. The horrors that Evergreed had passed through had finally made the familiar wonder about his master's sanity, his judgement. Orgoom said nothing, inwardly trying to convince himself that this was not a trap and that he was not one of the principal flies.

Scyllarza stood close beside the Voidal, though his tension had distanced him from even her. "Tell me, what will you do when you have won back what is yours?"

The Voidal had been studying the slumped figure of Xatrovul, now in the prow. The dark man's lips tightened, as if he fought to keep down his anger. "Shape my own destiny."

"The price may be terrible," she said, thinking of the countless souls who had poured into Evergreed, even after the slaughter of battle. She could not ignore the pangs of guilt that came with the thought of it. The darker side of her own nature, the demonic element, seemed to be ever subsiding. She welcomed that.

"I must have the truth. I must *know*," he insisted, resolute.

"Perhaps it is a path to madness —"

"The Dark Gods have brought all this to pass. Let them be judged," he said bitterly, directing his anger out at the starless darkness.

A cry from Vulparoon alerted them. He was pointing directly ahead to where clouds boiled out of the darkness, shredding to reveal what appeared to be a tunnel through the very fabric of the dimensions. "We must pass through the Hall of the Fallen!" the Asker cried.

"Keep course for Hedrazee," the Voidal called back. He studied the shifting clouds ahead as Evergreed sailed into the strange portal. Night gathered itself as the ship entered, thickening and cloying. Yet the deeper they went down this ever-widening tunnel, the more light began to permeate its curved sides, flickering as if it were born aloft on invisible wings. A fierce shout from the distance reached the ship and seemed to be taken up by many voices, all of them deep and stentorian.

As Evergreed sailed down the tunnel towards the growing light, his crew could now see that its walls were lined with rows of huge heads, all of them shouting, mouths stretched wide in fury.

The Voidal leapt up beside Vulparoon. "Keep this ship steady! Hold it in the exact centre of this tunnel. What devils are these?"

"The Fallen," the Asker told him. "Gods that have been chained here as a penalty for their sins. It is their everlasting fate to rant and roar. They curse all who pass them." *And you most of all.*

The ship was easing between the twin rows, the noise of their fury awful. Foul abuse was hurled at the travellers, striking at the ship in gales so that it rocked in the air as though the sounds would pull it apart or blow it off course and into the faces, like a wreck tossed on a reef. Great, baleful eyes widened and mouths gaped. The Fallen spat and hissed: Elfloq and Orgoom scuttled down a hatch to the safety of the hold. Every eye, however, was fixed upon the Voidal and necks craned to try and reach him, teeth flashing as if they would snap on his body or tear the ship apart to get at him.

For answer he stood high up in the prow, holding aloft the blade that held the twelve, which seemed to keep the Fallen back, although its presence served to madden them further.

"Voidal! Voidal!" they screamed in a maniacal chorus. "Most damned in all creation! Set us free and we will devour you a thousand times!"

The dark man looked down at Xatrovul, who had barely moved. But his eyes fixed on the rows of shrieking heads in horror. "Why do they curse me?" the Voidal asked him. "Who are they?"

"They are the ones who lost their godhead at the War of the Falling Gods. And in other wars."

"They shriek for my blood — why?"

"You made them what they are. You brought them all to this pass."

"How?" the Voidal shouted above the thunder of sound.

"They will tell you in Hedrazee."

The dark man would have demanded more of Xatrovul, but the ship had veered too close to one of the heads. Abruptly a tongue snaked out like some colossal sea serpent and wrapped itself about part of the vessel. At once the craft was drawn towards the line of heads and all mouths opened, teeth readying to bite into Evergreed and finish him. The Voidal rushed to the huge tongue and chopped into it with his sword. Great chunks of flesh thudded on to the deck as he cut, so that the tongue released its grip and flopped over the side, dangling from the mouth of the giant. Its eyes glazed over in pain, filling with tears of agony and frustration. But the wall of reverberating sound died at once as the others saw what had happened. The maiming of the giant seemed to have annihilated in an instant all their resistance.

The journey through the endless tunnel of the Fallen was now a silent one, for all eyes were downcast, full of misery, and all mouths were closed. The Voidal rejoined Scyllarza. "It seems that you are the only creature in the entire omniverse who does not despise me," he told her.

Her eyes flashed, the demon within her momentarily welling anew, eager to be one with him again. "They are afraid. In Hedrazee," she said.

When they at last emerged on the far side of the Hall of the Fallen, they drifted through another massing of dark clouds, beyond which there seemed to be no stars and no indication of where they might be. Universes and the voids between, the limbo outside the many dimensions, all meant nothing now as Evergreed went on his strange voyage, passing through realms that were no more than half-finished dreams. A kind of lethargy crept over the travellers, so that the Voidal and Scyllarza almost slept.

Elfloq and Orgoom had slipped back on to the deck. "Mad to begin this," muttered the Gelder.

"If I had known —" Elfloq whispered, seriously doubting the sanity of their having come on this voyage.

"Greed," said Orgoom, spitting noisily. "For power. All those gods, the same. Too much power. Ends same way. Like Ubeggi."

Elfloq could not argue. It seemed to be exactly so. Lust for power, even at second hand, had led him into many a predicament. But this was too terrible. He shuddered. Perhaps if he could find a bolthole here on the ship somewhere, he could hide away and not be seen at the end of the voyage.

"We're surely too insignificant to matter," he told Orgoom.

"You think so?"

Elfloq did not. But it reassured him to say so.

Below them was another weird landscape, a sea of frozen bones. These were strewn in all directions, millions upon millions of them, some rising up in gigantic structures, contorted and cracked, others sweeping to the horizon like frozen waves. There was no movement, not even a breath of air: a dismal aura of sadness rose up like a lament. Beyond this endless plain of bones were other freakish regions, all as despairing. One was choked with dead trees, leafless and rotting, while another displayed several immense cities, fused into one, as dead as the plain of bones. Evergreed had entered the wilderness of entropy.

Only the sudden light brought the numbed travellers out of their bemusement. It shone about them now, blotting out everything until they were totally immersed in it, drifting, ever drifting, across its shining nothingness.

"Where is this place?" the Voidal asked Vulparoon.

Surprisingly, the Asker left the helm and came down to the deck. He looked immensely tired, his skin cracked and parched, his face haggard, though the hint of madness that had threatened him in Cloudway had evaporated. "Evergreed has no power left. He has come as far as he can. He cannot take us beyond this point."

The Voidal glared at the Asker. "You have becalmed us. There is nothing here."

"No," said Vulparoon, apparently drained of emotion. "We are not alone."

"Evergreed will have to sail on," said the Voidal angrily. "Even if I have to feed him more souls."

Vulparoon gasped. "Have you not done enough!"

"Master!" shouted Elfloq, pointing out into the light.

They all turned to see what had snagged his attention. As one they drew back in horror. Rising up out of the light like some immense being from the depths of an ocean, was a hand, the proportions of which shook the mind. The Voidal instinctively looked at his own right hand, but it was intact. No one spoke as the hand moved sluggishly across the sea of light. Before it could reach the ship, it slipped down beneath the light billows and was gone.

The Voidal looked to Vulparoon for an answer, but the Asker had slumped down, head between his legs, utterly spent.

"What monsters live in this sea?" cried Elfloq. "Can we not rouse Evergreed and begone?" But as he spoke, the ship moved, in a moment recommencing its journey. Elfloq giggled with nervous glee. "You see! He hears us. Once more we are —" He got no further, for they all realised what had happened.

The tip of a huge finger rose up over the side of the ship. The hand was beneath it, *carrying* it across the limitless sea of light.

The Voidal reached down and gripped the robe of the Asker, shaking him until he stirred and gazed up at him pitifully. "What is this place? Tell me!"

Vulparoon's voice came out like the last gasp of a dying man. "The journey is over. We are on the threshold of Holy Hedrazee."

The Voidal released him and he toppled over, his eyes fixed on a point directly ahead of the ship. The others could see something beginning to materialise out of the light. It was as though they were coming to a misty wall of unimaginable proportions. From this projected a long ledge upon which sat pillars that rose up into infinity. Beyond these pillars the light intensified like a sun's heart.

As the Voidal looked, he realised that Xatrovul was gone: a quick scan of the ship's deck revealed that he was no longer here. He had either returned to dust, or gone over the side into the infinite emptiness. There was no time to consider it, for the ship was set down on the ledge before the great pillars, resting there, motionless. The dark man and his companions watched as the huge hand withdrew from beneath them and appeared to float away into the middle distances of the sea of light, before slipping down, down and away into depths that none of their minds could begin to fathom.

Beneath them, on the measureless stone ledge, great shadows had formed, thrown forward by the intense light behind them. But these were no giants. The Voidal could discern a group of figures, dwarfed like insects by the mighty pillars behind them. "It is time to leave the ship," he told the others.

"Surely it is not necessary for me to disembark," said Elfloq hopefully. "Would I not be better employed in remaining here to ensure that the treacherous Evergreed does not desert us?"

In spite of the situation, the Voidal grinned at him. "All of us will go down. We do not want to disappoint the Divine Askers."

Thus Elfloq and Orgoom followed the Voidal and Scyllarza down from the ship. Vulparoon did not stir and the Voidal made no further attempt to revive him. His fate no longer concerned the dark man.

As the four of them stepped on to the stone flags, they recognised the red-garbed figures coming to meet them. Elfloq let out a gasp. "Darquementi!"

"Greetings, little familiar! How busy you have been since last we met," replied the Divine Asker with an enigmatic smile.

The Voidal shot Elfloq a brief scowl, but it was evident that the familiar went in dread of the Asker. The dark man took out his sword slowly and rubbed his fingertips along the flat of its blade. He said nothing. They were all conscious of the immensity of their surroundings, the colossal vaults that stretched back towards the sun-blaze of light. When they did speak, their voices were like crystal bells, clear and precise.

"We have been awaiting your return, dark one," Darquementi told the Voidal. The scarlet hoods dipped as the Askers bowed, and the Voidal could sense the fear in them. He yet made no reply.

"It has taken many lifetimes," Darquementi went on, "the birth and death of many universes."

"I have not come to be judged," said the Voidal. "So be wary."

"You have come for what you believe is yours," the Asker agreed.

"Indeed, and I have not come to beg."

"No, that was never your way."

"Well?"

"The Dark Gods, for whom I speak, have instructed me. You have no need to unleash the powers you have already won back. Will you follow?"

The Voidal nodded. As the Askers moved away and out of the blinding light, the four companions followed cautiously. They went along the wide ledge, avoiding the great pillars and climbed a broad flight of stairs beside them to yet another wide area. Darquementi's companions moved back into shadows, but he stood with the Voidal and his companions. From here they could look out at the limitless sea of light.

Darquementi pointed to it. "The Dark Gods are watching."

The Voidal narrowed his eyes against the glare. Beyond he saw what he took to be the far walls of a vast circle, as though everything here was inside a ball of staggering dimensions. The curved walls of this ball were made up of shifting, concave surfaces that were impossible to fix on and define, but they gave a fleeting impression of faces. How many there were could not be estimated with any certainty, but the Voidal imagined that he could count thirteen of them. Each face appeared to be looking inward at something that rose up from the very heart of the shimmering sea of light.

"It begins," said Darquementi. "As you wish, the mystery is here."

While he spoke, the huge hand came back into view, having grown to an even more monstrous size. It held in its palm a glittering orb that shone and dazzled with myriad bolts of light and energy, proclaiming powers beyond comprehension.

"The prize," said Darquementi.

Each of the four travellers stared at this perfect sphere, wondering at its beauty, its power and its promise. It brought them all a longing such as they had never known before, a desire that threatened to engulf them. For each of them it had its own meaning, though none of them voiced it.

"There is One Prime God," said Darquementi. "This is the First Law. All other Gods are his servants. He is Power Absolute."

"Is that —?" spluttered Elfloq, unable to contain himself, but Darquementi shook his head.

Scyllarza and Orgoom were also transfixed by the distant sphere, but the Voidal remained on his guard, prepared for an attack which he was sure must come upon him at least. He knew that his presence in this place was a blasphemy to this Prime God. As he watched the vaults around him, he saw a movement that appeared to have gone unnoticed by the Askers. Below them, down on the wide ledge where Evergreed had come to rest, something stirred. It was Vulparoon. The discredited Asker was dragging something across the huge flagstones towards the very steps that led up to the huge pillars. Another cautious glance showed the Voidal that it was the rotting carcass of Xatrovul that Vulparoon was so laboriously pulling. For some reason he was anxious to get the carcass through the portal into the furnace of light. His wooden movements suggested that he was urged on by some outside force, his mind no longer his own. *But what could so move him?* the Voidal asked himself.

He turned his attention back to the gleaming orb, not knowing what it might be, but wondering if it could be his soul, or the remains of his stolen power.

"Everything was created by the Prime God," said Darquementi. "In His Creation, harmony is the law. But certain lesser deities envied the

Prime God His power. Some sought power for themselves. Into the great peace of Creation, there came discord and then a terrible conflict, for many of the lesser Gods joined together the powers that had generously been bestowed upon them and sought to use them to force the Prime God to accede to certain demands. Serving Him was not enough for them. They desired the power to create for themselves. But it was forbidden. None but the Prime God can create. That is the Second Law.

"The lesser Gods had to abide by this Law. Yet the mightiest of them, he who was the right hand of the Prime God, refused to accept this. He had always used the power devolved to him by the Prime God wisely, but in the using of it came to know the pangs of temptation. And he succumbed. He became the renegade, abusing his own powers and encouraging those who chose to put their faith in his rebellion. In secrecy he created what you see before you now — the glittering orb. See how it shines and seduces with its beauty! Who could not admire such a work? Who would not be dazzled by its splendour? But the Prime God was not pleased, for He has forbidden all such creations."

Again, Elfloq could not suppress his curiosity. "But what is it?" he blurted, at once regretting it.

However, there were no recriminations. Darquementi merely smiled. "You see before you the orb that contains the omniverse."

Elfloq gasped, as did Orgoom beside him and even Scyllarza looked uneasy.

"Everything is there," said the Asker. "The many dimensions, the countless universes, its gods without number, its demons and demi-gods, its swarming multitudes of mankind. The Rebel God took it upon himself to create it all, filling it with reason, order and beauty. But he balanced it with imperfections, madness and evil. Every god that dwells there, the very worms that crawl — all made by the renegade. And surrounding it, outside it, as you see, is Holy Hedrazee."

The Voidal listened as attentively as his companions, but saw also that Vulparoon had won his goal and had pulled Xatrovul's remains through the great pillars of the portal and into the white light beyond to whatever awaited them.

"And so the first flawed creation had come into being. Its perverse creator then fashioned thirteen servants for himself, to help him rule his omniverse. Inevitably, all were brought before the Prime God to be judged. And they were all punished, for the Prime God does not tolerate creation other than His own. Evil thrives in such dominions. The renegade God had created whimsically, randomly and without patience. He had laughed at the unbridled powers, amusing himself with the insouciance of a child. Harsh was the judgement of the Prime God.

"He stripped the renegade of all his powers and scattered them, for they could not be destroyed. He took from the disgraced one his soul, his identity and his memory and had them strewn throughout the unstable omniverse that he had created. He caused him to be in darkness, and of darkness. He caused him to wander endlessly throughout his warped creation, destroying the evils that abounded there in their many guises, as gods and beasts and demons. There were to be no friends, no allies and it was given to the Dark Gods, highest servants of the Prime God, to see that the wanderer in this void did not digress from the path forged for him.

"Yet such was the nature of the dark one that he has ever sought to regain his lost powers. There have been times when this unremitting drive has caused mighty conflagrations amongst the unwitting gods of the omniverse, both light and dark. It has always been through darkness that he has sought to regain his powers, seeking to overthrow light and plunge the omniverse into chaos. There were times when that darkness almost triumphed. At the War of the Falling Gods, the balance almost broke and only after the most violent upheaval was peace restored.

"And how often Man, puniest of all creations, has played a crucial role in the ebb and flow of power! How the gods of the omniverse use Man, fodder for their own struggles! Even now, it goes on. How many were sacrificed among the dead gods to feed the ship that brought you here? Who will mourn them?

"In the omniverse of late, darkness has indeed been gathering, amassing its energy. It is the irrepressible will of the renegade God, unifying all the evil that is in the orb to one purpose, uniting itself against the light that binds it."

"Yes, I have realised that much," said the Voidal, his voice resonant with a dreadful will. "*I* am that broken power, regenerating. I am here, in spite of any decree, with the powers I have won back, the allies that serve me yet."

Elfloq gaped. "Master! *You* are what mends itself —?"

Darquementi answered for the dark man. "He is. But evil begets evil. When the renegade was banished into darkness, his thirteen principal servants were subjugated. For their part in the perfidy of creation, they were made to serve the Dark Gods. They became the keepers of the Swords that locked up the soul of the dark one. The Thirteen Seneschals were your own servants, Voidal, that you had once set to oversee your creation for you. When you summoned them that last time and destroyed them, you were tearing apart your own powers, not those of the Dark Gods."

The Voidal stared at the Asker coldly. "Deceit was ever your tool."

"Your hand was ever the hand of destruction," Darquementi replied.

"What of the hand I was once forced to bear?"

"The Oblivion Hand, the hand of justice. Only you could have wielded it so brutally, yet so effectively."

"It was never me that used it. I had no control over it. Your Prime God knows that. And did he revel in its excesses?"

A deep silence followed. The companions were close to the edge of panic, sensing ultimate defeat for the dark man, and thus their own downfall.

The Voidal spoke at last. "I recall it all, now that you have said it. All that I did as the so-called renegade. All that I created and every step that I was forced to take in darkness as a result."

"And what have you learned?"

The Voidal thought for a moment, then laughed harshly. "That I was wrong? That I should have kept my place and never tested my powers to their full?"

"It is not for me to answer."

"No. You don't have the ability to think for yourself. You are greater pawns than I have been."

"We must all answer for the consequences of our actions."

"Why am I here?" the dark man suddenly snapped. "I did not win my way here. Evergreed did not fight off the terrors beyond the Crimson Gate and rupture a way through. It was made to look that way. The truth is, I was *brought* here."

Darquementi's cool resolve seemed shaken. "To learn the truths that you have sought. It was time."

"I had won that much back."

"Yes."

There came a sudden roar from beyond the pillars and they whirled as one to see flames lick out from the portal like writhing tongues. Standing in them was a figure. It stepped out of the furnace and climbed the steps that led up to the watchers, smouldering, white as an ember. In unified amazement they saw that it was Vulparoon, bleached and dead as stone. He moved like a machine, his eyes completely white, his face slack and expressionless. In his hands he carried a sword and crawling out of the flames beyond him was an even more frightful spectre.

Xatrovul. His body was almost completely wasted, rotting as the onlookers watched. Somehow the disintegrating Seneschal raised an arm and in a pathetic movement pushed Vulparoon forward, croaking out one word. "Master."

The Voidal was beside his dying servant before Darquementi could react. The others hung back in revulsion.

"Sword of Oblivion," hissed the Seneschal. "They didn't expect this. Took Vulparoon into the furnace with me to retrieve it."

The Voidal took the weapon from Vulparoon's limp fingers.

"When you destroyed them all, master," Xatrovul hissed, "I gathered up the dust of their remains. Enough to imbue me with the power to do this. Their will forced Vulparoon to act. Now you have all the Thirteen. The Sword of Shadows is within your grasp." He could say no more, for his body writhed a final time, crumbled and fell apart.

Darquementi's voice cut through the silence. "Faithful to the last. But returned to the primeval slime of the omniverse from which you raised him."

The Voidal held up the Sword of Oblivion in one hand and the twelve that were one in the other. Slowly he put them together. There was a bright flash, a sound like red hot metal being plunged into water. And then the Thirteen were one, the Sword of Shadows. Vulparoon's body collapsed in on itself like an empty shell, returned to ash in moments.

"My soul," the Voidal whispered, studying the blade. Yet the light had gone from it: it was dull, a seemingly lifeless blade like any other.

Darquementi, who had drawn back in fear as the blades met, stepped forward again. "The Sword of Shadows does not appear to be whole —" he began.

The Voidal scowled at him, but slowly a grim smile played on his face. He reached into his shirt and pulled out the sliver of madness, the fragment from the Sword of Madness that had been lodged in Orgoom. Like a magnet, the sword drew the piece of metal to itself in another flare of light. The Voidal could feel the blade, alive now. Alive and eager to do the work of such a weapon.

"The Sword of Shadows," said the dark man. "It is whole."

Darquementi nodded. If he was taken aback, he masked his feelings. "Now you, yourself, will be complete. So what will you do then?"

The Voidal scowled at him. "The Dark Gods have deceived me many times. I think your Prime God goes in fear of me. Perhaps he is jealous. And he could not prevent me from regaining my powers."

"That is in your hands, in the Sword of Shadows."

"My trapped soul? How am I to release it?" the Voidal demanded.

"Your coming here was as much the will of the Dark Gods as it was yours. As you have surmised, it was planned. You came here for the truth and you shall have it. Put the Sword into the stone at your feet and let the light from the portal bathe it."

The Voidal hesitated, but then did as the Asker told him. He found that the flagstone permitted the Sword of Shadows to slide into it like soft earth. He stepped aside and the light from beyond struck the weapon.

It cast not one shadow, but three. Each of them spilled across the stone, singling out Scyllarza, Elfloq and Orgoom. As a shadow touched each of them, they froze like statues, their expressions of shock held like solid masks.

"You have suffered for your sins," Darquementi told the Voidal. He pointed at each of the three trapped figures. "You were broken and scattered. In Scyllarza, you have found a part of yourself, the demon essence, which you have already shared again with her. And in the Gelder, who was once a man, lies the human part of you."

The Voidal's face clouded with a terrible apprehension.

"Without these things you are incomplete. And in this familiar," Darquementi went on, slowly walking towards the hunched figure of Elfloq, rigid as a gargoyle now, "is the last vital part of you. Your *soul*, Voidal."

The dark man gasped, too stunned to act.

"If you wish to be fully as you were, you must take back what is yours. From these three. Use the Sword of Shadows. Kill them and what they hold will be released into you once more."

"Do they know?" He studied their faces, the frozen looks of surprise.

Darquementi shook his head. "They cannot hear us."

The Voidal looked at the Sword of Shadows, his hands clenching.

"You hesitate, Voidal. You do not believe?"

The dark man shook his head. "I am certain that you do not lie. I have lived with the perfidy of your masters for long enough to know that."

"While you wandered the omniverse, you were used as a pawn to destroy evil. Yet there were many times when you opposed evil in all its forms without the prompting of the Dark Gods. You performed acts of justice and compassion and you turned the hands of others away from vile deeds. Your sojourn in darkness has not been wasted if it has taught you compassion. This is recognised. And because of this, you are given this opportunity to regain what is yours."

The Voidal was silent for a moment, considering the words of the Asker. Then he took the haft of the Sword of Shadows and slid it from the stone. He considered his companions and what they had come to mean to him. Scyllarza, who had revived the power of love within him and who had placed in him a deep trust that had overcome her own terror of darkness, her deep seated killing hatred. Orgoom, abused and betrayed by the evil god who had chained him, denied his own lost humanity, despairing of life, yet clinging to a last hope that the dark man would reward his service with protection.

Elfloq. Grasping, cunning, as deceitful as any of the gods who toyed with the dark man. If you knew what you held, the Voidal thought. What would you do with it, little familiar? Bargain with me? Or give it freely?

I see now why you have so tied yourself to me, though you could never have known why. You have been cheated and deceived, as I have. All of you!

In a few swift steps, he was beside Darquementi, who had time only to gasp, for the blade hissed in an arc. But it did not suck in the lives of the three companions. Instead it sheared the Asker's head clean from its shoulders. It bounced over the flagstones and out into the sea of light, leaving a thin trail of blood behind it. There were cries from the pillars, where the other Askers waited, but in a moment they had fled.

As Scyllarza, Elfloq and Orgoom broke free of the spell that had gripped them, they looked in shock at the fallen Asker, the pooling blood beside his decapitated corpse.

"We did not come here to be cheated!" the Voidal told them. "Grieve not for him. He has paid for all the deceits practised upon me. Stand with me now."

"Master," said Elfloq, ready to take to the air in an instant, certain that there would be a ghastly retribution for Darquementi's death. "What happened? You put the sword into the flagstones —"

"Have you won back what you desired?" said Scyllarza, as dazed as Elfloq.

The Voidal held up his bloody sword. *They will never have the truth from me.* "Yes."

"Where are we to go now?" Scyllarza asked him. Her own sword was poised, as if for any attack. But the air around them was utterly silent.

The Voidal pointed to the great portals, the blazing light. "I think we must face whatever lies through there. The Prime God, I suspect."

They began the climb up to the light, its heat intensifying, its roar growing. The Voidal alone was not dismayed by it, but as they reached the final steps, the others drew back in fear. As they stood on the threshold, a voice challenged them from behind. They saw nothing, but recognised the voice as that of Darquementi.

"Wait! Beyond the portal there is only the Prime God, nothing else."

"Why should I believe you?" cried the Voidal. "I have been tricked since the first day of my banishment. Where was your Prime God when I cut you down?"

"He felt that it was a just ending for the Divine Askers. For all the torment we have given you. We have served our purpose." The voice said no more.

Elfloq had flown back from the portal. The Voidal drew Scyllarza to him. "If the Asker spoke the truth, we cannot go through. It is not the gateway to freedom, only to a oneness that would be a prison of a different kind."

"You are right, master!" Elfloq called. "Do not be tempted!"

The Voidal turned away from the blazing portal and looked at his three companions, the three elements that would make him complete. He could let the Sword of Shadows do its bloody work at any time and he would be restored. A burden of a different kind. And no easier to bear.

"Then we were not brought here to be destroyed, or punished?" said Scyllarza, mystified.

"Not destroyed, no. I have been shown the truth and given a choice. But it is what I have always desired, to be able to choose my own destiny."

She sensed that there had been some inner struggle within him, though he seemed to have reached a calmness, a resolution. "What will you do?"

He walked down the steps and out to the ledge that overlooked the sea of light. At its heart, the immense hand still held up the gleaming orb that was the omniverse. "My sin was to create *that* and to allow evil its sway therein. I gave life to my wildest dreams and let them run freely. I understand now, through the paths I have been made to walk, the extent of that darkness.

"I could simply destroy that omniverse. Oh yes, I know that I have the power to do that. But there are thousands of universes and gods and creatures there. We know that they are not all deserving of such an end. Perhaps I should return and begin to put right the injustices, the cruelty, the evil practices. Ironically, I would be doing the work of the Dark Gods."

Elfloq had eased close to him. "It would take an eternity, master."

"Indeed. But we have eternity, do we not?"

"Then are we — *immortal*?" the familiar gasped. Somehow, the word did not appeal to him.

"Perhaps. Would you want to put it to the test?"

Elfloq drew back. "No, no. It's just — well, it's rather a complex concept —"

"I suggest that this is not the place to dwell on that. Take Orgoom and go down to Evergreed. Tell him to prepare for a new voyage. If he grumbles about payment, tell him I can always leave him here and find other ways of returning to the omniverse. Whereas he would not find it easy. I suspect he'll capitulate."

Only too relieved to leave this place, the familiar and the Gelder hopped across the ledge to the waiting ship. The Voidal grinned at their going. It would have been so easy to take back everything. *As you believed I would*, he thought, looking up at the light in the portal. *And then you would simply have dispersed me once more. But not this way.* And he knew, without an answer from the light, that he was right.

"Where in the omniverse will we go?" Scyllarza asked him. "Must we always be embroiled in conflict?"

He kissed her and smiled again. "We will find somewhere to rest for a while. Eventually I will be happy to let chance decide. I have been a prisoner of the gods for too long. Let there be a true randomness to our wandering."

"Is there such a thing?"

He indicated the vast ship below them. "Let us see."

>...And so it ended.
>
> The dark man, the enigmatic wanderer from the void between universes, learned the truth of his identity and the extent of his crimes. In considering these revelations, he would have time to reflect on his own nature and what it had brought to life in the rogue omniverse.
>
> Should we pity him? Was the uncovering of these truths the cruellest act of the Dark Gods? Was this bitter knowledge the unkindest cut of all?
>
> For myself, I envy the dark man! Unlike me, he is not shackled to inactivity, walled up with his thoughts and regrets. He was released, with the freedom to choose his own destiny, light or dark. Such possibilities! Such endless potential!
>
> When he left Holy Hedrazee in Evergreed, with his companions, the future was spread before him like a grimoire with blank pages, nay a library. His acts would be the ink to inscribe them and from which would spring a thousand new legends.
>
> And so it began...
>
> —**SALECCO**, recorder of the Forbidden Histories, seeker after truth, absolution and egress.

Lightning Source UK Ltd.
Milton Keynes UK
UKOW032110211111

182437UK00002B/169/P